ONE WINTER'S NIGHT

KATE FROST

Boldwood

First published in Great Britain in 2023 by Boldwood Books Ltd.

Copyright © Kate Frost, 2023

Cover Design by Alexandra Allden

Cover Photography: Shutterstock

A CIP catalogue record for this book is available from the British Library.

Paperback ISBN 978-1-80280-472-0

Large Print ISBN 978-1-80280-471-3

Hardback ISBN 978-1-80280-470-6

Ebook ISBN 978-1-80280-473-7

Kindle ISBN 978-1-80280-474-4

Audio CD ISBN 978-1-80280-465-2

MP3 CD ISBN 978-1-80280-466-9

Digital audio download ISBN 978-1-80280-469-0

Boldwood Books Ltd
23 Bowerdean Street
London SW6 3TN
www.boldwoodbooks.com

For my family, past and present
With love xx

1

Echoes of the past whispered around Molly as she walked through the house she'd grown up in. Any sense of it having been their family home had slowly been erased over the last year as her parents' belongings had been sorted and the furniture removed, leaving the rooms bare. Along with her thoughts, only her footsteps scuffing the flagstone floor and the wind rattling the single-glazed window panes kept her company.

Memories filtered in and out as she wandered. Trailing her fingers across the cold stone fireplace in the living room, she imagined the blast of heat from the flames devouring logs. It had been years ago when Christmas stockings had hung above the fireplace and the excited chatter of her nephew and niece, Finn and Alda, had filled the place.

Winter sunshine streamed through the dining room window, too weak to take the chill away. Molly shivered as she stood in the middle of the room, the ancient stone floor fully visible now the table was no longer there. It had been where countless birthdays and anniversaries had been celebrated over big family meals, when laughter had filled the room, a sound that had been missing for too long. With the fire unlit and only the picture hooks left on the walls, everywhere looked sad and drab.

She perched on the window seat and looked out over the lawn. The single glazing let in wisps of icy air and the grass and shrubs were covered with frost. They'd had a garden party out there for her sister Claudia to celebrate her moving to Iceland. It had been a perfect September day, on the cusp of autumn, with drinks and nibbles set up beneath a white marquee. It was hard to believe that was nearly twenty-five years ago. Much had changed, both in this house and with her family. Now the borders were overgrown with brambles twisting through the ceanothus. Her mum would have been horrified. When she'd been well, she'd been out there in all weathers: sunhat and shorts in summer, woolly hat and a well-worn Burberry body warmer in winter. Everything had been neat, tidy and contained; it had been the same inside too. She had been house proud and had the time to keep on top of everything. A large draughty Grade I listed house could have felt cold and unsettling, but she had turned it into a warm and inviting home.

Molly didn't want to entertain sad memories but it was hard not to. She'd been building up to this day for months, desperately wanting to be rid of the stress involved in probate, going through the will, selling the house, sorting out inheritance tax and all the paperwork. The whole process had been long and drawn out, much of the past year spent dealing with the house sale, going through her parents' belongings, sitting through video calls with her sister in Iceland, trying to work out what should be kept, chucked, recycled or sent to charity. They'd kept very little; there was only so much Molly could take back to the three-bedroomed townhouse in Cheltenham she shared with her boyfriend Howard, particularly as he rolled his eyes every time she returned with a boot load of stuff. Most things had been stored away in the attic, along with some of the things Claudia wanted but needed to organise getting shipped to Iceland. It had been emotionally exhausting, stripping Ashford House of everything that had made it a home.

Even if she could afford to keep the place, it wasn't somewhere she could live, not with the memories. Not that Howard would want to live here either. He preferred clean lines and a modern look. They'd compromised over their Georgian town house, blending modern with the period detail she loved. Keeping this house would never work. A clean break from the past was what she needed even if she didn't feel that way right now. The last couple of years had been filled with constant change and upheaval, leaving Molly feeling as if she was running from one crisis to another, her insides in turmoil. She was desperate to escape, for time to pause to allow her to get a grip on her emotions. But of course, life wasn't like that. When she was down, something else inevitably happened to send her spiralling further.

Molly shivered and pulled her forest-green coat tighter around her. With no heating, her breath streamed white into the air. She stood up, feeling the need to move and keep warm. She'd do one last sweep of the house and then leave. It was time to let go. Later, a new family would be moving in to create their own memories, breathing new life into the place. It was just a house, she tried telling herself, not a home any longer, and yet sadness curled around her. She had this desperate need to hold on to the place she loved, that reminded her of happier times despite the last couple of years having been threaded with heartache. It was the finality that upset her the most. Being here made her focus on the reality of her loss, while her coping mechanism had been to try not to think too hard about it all.

As she headed upstairs and poked her head into the damp

bathroom, she acknowledged that however hard it was to let go, she couldn't cling to the past. The memories of her parents would remain, yet there was something about no longer being in their home that tugged at her heart. Claudia, more practical and less sentimental, would tell her to pull herself together. But Claudia wasn't here. She wasn't the one who'd had to deal with all of this on a daily basis.

The sound of Molly's phone ringing was loud in the quiet stillness and made her jump. Claudia. It was as if she somehow knew Molly had been thinking about her.

She forced down a sigh, pushed open the door of her old bedroom and answered.

'Hi, Claudia.'

'Hey, are you at the house?'

'Yes, just checking the place and walking round one last time.'

There was a pause. Molly drew back the curtain and peered past the condensation at the garden view she'd grown up with. She caught sight of her reflection, her long chestnut-brown hair, now straightened rather than wavy as it had been in her childhood. Her delicate features, pale skin and button nose, so cute when she was younger, made her looked washed-out and tired in the grey light. Her happy-go-lucky side that had continued into adulthood had slowly been chipped away, making her wonder if she'd ever get that side of herself back.

'I'm sorry I'm not there.' Claudia's voice suddenly filled the quiet. 'At least you have Howard with you.'

Molly glanced around her childhood bedroom and remained silent. The floorboards were bare, the furniture gone, the creaks and groans of the old house accentuated by its emptiness.

Claudia made a knowing huh sound. 'He's not there, is he?'

'He needed to work.'

'Of course he did.' Claudia had used that tone many times before when talking about Howard and it grated on Molly.

'Not everyone can just take time off whenever they want, you know,' Molly said cuttingly. She ran her fingers along the top of the fireplace. It had never been lit and when she was little she'd stored cuddly toys in the grate. In her teens she'd swapped them for twinkling fairy lights. 'I'm used to doing things on my own.'

If Claudia took offence to that, so be it.

'Well, you'll be here soon enough. Proper quality family time...' Claudia trailed off. A lump caught in Molly's throat. She knew what they were both thinking; just how much their family had changed, losing both of their parents within a year of each other. Molly didn't want to focus on any of that now. Selling the family home was the last of the past. She couldn't wait for today to be over despite a part of her wanting to never let go of Ashford House and the memories it held.

'We can't wait to see you,' Claudia continued gently. 'The kids are actually really excited about Christmas for once. Even Finn, who's way too old for all that festive nonsense. I think the last couple of years have made us all appreciate what's important; spending time with family being top of the list.'

'I can't wait to see you all too. This whole house sale has dragged on for so long; I hadn't anticipated I'd still be dealing with this so close to Christmas.' Although she was on the phone, Molly wafted her hand around as she headed on to the landing, swallowing tears at the thought that it was the last time she'd set foot in her old bedroom. She hadn't lived at home for a good fifteen years and yet...

'Are you okay, Moll?'

No.

'Yes.' She breathed deeply. 'I'm focusing on the eighteenth, getting to Iceland and seeing you all.'

'It will do us all good,' Claudia agreed. 'And we'll get to cele-brate your birthday too. It'll be nice to have happy things to focus on.'

Molly hmmed in reply as she headed for the stairs but paused to glance back along the landing, dimly lit in the grey December light. 'I'd better go. I've got to be out of here by midday before the removers and the new family arrive. I just wanted to see it one last time.'

'Of course.' Was there a hint of sorrow in Claudia's voice? She couldn't tell. 'We'll see you in ten days. It's not long.'

Molly said goodbye and clutched her phone to her chest. At least there was Iceland to focus on. How she would manage to feel festive, get through Christmas or feel like celebrating her thirty-fifth birthday was a whole other matter, but seeing her sister, her brother-in-law, niece and nephew and immersing herself in the joyfulness and adventure of being back in the land of fire and ice was sorely needed.

Instead of going downstairs, Molly headed to the room at the far end of the hallway. It was the only room she hadn't looked in; why she was putting herself through it, she had no idea, but she felt compelled to. Once a guest room, it had been turned into a bedroom and a haven for her mum when she'd deteriorated too much to get up and downstairs safely. Molly had filled the room with plants, books and pictures to take away the clinical-ness of the adjustable hospital bed, the hoist and the portable toilet. It was the room in which her mum had taken her last breath; the room in which Molly had said her final goodbye.

The emptiness where only the stirrings of sad memories remained was heart-breaking. Molly steeled herself, whispered 'goodbye' and closed the door firmly on the past. She went down-stairs, through the kitchen that had always been filled with life, and out into the once beautiful garden. Even overgrown and in the depths of winter, the magic remained. Molly's eyes traced the borders, the purple heather catching her eye. She plucked a handful of fronds and with a deep breath of fresh, cold air, returned inside. Clutching the heather to her chest, she marched along the empty hallway, tears blurring her vision, a sob ready to erupt as she took a quick, final glance in each room. Their bareness mirrored her own feeling of desolation, making her question if she'd ever be happy again. She pushed open the oak front door, stepped outside and shut it behind her for the very last time.

2

Tears streamed down Molly's face as she drove through the picture-perfect Cotswold village she knew so well. Even the Christmas trees glinting in cottage windows did little to raise her spirits.

The church where her parents were buried was on the edge of the village, a serene and peaceful place, its Cotswold stone casting a golden hue among the winter-tinged greens and browns of the churchyard. The place held happy memories too; it was where Claudia had married Elvar on a sunny spring day twenty-two years before when twelve-year-old Molly had revelled in being a bridesmaid. Molly had visited during all the seasons, but it felt particularly bleak today as she laid the heather on the grave. There was so much she wanted to say, but emotion choked her; there was nothing good she could tell them, so she remained quiet, silent tears running freely down her cold cheeks.

Despite the ache in her heart, the forty-minute drive back to Cheltenham allowed her the time to process her feelings. It was a journey she'd driven on nearly a daily basis for months on end when her mum was ill. She'd stayed over most weekends, particularly after her dad had died of a heart attack just four months after her mum's terminal diagnosis. Molly swiped angrily at her face, wiping away the tears. She knew she couldn't continue to torture herself, reflecting on the sad events like this. Everything had been leading up to today; saying goodbye to the family home had closed the door on the past. It was time to move on and focus on the future.

Her and Howard's period townhouse on a leafy street in Cheltenham was very different to her parents' sprawling mid-seventeenth-century house. It was home though, even if she'd spent far less time here than she'd wanted to recently. It was also a house she and Howard could grow into. With three bedrooms there was enough space for a family – not that they'd explicitly talked about it; they hadn't even got to the point of discussing getting married, and a proposal from Howard seemed a distant dream, but she'd occasionally imagine what their future would look like. Buying a house together had been commitment enough and both of them were busy; Howard mostly with work, while the last couple of years for Molly had been spent juggling her own work, supporting her parents and dealing with her grief.

Unlike the empty shell of Ashford House, her house was filled with belongings and yet, somehow, it felt just as empty. Molly put it down to her mood. With Howard at work and the heating on low, she shivered in the dark hallway. Feeling the need to fill the space and rid herself of the gloom, she bustled about, switching on lights and the radio. Chris Rea's 'Driving Home for Christmas' filled the silence, which only accentuated her sadness. There were no Christmas decorations up. Normally Molly would have decorated the house by the beginning of December, but eight days in and the Christmas box remained in the loft.

The last two Christmases had been consumed by sadness as well. Last year, it had been their turn to spend it with Howard's parents and, after the loss of her own parents and with Claudia in Iceland, there had been no reason not to. Molly had gone through the motions, pretending to be okay while breaking down in private. The Christmas before that at Ashford House had been the last with her mum and the first without her dad, all of them reeling from her dad's devastating heart attack just a few weeks before. Even with Howard, Claudia and her family there, it had taken all of Molly's resolve to put on a brave face and give everyone the best Christmas possible. Molly had felt adrift in a house that had no longer felt like a home, and her mum had been overcome with grief from the sudden loss of her husband and deeply depressed by the rapid progression of the motor neurone disease cruelly consuming her body.

Molly stopped her thoughts in their tracks. Although her grief counsellor had suggested it would be good to think back on painful times to try and process her feelings, it wasn't helpful today. She knew the grieving process was long and often unexpected. So many times, a wave of sadness would hit, often after she'd been feeling upbeat for a while, as if toying with her, whispering in its cruel little voice 'you didn't think it would be that easy, did you?' She couldn't allow her thoughts to spiral like this; she'd made a promise to herself to look forward rather than back on events she couldn't change.

After forcing herself to eat a sandwich and at a loss for what to do, Molly reflected that taking the whole day off work might not have been the wisest idea. She needed to escape, to clear her head and let all of the upset ebb away before Howard got home.

She drove out of Cheltenham to Lineover Wood, parked up and put on wellies before navigating the well-trodden, muddy paths. Pale winter sun strained through swirls of white cloud, the patchy blue sky beyond the bare tree branches just as insipid. Where the sun hadn't reached, frosted leaves crunched underfoot, a satisfying sound against the constant background noise of traffic on the A40.

Going to Iceland felt like a slice of normality, a chance to try to forget and move on from her heartache while immersing herself in fun and adventure. The idea seemed out of kilter with how she was feeling and everything she'd been through, but Claudia's life had continued, looking after and entertaining guests at their Icelandic lodge, so perhaps Molly's guilt wouldn't surface while there. On the rare occasion Molly had gone out with friends over the last year, her grief had rumbled on in the background, never allowing her to have fun. She desperately hoped she'd feel differently in Iceland.

The pacy walk and the refreshingly chill air – if damp and rather miserable by the time she made it back to the car – did at least revive her even if it didn't erase the sadness. She switched on the engine and let the car warm up as she stared in the rear-view mirror at her red-rimmed eyes, smudged eyeliner and tear tracks down her cheeks. She wiped away the evidence before heading back. Howard would be home soon.

He wasn't. Not that it was unusual for him to be late, but his phone call an hour after he should have got home did nothing to make her feel any better.

'So sorry, Moll, things got hectic at work sorting out an issue and I didn't have time to call.'

Or apparently text.

'That's okay.' Her way of saying *I'm used to it.* 'Are you on your way back now?'

'About that.'

Molly held in a resigned sigh but she did wonder if Howard would hear the upset in her voice. 'I was hoping we could get a takeaway and watch a movie. Take my mind off things.'

'Sorry, I completely forgot I'd said yes to having a drink with

Darren. He's in a really bad place at the moment with his crazy ex-wife and custody issues with his kids.' He paused. Molly wondered if he was turning over what he'd just said. Yes, other people's lives were shit too, but even so... Today of all days. 'Look, we'll do something tomorrow evening. I'll book that French bistro you love. I won't be home too late, I promise.'

Molly couldn't help but think he was avoiding her. She didn't say that though. She never said what she was really thinking, at least not recently.

'Are you okay though?' Howard's voice interrupted her thoughts.

Finally, he was asking after her.

'I'm fine,' she said firmly as if saying it with such certainty would make it true. 'Just been a bit emotional, that's all.'

Now that was an understatement, but it was all she was willing to say, at least over the phone. The last thing she wanted after the day she'd had was a confrontation. Better to let it slide. They said goodbye instead. She was desperate for company though, for a hug and for someone to tell her it was all okay, even if it wasn't. And she was certain the real reason he was going out was less about being a sounding board for his mate and more because he didn't know how to deal with her and her sadness. He'd found it hard over the last couple of years, of course he had. Life had been far from a bundle of laughs.

Claudia's earlier comment about Howard not being at the house twisted in her mind. To be fair, she hadn't explicitly asked him to be there, yet she'd hoped he'd offer. If it had crossed his mind that she'd need his support and company on one of the hardest days beyond the funerals, he hadn't acted on it. Him being there with her would have meant everything. To know he cared, to know he had a small understanding of just how hard it had been. Yet another goodbye. Once again, she cut her thoughts short. No, she wasn't going to go down that road this evening; she wasn't going to cry her eyes out again.

She scrolled through Deliveroo but her appetite had deserted her. It would have been different if they'd been eating together. Cooking was her passion and normally an escape, but recently it had felt like a chore, so she raided the fridge instead and found a bowl of leftover macaroni cheese. After changing into her pyjamas and snuggling beneath a throw on the sofa, her thoughts strayed to Howard and what had become of their relationship. When was the last time they'd done something together that hadn't involved a work do or mutual friends? Something nice and romantic. Something where they were able to spend time together. She'd see if his promise of dinner out tomorrow evening materialised. When was the last time they'd had sex? Molly scrunched her nose; she honestly couldn't remember. How awful was that. There was always an excuse and it wasn't just her not being in the mood. She couldn't even remember the last time he'd properly held her.

Everything had been pushed away to deal with later: her emotions, her grief, her relationship. Absolutely everything.

Escaping to Iceland for two weeks with Howard, far from the reality and stress of home, was what they desperately needed. The thought had kept her going for months. Claudia had suggested it when she'd come over in the summer to help sort through the house and Molly had jumped at the chance; the idea of her and Howard spending Christmas at home or going to his parents again because hers were no longer around had filled her with fear. This Christmas needed to be different and she was determined it would be.

In an attempt to make herself feel festive, Molly watched *Love Actually*, but all it did was make her cry; both the sad and happy parts. Yet, the underlying message of giving yourself a chance at

happiness and the importance of loved ones left her with a
renewed feeling of hope. After focusing all her love and energy
on her parents and the aftermath of losing them, it was time to
put herself first, to piece her heart back together as much as her
damaged relationship with Howard.

He messaged when he was on his way back, but she decided
not to wait up. Not only was she emotionally drained and physically wrung out, but she'd gone past wanting to talk to him – for
tonight at least. Apart from briefly talking to her sister, she'd dealt
with the day by herself. If she'd wanted to, she had close friends
she could have called. They'd messaged earlier, asking how it had
gone and she'd replied with a simple *glad it's over*. It was impossible to put into words the enormity of the day. Tomorrow would
be a fresh start.

As she wiped away her make-up and brushed her teeth, she
imagined the new family doing the same in her parents' old bathroom with its creaky floorboards and rolltop bath, the icy air
seeping in through the window. A young family would fill the
rooms with laughter and much needed happiness. For them it
would be an exciting new chapter, just as this chapter of Molly's
life was finishing.

She heard Howard come in, but he didn't come upstairs
straight away. She wondered if he was trying to avoid her as much
as she was avoiding him. Because that was what she was now
doing; she'd already decided to pretend to be asleep when he
came to bed. As it turned out, he took so long, she didn't have to
pretend.

* * *

There was little time to chat to Howard before work in the
morning as he was up and out early. For so long her focus had

been on Ashford House, that with the sale having finally gone through, she felt lost. At least she had work to take her mind off things, even if it felt as if she was going through the motions. Working as an HR Manager for a large entertainment group was a job she knew inside and out, which was just as well given how little she'd focused on it recently.

Howard stayed true to his word and booked the restaurant. Molly had been there a few times before, but only once with Howard. She was pleased he'd remembered how much she'd liked it, even if it felt odd being out alone together. They'd met through mutual friends seven years ago and used to have so much to talk about, but back then they'd been carefree, bonding over a shared love of crime dramas, live comedy and paddle boarding. Now it was an effort to find something to say beyond the sad events of recent years.

They ordered and chatted about work and Howard's promotion at the beginning of the year to senior project manager, safe and easy subjects as they shared a bottle of Sancerre. By the time they'd finished their starters and their mains of chicken ballotine with wild mushrooms and moules marinière were brought out, they'd run out of topics to talk about. When had things got so awkward? They were out of practice, Molly reasoned, both at going out and spending time together. They used to enjoy spontaneous weekends away paddle boarding in Devon or having cocktails with friends in London. Sunday mornings used to be spent lazing in bed, having sex and chatting about anything and everything before Molly would make brunch, experimenting with new recipes to try out on Howard. Perhaps it was best to acknowledge the awkwardness rather than ignore it?

'It'll be good to go away together after so long,' Molly finally said to fill the growing silence. The reason why they hadn't been away together remained heavy and unspoken between them.

Their lives had diverged. Howard had gone on a stag weekend in Prague, plus he'd been away for work a few times, while Molly's life had revolved around her parents and then their house. It was strange to be able to think of herself for once. Not just herself; her and Howard.

'I can't think further ahead than the next day at the moment.' Howard loosened his tie and stabbed a mussel with his fork. 'I have too much work on that needs my focus.'

Molly bit her lip. She felt the opposite; yes, work had been a good distraction and escape, while keeping busy had been an essential part of her being able to function, but she didn't love her job. She didn't live for work like Howard did. Her ambition and dreams had been put on hold and she was desperate to focus on Christmas and Iceland. She *needed* to focus on something positive, something she was actually looking forward to.

Howard reached across the table and put his hand on hers. She met his hazel eyes, which were framed by thick dark eyebrows that always made him look serious. Perhaps he sensed her upset. 'Honestly, I am looking forward to Christmas. There's just lots to do beforehand.'

'I know, I'm sorry.' Molly dropped her eyes, focusing on his neat nails and the dark hair on his fingers as she pushed the remains of her crispy-skinned, succulent chicken around her plate. She didn't want to show her disappointment about his lack of excitement for their upcoming trip. 'It's just, for me, for the first time in, well, what feels like forever, I'm actually looking forward to something. Selling the house and sorting out that side of things has been all-consuming and it feels a little like a weight has been lifted, you know?'

'Yeah, I get it.'

Did he, though?

'You've had a shitty couple of years,' he continued, 'so you absolutely deserve to get excited about seeing your family again.'

'Okay good, as long as you don't mind me banging on about it.' She smiled tentatively. She knew she struggled to talk to him about losing her parents, but if she couldn't talk about something as uplifting as Iceland with him, what else did they have to talk about?

'It's hard to believe it's been nearly three years since I was last there.' Molly sighed. 'And that was in spring. I can't even remember the last time we went in winter.'

'That Christmas before we bought our house. Snowmobiling with Elvar was pretty cool.'

'Oh, I remember. Finn was adamant he was going to lead the trip but he was only fourteen at the time.' Molly smiled at the memory of her headstrong nephew. Even back then he was capable, although his dad Elvar had been right not to give him free rein, at least when there were guests around.

'That was my highlight of Iceland.' Howard finished his last mouthful of moules marinière and sat back, clasping his wine.

'Well, maybe we can do it again this time.'

Howard ran his hand down his clean-shaven cheeks and crinkled his lips.

Not that Molly was convinced by her own suggestion either. Four years ago she'd jumped at the chance to snowmobile across Langjökull Glacier. It wasn't that she'd mellowed, it was just her adventurous side had slowly been sucked from her with responsibility and uncertainty. The idea of soaking in the Blue Lagoon appealed more than bombing it across a glacier far from civilisation.

Molly took a final bite of the chicken ballotine, relishing the flavour and promising herself to try the recipe out at home. She put down her knife and fork and looked at Howard. 'I'm going to go into town tomorrow, get some more thermal socks. Do you need anything? I know you're focused on work, but time's running out if you need anything extra. It's going to be absolutely freezing, you realise.'

Still clasping his wine, he met her eyes, his mouth pursed and nose wrinkled. 'About that. You know what I said before about work...'

Molly's heart sank; she had a horrible feeling she knew what was coming.

'I understand you're busy,' she cut in before he could say anything else. 'But they can't expect you to work over Christmas, so what's the problem?'

'The eighteenth is too early; I did tell you this when we were booking the tickets. The flight on the twenty-second would have been better, it would have meant only having to take a couple of days off that way.'

Molly frowned. 'Well, I'm sorry, it's too late now.'

'It's not actually, I checked.' He held her gaze as he put his wine down. 'There are still seats and only an admin fee to pay to amend the booking.'

'What are you saying?'

'I'm saying I need to work, so I've changed the ticket and will fly out on the Thursday instead.'

'You've already done it and didn't think to discuss it with me first?'

'I didn't want to risk losing the seat. It's only four days later.' He shrugged as if it was nothing. 'Let Claudia know; I'm sure it would be good for you guys to spend some time together without me. You're always going on about how little you see of each other. This is the perfect solution.'

For you, maybe. Molly held her tongue. If he'd wanted to, he would have talked to her. What he'd done was taken away her say in the matter. They'd once been a team and extra time away together would have trumped staying home to work, but then lots had changed. Her appetite for pudding deserted her. What upset her the most was the tiny part of her that was relieved to have a bit of time in Iceland without him. A few days where she wouldn't have to worry if he was enjoying himself, if he and Claudia were getting on, or where she'd have to consider what to say and how to act around him. It was crazy, she knew, to feel this way, which was why the time away to focus on their neglected relationship was needed. And they would get that chance; she just had a few days' grace first to focus on herself and her sister.

3

Molly packed away her worries about Howard having to work and his delay in joining her in Iceland, but the niggling feeling of uncertainty about their relationship gnawed at her subconscious. Although, with the last-minute shopping to fit in between work and packing, there wasn't much time to dwell. Going away for two weeks over Christmas and New Year meant she had extra to do at work and it seemed Howard was being truthful about how busy he was, getting home even later than she did most days. One of them would cook and they'd eat together in front of the TV watching *Line of Duty*, which of course meant they didn't actually have to talk to each other. Any conversation they did have was about work, what they were watching and getting Christmas presents to family and friends. Perfunctory, boring chatter. She wanted to remind him of the times when their relationship had been filled with laughter and fun, when they couldn't keep their hands off each other and they were excited about the future, but she didn't know how to begin. What worried her was not really knowing how Howard felt. Did he feel the same: bored and stuck in a rut? She made a silent promise to spend the holiday together concentrating on getting the spark back. With her thirty-fifth birthday looming, she was aware that time wasn't on her side; she needed to be brave and initiate the conversation about their future, about starting a family. And she would, as soon as they were in Iceland.

Molly's last day of work soon came round and the Saturday was spent washing and packing. The Sunday flight was early but Howard's decision to go separately had messed up the logistics. He insisted she still drove and he would get a friend to take him to the airport.

After a fitful sleep, Molly woke before the alarm and tried not to disturb Howard as she got dressed in the dark. She crept into the bathroom to clean her teeth, splash water on her face and put on a bit of make-up before heading downstairs. Her suitcase and rucksack were already packed and in the hallway. As she made a flask of coffee for her journey, a second alarm went off and she heard Howard drag himself out of bed. With a jumper thrown over his pyjamas, he joined her in the hallway, rubbing his eyes.

'Couldn't let you leave without saying goodbye.' He gave her a hug and kissed her gently.

'Thank you.' She really meant it because the gesture was unexpected but welcome.

Howard slipped on his trainers and dragged her suitcase outside while she hefted the rucksack on her back.

It was a quarter to four on a Sunday morning, quiet and dark apart from the streetlights. Fine drizzle made it feel colder than it probably was and Molly was glad of her insulated coat with its faux-fur-trimmed hood. Knowing she'd get hot on the flight, she hadn't put thermals on and once she was in Iceland, she wouldn't be outside for long.

They loaded the luggage in the boot and Molly turned to

Howard. He was shivering, his dark hair already damp, his eyes just black pools in the dim light.

'Go on in before you get soaked.' Molly gave him another hug, holding on until he let go. 'See you on the twenty-second. Don't work too hard.'

'I'll try not to. Safe flight.' He faltered, as if to say something more but then gave a weak smile and headed up the garden path.

Molly shrugged out of her coat, slipped into the car and started the engine. As she reached for her seatbelt she went to wave at Howard but he'd already gone. The porch light switched off, shrouding the front garden in darkness.

I did tell him to go inside, she reflected as she pulled away. What had she expected? For him to stand shivering in the doorway blowing kisses? At one time, perhaps yes.

Molly turned the heater up, put the radio on and headed for the M5 and Bristol Airport.

* * *

Cocooned in the window seat with her coat over her lap like a blanket, Molly yawned, desperate for sleep but only managing snatched moments with her head lolling against her blow-up pillow. The hushed but excited chatter of the couple next to her kept disturbing her – she gathered it was their first time to Iceland and they were celebrating their first wedding anniversary with a whirlwind few days. When she did finally nod off, the refreshment trolley wheeled by, waking her again.

What she was conscious about, as she tucked into a nonde-script toastie, was that she was alone, which was accentuated by the loved-up couple. It was a feeling that had weaved around her for months on end. Thinking back, she wasn't really sure when it had started, but her mum's diagnosis had been the catalyst. Any spare time had been spent caring for and being with her mum. Not that she resented it one bit, but she'd neglected Howard. Although, it hadn't been down to just her; they'd both neglected their relationship.

Was Claudia right, though? Did Howard always let her down? She shouldn't feel lonely, not when her sister would be meeting her in Reykjavík. She'd soon be ensconced in the warm embrace of her Icelandic family, but it was hard to not be disappointed over Howard's decision, even if she would see him again in a few days. It wasn't as if this was the first time he'd changed their plans at the last minute.

Molly finished her toastie and cupped her hands around her hot coffee. The woman next to her kept leaning closer, trying to peer out of the window.

Molly smiled at her. 'We're sitting on the right side of the plane to see the south coast as we fly in.'

The woman swallowed her mouthful of food. 'You've been before then?'

Molly nodded. 'Many times. My sister lives in Iceland with her family. They run a friendly boutique lodge specialising in small group tours with a good dose of adventure thrown in.'

'That sounds wonderful. We're staying in Reykjavík but have a Golden Circle and South Coast Adventure tour booked – I hope they're the best things to do?'

'To be honest, any of it is.' Molly shrugged. 'It's truly wonderful in winter, with the guarantee of a white Christmas.'

'Oh, we'll be home by then but the whole trip is putting us in the festive spirit.'

Holidays in Iceland had been a part of Molly's life ever since Claudia had moved there to live with Elvar. After university, Claudia had taken a gap year and travelled all over the world but her week in Iceland had changed her life. Elvar had been one of the guides on a three-day adventure tour Claudia had taken from Reykjavík and by the time they'd returned to the city, they'd fallen in love and Claudia had never left – except to briefly return to the UK to pack up and move out of the family home. Molly had visited at every time of the year, but there was something extra special about winter.

The dull, drizzly day they'd left behind continued as they flew north. The Atlantic Ocean was whale-grey and rough, peaked with flurries of ash-white foam. The wild remoteness was what made Iceland so special and as they neared the coast, Molly crammed herself to the side of the window, allowing the couple their first glimpse of Iceland.

The black sand beaches that studded the southern coast were stark against the white snow that spread inland. The golden glimmer of the wintery sun made the ice glow. She usually felt uplifted arriving in Iceland, the magic never having dispersed since the first time she'd visited, but that spark had been lost this time, not because of the place itself – she didn't think she'd ever take the desolate beauty for granted – but because life had worn her down. Everything felt an effort, even the idea of talking to her sister, brother-in-law, niece and nephew. Maybe it would be different when she saw them. Apart from her sister, the last time she'd seen Elvar, Finn and Alda was at her mum's funeral four-teen months ago. Not only did it feel longer than that, but the time they'd all spent together had been fuelled by sadness and her own stress at being responsible for organising it all.

Would she have felt differently if Howard had been sitting next to her? She wasn't sure, but she was disappointed by his decision and certain that when he did arrive, having time together and embracing all the delights Iceland had to offer would do them good.

The plane changed course, heading away from the snarling

foam-tipped waves and inland across the snow, leaving behind the smudge of black edging the island as they began to make their descent.

* * *

Freezing air blasted Molly as she stepped outside the airport terminal and pulled on her hat and thermal gloves. The hit of cold was bracing, a reminder of happy times when she'd been here before: days filled with adventure, exploring ice caves and snowmobiling, then summer hikes when the white landscape dramatically changed to moss-covered terrain, the greens vivid against black rock and grey mountainous backdrops. Long days spent outside would be rewarded with cosy evenings in. Even in summer, the fires were lit at Claudia and Elvar's aptly named The Fire Lodge and the midnight sun would keep them company as family and guests would tuck into home-cooked food washed down with home-brewed beer. Molly craved that hygge vibe at home but somehow missed the mark, whereas her sister and brother-in-law had nailed it.

The Flybus was warm and filled with the chatter of holiday-makers. The drive from Keflavik Airport to Reykjavík was familiar to Molly, the landscape blanketed with snow, only an occasional rock poking through, its stark black surface disturbing the uniform white. Then they passed blocks of square buildings, the splashes of red and yellow surprising among the muted white and grey. The gusty wind churned the sea, grey peaks rolling towards the shore, hidden by banks of snow.

Molly wondered what Howard was doing and if he was working today, rushing to get everything finished before joining her. She messaged him to let him know she'd arrived safely and was on her way to meet Claudia. The closer they got to Reykjavík, the more upbeat she began to feel, the relief at finally being back in Iceland and about to see her sister immense.

As the bus pulled into the station, she spotted Claudia leaning against the side of her solid black 4x4. Claudia was tall and wiry and had studied sports science. She always had been active and her life in Iceland had only fuelled her love for sport and the outdoors. A head shorter, Molly was slender but curvier, her passion lying in creative pursuits such as art and cooking, although she had reluctantly done a business studies degree. Both sisters were drawn to wild open spaces though, happiest trekking for miles before heading home to tuck into a home-cooked meal. The other thing they had in common was their chestnut hair – Claudia's pixie cut was now flecked with grey, while Molly's was long with a choppy fringe.

Molly's happiness at seeing her big sister overwhelmed her, momentarily pushing away the grief as they hugged each other. Not only were they different in looks and personality, but the divide of eleven years made her sister sometimes feel more like an aunt. They hadn't really grown up together either; by the time Molly was seven, Claudia had gone off to university. In many respects she'd grown up as an only child, just as her sister had done in the eleven years before Molly was born.

Molly shed happy tears, while Claudia's cry of 'It's so good to see you!' rang into the icy air.

Claudia's 4x4 wasn't necessary in the city, but Molly felt warm and safe as she gazed out of the window on the short drive from the bus terminal to the centre. Although Claudia and her family lived a forty-five-minute drive outside of Reykjavík, the city was familiar from numerous visits. With snow everywhere, the winter light was soft even in the middle of the day. The sun had only risen a little after eleven and would be making its descent later that afternoon. The trees in front of the houses lining the far side of the frozen lake were lit with tiny warm lights that glimmered in the half-light.

'We're going to the usual place?' Molly asked as they parked in a quiet side road.

'Of course.' Claudia crunched through the snow and joined her on the pavement.

She hooked her arm in Molly's and they set off towards the busier heart of the city. It was a fully functioning winter wonderland with the roads clear of snow in the centre and piles of pristine white coating everything else. Molly knew if this much snow fell in Cheltenham, everything would grind to a halt.

It was a few degrees below freezing but the wind chill made it even colder as specks of snow drifted and the icy wind twisted around Molly. She had long socks on beneath her jeans but she wished she was wearing the thermals that were packed in her suitcase. It was a short but brisk walk to the cafe, past festive shop windows and the typical corrugated iron clad buildings which were colourful in the gloom with warm light spilling from windows and trees entwined with lights. Molly couldn't help but feel revitalised at being here, particularly in winter when everywhere seemed even more beautiful and otherworldly. She envied Claudia's lifestyle. Molly often felt as if she'd missed her chance to shake up her life, particularly in recent years. It had fallen to Molly to support her parents and look after her mum alongside the carers because she was the one close by. While Molly had been juggling her mum's hospital appointments with her own job, Claudia had been taking guests out on adventurous glacier hikes or horse riding to breathtakingly beautiful waterfalls. But however hard it had been, Molly had been there for her mum unconditionally and would be so again in a heartbeat. She would treasure that time forever and, despite the painful loss, there was relief too that her mum was now at peace.

Molly's jealousy of her sister's unique life had seeded itself long before her own life had been consumed by supporting her parents, though it had always been easier to visit them in Iceland than for Claudia's family to come to the UK and they only did when they shut down the lodge for a couple of weeks in early spring and occasionally over Christmas. Even if they didn't leave Iceland often, their whole life was an adventure. Molly's job helped to pay the bills and she and Howard had a nice house in a decent part of Cheltenham, but she'd never taken a chance on anything, never thrown all caution to the wind and done anything as exciting or dramatic as her sister. It was about time she took inspiration from Claudia and changed that.

4

The Reykjavík Street Food cafe on Rainbow Street was compact, with a couple of tables squeezed next to the ground floor window. Molly and Claudia timed it perfectly, with people leaving just as they arrived.

They were welcomed and Claudia chatted in Icelandic to the man behind the counter, while Molly settled herself by the window, looking out at the colourful rainbow stripes that ran the length of the pedestrianised street.

Only a couple of minutes after Claudia sat down, two cardboard trays with crispy fried fish and chips were placed in front of them along with two cups of coffee. For as long as Molly could remember, it had been a tradition to eat here whenever they were in Reykjavík.

Claudia squeezed lemon over her fish, stabbed her fork into it and grinned at Molly. 'I'm so glad you're here.'

With a mouthful of moist fresh fish and tasty batter, Molly nodded in agreement. The tension after months and months of heartache and grief hadn't completely abated, but the coil in her stomach began to loosen a little as they chatted about Finn and Alda and the plans Claudia and Elvar had for them and their guests over the festive period. As jobs went, her sister and brother-in-law had the perfect work-life balance, managing to work hard and play hard. They didn't always keep the lodge open over Christmas but this year it had been at the special request of two of the guests staying and, being the friendly and open people they were, they always included the guests in their festivities.

Molly and Claudia had always had an interesting relation-ship. By the time Molly had reached adulthood, her sister had made a life for herself away from Molly, their parents and the UK. When university, dating and having fun was at the forefront of Molly's mind, Claudia was focused on her marriage to Elvar, building their business and raising kids. Time with Claudia had been fleeting, usually in the form of holidays in Iceland, occa-sional ones in the UK and then in recent times, bereavement had brought them together.

Molly steered her thoughts away from the part of her life she couldn't change and watched the tourists outside, battling against the icy wind as, wrapped in winter coats, hats, gloves and scarves, they made their way up the street. She turned back to her tray of fish and chips and met Claudia's intense gaze from across the table.

'Why's Howard not with you, Moll? Tell me honestly.'

Molly could barely look her sister in the eye. Claudia had never warmed to him. For whatever reason, Molly had always sensed that her sister had never thought he was good enough for her and, once again, he'd let her down and proved Claudia right.

'You know why; he had to work.'

Claudia scrunched her lips.

Molly sighed and skewered a chip. 'He'll be here soon

enough.' She reached across the table and put her hand on Claudia's. 'It's meant we can spend some proper time together, so it's not all bad, is it?'

She was using Howard's own reasoning to pacify Claudia. She desperately wanted her to agree, if only to make herself feel better.

'I'm just worried. I've not been there for you—'

'With good reason.' Molly's insides clenched.

'Yes, maybe, but Howard should have been.'

'He has, in his own way.' Molly's own words sounded false as she caught Claudia's raised eyebrow. 'It's not been easy for him either. Both of our lives have been turned upside down since Mum...'

'I know.' Claudia took Molly's hand and squeezed it. Her reasoning didn't need to be spoken out loud.

'Howard's never been one for showing his emotions and it's hard for him to deal with mine. It's been an incredibly shit time. He's had a new promotion at work, more responsibility, more travel. There's been lots going on and a lot to deal with.'

Molly knew she was making excuses for him. How often had she felt neglected emotionally and physically while dealing with this incredibly emotive and difficult period of her life?

The tension coiled tighter in her stomach. She grimaced, wanting to rid herself of the stress, the anger and the sorrow she was holding on to. She willed her worries to melt away. The heater flickering with flames behind her warmed her back and through the window was Rainbow Street. She focused on that, a sight that always brought a smile to her face.

'Can we not talk about Howard?' Molly put the last bit of flaky fish in her mouth. 'He'll be here in a few days. It'll be fine.'

'You're right, I'm sorry.' Claudia sipped her coffee and rested her arm along the back of the seat. 'You're probably not going to want to talk about this either, but I'm interested, so I'm going to ask anyway about the money from the house sale.'

'Oh that.' Molly sighed, yet she knew lots of what they would talk about would be difficult and emotional; it didn't mean they shouldn't talk about such things.

'It's a significant amount of money, Moll, even after the inheritance tax, solicitor fees, all that malarky,' Claudia said. 'What are you going to do with your share?'

'I have no idea.'

'You must have at least thought about it?'

'I haven't really had the time.' Molly cupped her mug of coffee, fingers tense. Of course she'd thought about it. She had dreams, but saying them out loud meant her sister would berate her for not doing something about them years ago. That was the last thing she wanted to hear right now. 'Have you thought about what you're going to do with yours?'

'Oh, there's a million things we can use it for. First and foremost, we're going to give Finn and Alda a decent amount each to help them out. We're pretty certain Finn's going to stay in Iceland and continue working with us – I mean, he loves all the adventure and taking guests out, but Alda is talking about going to university in the UK. She'll definitely spread her wings. She loves Iceland but I know she feels constricted. She wants to live a little – beyond our adventures in the great outdoors. As for me and Elvar, we have so many ideas for our lodge and on the land where we opened The Star Lodge – there's so much more we can do. The possibilities are endless. We've done lots since you were here last.' She trailed off. 'Well, you'll see soon enough.'

Once again, the reason Molly hadn't visited for so long was left unspoken.

Molly drained the dregs of her coffee. 'What's the plan for the rest of the day?'

'Sorry to mention him again, but if Howard had given me more warning, I would have planned for us to go to the Blue Lagoon; perhaps we could even have stayed overnight.' Claudia raised an eyebrow. 'As it is, we've got a group tour first thing tomorrow to prepare for and more guests arriving on Tuesday. I say guests, one of them is a good friend of Leifur's.' She met Molly's eyes and Molly willed herself not to blush. 'They've known each other for years. Me and Elvar have met him before too.' She nodded towards the queue forming at the door. 'Let's pay and walk off lunch.'

After the warmth from the heater, emerging from the cafe into the glacial air was a shock. Molly pulled her hat down over her ears and tugged on her gloves as they walked up Rainbow Street, avoiding tourists taking selfies. Claudia was kitted out in Icelandic branded thermal walking trousers and a windproof coat and looked far warmer than Molly was feeling.

They made their way up the hill, the long straight road allowing them an uninterrupted view of Hallgrímskirkja. The iconic church soared into the sky, its grey stone and jutting edges silhouetted like pillars of basalt, winter sun straining through the bank of clouds studding the sky behind.

'Leifur's back working with you?' Molly asked once they'd escaped the bustle of people further down the hill. 'I thought he lived somewhere in the north?'

'He did, but he came back earlier this year. I thought I'd told you?' Claudia glanced at Molly as they continued up the road. 'His ex-wife moved back south with their daughter to be closer to her parents and he followed. He's been living with us at the lodge while he finds his feet.'

Molly suddenly found the shop window they were passing incredibly interesting. She was only half-feigning as she paused to gaze at the pottery houses, distinctive square buildings that echoed the equally distinctive houses lining the road.

'Mum would have loved that one.' Molly gestured to a dove-grey house.

'Yeah, she would have done,' Claudia said sadly. She breathed in deeply. 'I always wondered if you'd end up with Leifur. You had a bit of a thing for him a long time ago, if I remember rightly?'

'Not really, no.' She looked firmly at Claudia. 'Anyway, I'm with Ho—'

'Yeah, yeah, you're with Howard.' Claudia paced ahead to the top of the road where the church dominated the skyline, its jagged, striking shape oddly beautiful.

Molly let out a sigh, which turned into a puff of icy breath as she followed after Claudia. She was glad to be moving again as the freezing wind wrapped itself around her, seeping through her jeans. Her thighs were beginning to feel like blocks of ice and now she was finally in Iceland, her stomach full of delicious food, she was longing to get to the welcoming warmth of Claudia and Elvar's lodge.

Molly knew she'd held things back from Claudia for fear of unlocking her emotions and not being able to control them, but as they walked together past the banks of snow surrounding the spacious concourse in front of the cathedral, she wondered if it wasn't a new thing to not confide in her sister. The problem with withholding things from Claudia was that she made assumptions. Although to be fair, she was right about this; Molly did once have a huge crush on Leifur, but that was way in the past. She certainly hadn't anticipated he'd be back at the lodge, though. Then again, if she'd ever talked to Claudia properly about things such as crushes and feelings, then maybe she would have had prior warning. Had she ever really opened up to her sister? Not that she could remember. That was something else that might need addressing, along with fixing her relationship with Howard.

5

By the time they'd driven through Reykjavík, what little daylight remained had seeped from the sky, plunging the horizon into darkness. Once they were past the outskirts, the pristine snow spread away from the road with only occasional dark bushes poking through to taint the white. The headlights of oncoming cars and coaches cut through the dusk. Molly knew the route by heart and she'd driven it too, but she was glad to be a passenger as the snow got heavier.

They reached a long, wide curve in the road where a stream of vehicles wound their way down the valley to the village of Hveragerði. Its golden lights were an oasis in the gloom of the vast snow-covered wilderness. Molly got a fizz of excitement as she always did, but it was more to do with knowing that they were getting close to warmth and safety. Usually her excitement stemmed from the anticipation of adventure, but this time the drive through the dark with the swirling snow and her newfound understanding of how unpredictable life could be had erased her usual confidence and love of adventure. She was craving home comforts and wanting to be inside looking out on the wild beauty.

The Fire Lodge was like a beacon in the darkness, dipping in and out of sight as they drove deeper into the valley along the narrow winding road away from civilisation. As they neared the lodge, warm light spilt from the picture windows on to the surrounding snow. It was difficult to see the river that ran past it, but a dark glistening line cut through the white, snaking like a scar through the pristine landscape. At night it seemed wild and unfriendly, but by day Molly knew the river, nestled between geothermal hills, would look completely different, its clear, warm water enticing.

Claudia pulled into the small parking area at the rear. In front of them was the main two-storey lodge, which had a communal living area and a first-class restaurant on the ground floor, while the family apartment was above. A glass walkway, which made the most of the view, linked the lodge to a series of low buildings perched on the riverbank, which housed the guest suites. Work, play and family life went hand in hand.

Candles within intricately decorated floor lanterns flickered around the entrance hall and gave off a nutmeg and cinnamon scent. It smelt of Christmas. Through an open doorway, Molly spied the dining area with its central open fire and the tables dotted in front of the two picture windows that framed the view to the river.

'Welcome home,' Claudia said with glee. She was unbelievably proud of the place and rightly so. 'I think everyone's still out but they'll be back for dinner. Speaking of which, I need to check everything's in hand. Do you mind showing yourself to your room?' Claudia handed her a key. 'Suite two. Get yourself settled. I'll see if Alda's around.'

Molly usually stayed with them in their apartment, but Claudia had insisted on treating her and Howard to the luxury of a guest suite. Not that where Claudia and her family lived was

shabby in the slightest, but the suites, perched on the riverbank
with a private outside deck and a path that led to one of two hot
tubs, were something else entirely.

As Molly headed along the glass walkway towards the suites,
she reflected again on her feeling of relief at having time to
herself.

She opened the door to her room and was greeted by a blast
of heat. A central wood burner divided the suite in two, sepa-
rating the bed from the living area, its flames sending light
dancing across the linen-toned walls. Molly left her suitcase and
rucksack by the door, squeezed out of her boots and dropped her
gloves, hat and coat on the end of the bed. Every detail had been
carefully thought through from the comfy sofa next to the wood
burner and the wall of glass allowing an unrivalled view of the
river, to a mini Christmas tree by the window and the en suite
with its large skylight above a freestanding bath from which to
stargaze.

Claudia was always busy, always thinking about something,
always on the go; Molly imagined she was liaising with their
housekeeper and checking in with the chef about dinner prepa-
rations – it wasn't just guests they catered for. Six evenings a week
they opened to the public and were renowned as one of the best
restaurants in the area.

'Be more like Claudia' had been their mum's catchphrase
when Molly was growing up. She'd never meant it in a negative
way or that Molly was lazy, she just used it jokingly when she
needed to get stuff done. It had etched itself on Molly's subconscious though, the difference between her and her 'do it all' sister.

Molly wandered over to the large window that overlooked the
river. The sky was colourless and the blanket of cloud allowed
little opportunity of seeing the northern lights tonight. There
would hopefully be plenty of chances to see them once Howard

arrived. What a welcome that would be. At the moment, the dark, desolate quietness suited her.

The room evoked warmth, luxury and comfort, contrasting with the white of the stark landscape outside. Snow covered the hill on the other side of the river, pristine apart from melted pockets where steam escaped into the air from the boiling water running below the surface. Just outside was a small deck to brave the winter weather, to stargaze or watch for the northern lights, along with the two hot tubs spaced along the riverbank. It was perfect in every way.

A knock on the door stirred Molly from her thoughts. She opened it and came face to face with her fifteen-year-old niece's smiling face.

'*Hæ*, Molly.'

'Alda! Oh, it's so good to see you.' Molly pulled her into a hug. She'd grown taller since she'd last seen her at her mum's funeral, but her heart-shaped face was still framed by long, light-brown hair.

'Mamma said you'd arrived.' Her English was faultless with only a hint of an accent. She had the same delicate features that Molly had inherited from her mum. Claudia looked more like their dad; tall and strong rather than slender and elvish.

'You didn't go out with Finn and your dad today?'

Alda wrinkled her nose. 'I had homework to finish.'

'Your mum said you might want to go to university in England.'

Alda shrugged shyly. 'If I'm good enough.'

'You will be; any university will be lucky to have you.'

'That's why I'm doing my homework. Then I can enjoy Christmas. Mamma also said Howard's not coming?'

Molly smiled wryly at her niece's directness. 'He is, just a few days later than planned.'

Alda looked as if she was going to say something else, but stopped herself. She flung her arms around Molly again and hugged her tight. 'I'm really happy you're here.'

The lump in Molly's throat was testament to how much those words and that hug meant. Alda was a sensitive soul, more like Elvar in that respect and a hugger unlike Claudia, and Molly appreciated it. She'd been dealing with everything on her own for so long that it was refreshing to finally be surrounded by her loved ones.

* * *

After unpacking her thermals and layers of leggings, trousers, tops, tights and a couple of dresses for cosy Christmas nights in, the arrival of other people enticed Molly back towards the communal heart of the lodge.

Leifur took her by surprise as she entered the entrance hall. Her heart thudded – only from surprise, she told herself. Kitted out in a black all-in-one snowsuit, his hair shaved at the sides and spiky on top, he was familiar even with the addition of a beard, and still ruggedly handsome. He spent his days outdoors 'adventuring' as he'd once told her. The first time she'd met him in her early twenties, they'd both been up for an adventure as much as each other, but that had been a long time ago.

'Hey!' His grin lit up his face as he clocked her. 'Elvar said you were arriving today.' He glanced behind her. 'You're on your own?'

'For the time being, yes,' she said, returning a smile. 'My boyfriend's joining me in a few days.' She silently cursed having to repeat the same thing because of Howard's decision.

'Ah okay. We get you to ourselves for a time then.' He flashed another grin. 'I need to change, but um, see you at dinner.'

Molly watched him stride away. She remembered the effect he'd once had on her back in her twenties, before either of them were in a serious relationship. Howard liked going to the gym and kept in decent shape, but Leifur lived and breathed adventure and the outdoors, never happier than when he was hiking up a mountain, traversing a glacier or exploring an ice tunnel. Howard enjoyed his home comforts a bit too much; not that there was anything wrong with that as she did too, it was just Howard and Leifur were incredibly different which made her wonder what it was that had attracted her to them both.

Molly grimaced as she headed into the dining area. What she'd seen in Leifur was a fit, young man who'd flirted outrageously with her when she was as young and single as he was. Lots had changed since then and this weird discomfort in the pit of her stomach was because Howard wasn't with her yet. She was alone but not on her own.

Elvar was a welcome sight, entering the firelit restaurant and striding towards her. On the cusp of fifty, and a good deal older than both her and Leifur, he had something of a wild man about him, with dark shaggy hair and a beard flecked with white like it was permanently dusted with snow. His grey eyes were piercing but warm as he wrapped her in a bear hug.

'It's been too long, Moll.'

A strange mix of relief and sadness washed over her as he released her, emotion tugging at her heart at finally being back in a place she adored with the people she loved.

He clamped a reassuring hand on her shoulder. 'I know it's hard to be here after everything. We miss them too.'

In many ways, Molly had an easier relationship with him than she did Claudia; he seemed to understand her more and appreciate her sensitivity, and yet with his love of adventure and the outdoors, he perfectly matched her adrenalin-loving sister.

As Finn, her eighteen-year-old nephew, joined them, she relished being swept up in family life. This was what she'd been longing for, to be somewhere far removed from the challenges of everyday life.

Molly loved the set-up at The Fire Lodge, with just five suites ensuring Claudia and Elvar could really focus their time and attention on each guest. Although they had luxurious, private rooms to escape to, guests were encouraged to join the family each evening for dinner at the communal table, to share stories, laughter, food and drink, whether they were newlyweds or a couple celebrating their twenty-fifth wedding anniversary. And it was usually couples – the lodge was the epitome of romantic luxury, but occasionally there were friends, which was true this time as Molly discovered once they'd all been seated at the long table in front of one of the floor-to-ceiling windows.

Claudia was a brilliant host, confident and the queen of small talk. She effortlessly put everyone at ease as she introduced Molly to their guests.

First up was Kat and Lils, two friends in their late forties, Kat with bobbed dark hair, Lils's short and grey, both single, both divorced and both sworn off men – or so Kat said, laughing. They were friendly and upbeat as they happily took over from Claudia and introduced themselves.

'I'm Kat and I'm not an alcoholic!' She giggled. 'Sorry, for a moment it felt like we were about to start an AA meeting. Which I've never been to, I should add. But seriously, I'm Kat and this is Lils and we've been best friends practically forever.'

They were the perfect contrast to the quieter but equally friendly older couple who happily announced that they were on a holiday of a lifetime to celebrate their thirtieth wedding anniversary.

'Iceland is one to cross off our bucket list.' Graham squeezed his wife Maggie's hand.

'And of course,' Claudia said, glancing around the table, 'Molly's partner Howard will be joining us later in the week, while the day after tomorrow we'll have two more guests arriving in time for Christmas.' She raised her glass of their home-brewed ale and waited until everyone had followed her lead. 'To festive fun and adventure!'

Glasses clinked together before spoons were eagerly dipped into the steaming bowls of lobster soup. A hush descended with just the sound of satisfied sighs and the gentle background chatter from the other diners in the restaurant around them before conversation began to start up again around their table. Claudia had a central spot, ensuring everyone was okay and no one was without someone to talk to. Finn and Alda had grown up with their home filled with strangers who soon became friends and so were at ease chatting to guests. Molly was happy to just sit and listen as she savoured the warm, delicately spiced soup, which left her intent on getting the recipe from the chef to try out at home.

Her thoughts returned to Howard and how he should have been there, enjoying all of this. The room alone, even without the incredible setting, would surely inject some much needed romance back into their lives. Her neck grew warm at the thought. Why was she flushing thinking about him in that way? Perhaps it was because she hadn't in a long time, being preoccupied by other more serious and pressing matters.

She reached for her glass of ale and met Leifur's eyes across the table. He smiled at her before continuing to chat to Kat who, with a grin plastered on her face, seemed rather enamoured by him, despite her pre-dinner comment about being sworn off men.

Molly savoured the food, from the lobster soup starter to the main course of melt-in-the-mouth grilled lamb with pumpkin and potato gratin, carrots and leeks. Tiny Christmas lights decorated the edges of the windows, reminding Molly of twinkling stars. She soaked up the atmosphere, the conversation and laughter mixing with the chatter from the other tables filled with tourists and locals.

In between mouthfuls of food, Alda was telling her all about school and the plans she had for the future, about how she still loved art but was considering doing an environmental science degree. It was good to listen, to be drawn in by someone else's happiness, her youth untainted by the awfulness of real life.

'Maybe if I go to university in England I can see more of you.'

'That would be wonderful,' Molly said, and truly meant it. Her family in England had diminished; there were cousins and a couple of aunts and uncles but she didn't see them often.

Alda scooted off to her room before the Skyr crème brûlée was served; Molly adored how involved the kids were, but she understood they still liked their own space. She thought of how she was at fifteen, either holed away in her room or out with friends. The only time she'd not liked living at Ashford House was as a teenager – a picturesque Cotswold village miles from anywhere with a bus only twice a week hadn't exactly been a social hub.

'You're quiet this evening, Moll.' Elvar's voice was deep and gentle next to her. Claudia's chatty confidence with the guests was offset by Elvar's quiet and steady presence. He had an effortless way of encouraging guests and his own friends and family to get out of their comfort zone and try new things without ever pressuring them.

'Sorry, I'm just tired after an early start.'

'You don't have to apologise. I only want to make sure you're okay?'

Molly nodded. 'I am, it's just overwhelming being back here after so long and with all that's happened.'

'I understand how hard it is. But I'm glad you're here. We all are. And you need this, this um, break shall we say, to recharge. It was a privilege to look after my own parents before they died, but it was the hardest thing I ever did and they were just elderly, nothing like the awful disease your mother suffered.'

He suddenly stopped as if sensing the sorrow building in Molly at his words. He picked up his glass. 'We toast family tonight, Moll. Those who are with us and those who aren't.'

Molly forced back a flood of emotion. Elvar's sensitivity and his gentle understanding had always been a blessing.

Elvar squeezed her arm and raised his glass.

'To Alan and Gertrude,' he said.

'Mum and Dad,' Molly whispered as they knocked their glasses together. She took a gulp of the smooth yet refreshingly bitter ale, wanting to drown the wave of grief.

'I don't want to upset you, but we should always think and talk about them. Keep their spirit alive.'

Molly nodded and took another sip. 'I've wanted to, desperately, but it's still so raw. I can't seem to speak without...' She flapped her hand in front of her face in an attempt to indicate that she was trying hard not to burst into tears. She glanced around the table at the happy faces of her family, of the guests, of Leifur chatting to a rather rosy-cheeked Kat. 'Mum would have loved this – she did love it. Dad too in his own way, but they hadn't been over here for such a long time.'

'That was a great shame and something Claudia regrets, not making them visit again.'

'That was out of her hands. Dad was steadfast in what he liked and he didn't like flying. Mum always went along with him. And it wasn't as if it was easy for Claudia to drop everything and visit. Until she had to.' Feeling heat rising in her chest, as it always did when she talked about the recent past, Molly cupped her hands around her glass and focused on it rather than the heartache.

Perhaps Elvar sensed this and decided not to push the conversation further. Despite his rugged appearance, he was a gentle soul and an antidote to Claudia's directness. They matched each other perfectly. She wondered if people thought the same about her and Howard.

6

Molly was rather glad that the aurora borealis forecast wasn't good as it meant Elvar and Finn, ever eager to head out in search of the northern lights, didn't even suggest it. Usually she'd be the first to jump at the chance of heading out into the night, but not this evening. After being constantly on the go for months on end, the adrenalin that had kept her going had now deserted her.

After finishing dinner, almost everyone went to the lounge to relax with a drink and continue chatting. It was a large but cosy room off the dining area, a private space for the guests to use, with book cases covering most of the midnight blue walls, and chesterfield-style sofas and armchairs draped with insanely soft faux-furs, arranged around a roaring fire. In the corner, next to the window looking out on the snowy wilderness, was a huge Christmas tree strung with lights.

Molly snuggled on a sofa on the periphery, happy once again to listen to everyone else chat about their plans for the rest of the week in the lead up to Christmas. It was always special here, but the festive season was extra special. Sadness twisted around Molly's heart; this time of year would be forever changed for her.

She would never again be able to buy her parents a present or talk to them or include them in her plans. She'd never be able to make her mum's favourite cranberry ripple cheesecake and watch the delight on her face as she took the first bite. Even when they'd had Christmas at her parents', she'd been in charge of food, revelling in experimenting with Christmas dinner and cooking for lots of people. As she'd said to Elvar earlier, her mum would have loved all of this. Kat and Lils's jolly chattiness would have appealed to her and she'd have got on with Graham and Maggie too.

'Hey sleepy head.' Claudia disturbed her thoughts as she handed her a mug and flopped next to her on the sofa. 'Try this.'

'What is it?' Molly cupped the warm mug.

'Hot chocolate heated in the hot spring – our secret festive recipe.'

Molly took a sip and the rich chocolatey warmth with a hint of orange and nutmeg rushed through her. 'That's seriously good.'

'Everything cooked in the hot spring is.'

'Please tell me you're still baking rye bread like that.'

'Oh yes, freshly baked and ready to retrieve in the morning for breakfast.' Claudia sipped her drink, leaving her lips coated with the thick creamy hot chocolate. She licked it off with relish. 'Our chef is wonderful, but I'm sure you'd be able to put your own twist on this. Have you been cooking much at home? Or should I say experimenting?'

Molly breathed in the spiced chocolate scent and shook her head. 'Not beyond everyday meals; I just haven't had time.'

'Apart from when we close for Christmas, this is the kitchen's busiest time of year.' The corners of her eyes crinkled as she smiled gently. 'You always used to be itching to help in the kitchen and try things out – you've not lost that passion, have you?'

The burning sensation returned to Molly's chest. Thinking about her hopes and dreams was difficult, mainly because she'd put things off for so long. Claudia was wise to it. 'No, it's not lost, just diminished; nothing's been easy.'

'I know, which is why tonight it's time to relax.' Claudia tucked her legs beneath her on the sofa and shuffled closer to Molly. 'And also, I want to know the truth.'

Molly frowned. 'About what?'

'About you and Leifur. You brushed off the question when I asked earlier. So, did you? Have a thing for him?'

Even though her voice was low, Molly glanced around, worried about someone overhearing. 'I never had a thing.' That was a blatant lie, but considering she'd never confided in Claudia about her feelings for Leifur, she certainly wasn't going to start now. Perhaps she'd heard things about her and Leifur from Elvar. She wrinkled her nose, stalling as she sipped her hot chocolate. If Leifur had talked to Elvar then of course he'd talked to Claudia. 'It was a long time ago. We kissed and it was well before I met Howard.' She lowered her voice even more. 'So talking about it now isn't really appropriate.'

Claudia watched her coolly. 'Because you don't want to talk about it? Or because you still like him?'

'Because I'm with Howard,' she hissed.

'Don't be such a prissy.' Claudia practically rolled her eyes and gestured in Leifur's direction. 'He can't hear anything – his attention is on our guests who can certainly see his charm.'

It felt uncomfortable to Molly, the idea of sharing her feelings and innermost thoughts with her sister. They weren't close enough in age to have ever confided in each other in this way.

Molly gripped the edge of a cushion. 'I don't want to talk about him.'

'He is single, you know,' Claudia said pointedly.

'And I'm with Howard and have been for seven years.' The annoyance that occasionally flared in Molly when Claudia mentioned Howard manifested itself now. While Howard and her dad had hit it off from the beginning, Claudia and Howard, although perfectly civil towards one another, had never clicked. But then Claudia and their dad had rarely got along either, so perhaps that was the reason why. It irked her no end the way Claudia so easily dismissed her relationship with Howard. They lived together; they'd bought a house together. Wasn't that commitment enough?

Perhaps this line of questioning was Claudia's way of avoiding talking about the loss of their parents and the things that Molly knew were really playing on both of their minds. Claudia was focusing on stuff that wasn't important. No; irrelevant. Leifur was irrelevant, both what happened between the two of them years ago and him being here now. So what if he was single? He had an ex-wife and a daughter, while Molly was in a committed, albeit strained, relationship with Howard.

It'll be easier once he's here. If she kept telling herself that, perhaps she'd begin to believe it. Although, the underlying tension with Claudia still needed to be addressed, even if it meant opening up and actually talking, something Molly had been avoiding as much as possible.

For once, Claudia didn't push things; perhaps after nearly twenty-five years with Elvar, some of his patience and diplomacy had finally rubbed off. Molly was relieved when Graham and Maggie pulled Claudia into a conversation about the places along the south coast they were going to visit, allowing Molly to finish her hot chocolate in peace.

It felt later than it actually was because it had been dark for so long. There was no time difference with the UK, but the days this far north were much shorter. Molly had also been up since the early hours and by ten she found it impossible to stifle a yawn. She wasn't the only one struggling; Graham and Maggie said good night and Leifur headed off with a wave, leaving Kat and Lils chatting together.

Claudia turned back to Molly. 'Time to light the candle. Finn, Alda.' She beckoned to her children, both ensconced on a sofa.

How many teenagers back in England would be content to spend a Sunday evening lounging by the fire reading? She knew it was a completely different way of life and it wasn't always this rosy; Finn had certainly had his moments of rebellion over the years and enjoyed the nightlife in Reykjavík whenever he got the chance. The lodge was their life though and Molly loved how involved the kids were. At eighteen and having left school a few months before, Finn worked as hard as his parents. This had been his life since he was little.

Molly joined them by the bookshelf next to the Christmas tree. The festivities in Iceland stretched for twenty-six days and featured thirteen Yule Lads – mischievous elf-like gift-givers and the sons of a troll called Grýla – the first one arriving thirteen days before Christmas Eve. One tradition they followed was to light an advent candle on the four Sundays before Christmas. Claudia handed Molly the matches. The Christmas wreath surrounding the candles was a deep forest green, its freshness complemented by pinecones sprayed gold and a pop of Christmas red in the berries. Their mum, who loved gardening and the outdoors, had taken up the tradition back home, foraging in her garden and the local wood for berries, evergreen branches and holly to weave into a wreath, adding sprigs of dried lavender and cinnamon sticks tied with ribbon before placing it around the four candles as a centre piece on the dining table.

Molly struck the match. The flame burst into life and she held it to the candle.

Claudia squeezed Molly's arm. 'For Mum and Dad.'

More was said in that moment than either Molly or Claudia had been able to put into words. Everything had changed and yet, by holding on to the traditions that they'd cherished over the years, they managed to balance the past and future with the present, enabling them to enjoy the peace of the moment. With their arms linked with Finn's and Alda's, they watched the flames flicker to life.

Molly woke late to darkness but a clearer sky than the day before. It would be a while before a short-lived sunrise, but the festive lights decorating the lodge hinted at the view, the beginnings of a glimmer on the horizon catching the glistening flow of the river.

This was the first day for as long as Molly could remember where she had nothing to do: no work, no stress over the house sale, no paperwork or never-ending phone calls to make. Time to herself was a strange sensation, welcome yet unsettling. The only trouble with stopping was the exhaustion. After a proper lie-in, she still felt wrung out, although strong coffee and a breakfast of the deliciously warm, sweet rye bread that had been baking in a tin submerged in the hot spring for close to twenty-four hours made her feel a whole lot better, particularly as it was slathered in butter and served with copious amounts of birchwood smoked salmon.

Molly decided not to join Claudia and the guests for a day out exploring the Golden Circle with stops at Gullfoss waterfall and

Þingvellir National Park, places she'd been to many times before. Instead, with Finn out with his mum and Elvar busy with jobs, she spent much of the day with Alda, chatting, reading and having a brisk walk in the snow together before they headed to the apartment to bake a coffee and walnut cake to share with everyone when they returned. Leifur had gone on an overnight tour to The Star Lodge taking a small group from Reykjavík, so he wasn't around either. Molly wasn't sure if it was relief she felt at his absence, but it certainly felt easier not being in his presence.

After a blissfully chilled out day with Alda, Molly enjoyed everyone's company at dinner, listening to Kat and Lils talk non-stop about the incredible sights they'd seen, with Graham and Maggie occasionally chipping in. Feeling sleepy and full, Molly retreated to her room to phone Howard and had a short conversation about what they'd been up to, although with him working, she had more to talk about than he did.

After another good sleep, she felt revived, and with Howard arriving the day after next, she was ready to embrace the experience. In the afternoon, she made the most of what remained of the winter sun and layered up before heading out for a walk along the river. In spring and summer it was possible to walk for miles, but the winter landscape was unforgiving, the snow deep, compacting with a satisfying crunch beneath her boots. The fading sun, low on the horizon, turned the snow a glittering gold. Ensuring the lodge remained in sight, she walked as far as she dared across the stark, white landscape. The wind whistled into the gullies, wrapping around her and attacking her exposed cheeks. At least it was impossible to get lost with the river a constant companion, its warm flowing water and the occasional steam rising from the dark patches where the snow had melted on the hill opposite, reminders of the fiery rage and power beneath the surface.

The return walk seemed easier, following her compacted footsteps towards the lodge, sparkling silver in the dusk. It had hardly felt like any time at all since the sun had risen and now the landscape was about to be plunged into darkness again.

As she left the riverbank and cut past the guest suites, a vehicle pulled into the parking area. Elvar and the two new guests emerged from the jeep, the doors slamming closed, loud in the quiet stillness. By the time Elvar had dragged the suitcases out, Molly had almost reached the main path to the lodge.

Elvar gestured for the guests to go in front and Molly almost saw it happening in slow motion. As she joined the path, one of the guests, a tall man with a few days' worth of dark stubble, black-rimmed glasses and a stripy woolly hat stepped to the side to let the woman go ahead. Losing control of the suitcase and his footing, he staggered backwards. The woman yelped, while Elvar grabbed the handle of the freewheeling suitcase. Molly launched herself towards the dark-haired man just as he crashed with a thump into the snow.

'Oh my goodness! Are you okay?'

The man looked up and met her eyes. His were wide beneath his glasses and a piercing ice blue. He had a look of shocked confusion. He stared at her for a heartbeat before he beamed then moved his arms and legs up and down to make a snow angel.

Molly laughed and reached out her hand.

'I always like to make an entrance!' he said with a gentle Scottish accent as he took her offered hand.

Molly frowned as she helped him back to his feet. 'You look familiar.'

'Aye, and so do you.' His smile grew wider and dimples appeared on his stubbled cheeks. 'Molly Bliss. Elvar's sister-in-law, right? It's been a while. I'm James, Leifur's friend, and I'm familiar because we first met here in Iceland, what, ten years ago now? We went camping together, although er, your memory of me might be a wee bit vague because you and Leif were, let's say, rather infatuated with each other.'

Despite the swirling cold, Molly's cheeks flushed hot. 'Oh, that summer.'

James laughed and turned to the blonde woman. 'This is my fiancée, Jen.'

'Hi there. Lovely to meet you,' Molly said, shaking her gloved hand.

'Making an entrance is one way to put it.' Jen raised an eyebrow. Shivering and with a stern expression, she didn't seem amused.

'That was definitely a memorable arrival, James!' Elvar grinned and thumped his back, dislodging some of the powder stuck to him. A snow angel-shaped dent remained in the otherwise pristine snow. 'Let's get inside before there are any more accidents!'

James and Elvar, who was firmly clasping the handle of the runaway suitcase, laughed together as they made their way up the path. Molly followed behind with Jen. The light was fading fast, the Christmas lights twinkling in the dusk.

'Is this your first time to Iceland?' Molly asked as they reached the lodge.

'Yes,' Jen said through chattering teeth. 'It's even colder and darker than I imagined.'

Molly held the door open for her and hoped her negativity was down to being cold and tired – there was plenty of time for Iceland to work its charm.

'It's nice though,' Molly said, wanting to put a smile on Jen's face as she followed her into the warmth, 'to be able to come here and have a guaranteed white Christmas.'

'I guess there is that,' Jen said with a resigned tone that sounded as if she wasn't convinced. 'Sorry, I don't mean to sound ungrateful to be here, I'm just exhausted. I've had a tough work schedule to be able to take time off.' She glanced at Molly. 'I'm a solicitor specialising in property and conveyancing so have clients relying on me. Sorry to moan.'

'Oh don't apologise. It sounds like you could do with a break,' Molly suggested, not really knowing what else to say.

The lodge's entrance hall was soon filled with the sound of snow being knocked off boots and Elvar and James chatting as they removed coats, hats and gloves. Claudia joined them, her voice rising over the commotion as she welcomed James and Jen with the promise of a roaring fire and mulled wine.

Jen looked pristine in a cream and pink turtleneck jumper and black leggings which Molly hoped were fleece lined. Travelling could be exhausting, particularly if you were already tired; it had taken Molly a good forty-eight hours to begin to feel alive again, so it was unsurprising that Jen's delicate features were pinched into a frown. Meeting new people when your partner knew them but you didn't could be challenging too. Molly always felt that way at Howard's Christmas work dos when partners were invited, although she'd skipped the last couple and Howard had gone without her.

Molly hung up her coat and tuned back in to the conversation.

'Leifur's not long back. He should be down in a minute,' Claudia said to James, while indicating to Jen to leave their suitcases in the hallway. 'He's been looking forward to you arriving – a chance to reminisce over your uni days.'

'God, yeah. Hard to believe it was twenty years ago that we were fresh-faced freshers.' James already looked at home. He'd had a permanent smile on his face from the moment he'd scooped himself up out of the snow. He beamed at Claudia now. 'And it's been what, six or seven years since I was last here.'

'Too long!' Leifur appeared with his arms wide open and they greeted each other with a hug. 'It's so good to see you!'

'You too,' James said, motioning across the entrance hall. 'This is Jen. Jen, this is Leifur, my best friend from university.'

Leifur greeted Jen with a handshake and a kiss on the cheek. James's Scottish accent was soft and lilting, perfectly suiting his warm and friendly demeanour. Molly did remember him from that summer ten years ago; he'd been just as friendly and chatty and as up for an adventure as everyone else. He'd come alone, but if she'd remembered correctly he'd had a girlfriend back home, although it definitely hadn't been Jen; she was far too young. Molly grimaced, knowing now how obvious her attraction to Leifur had been; she really had been infatuated. Seeing James and Leifur together now took her right back. James seemed more and more familiar, a similar age to Leifur with dark curly hair speckled with grey. A smattering of freckles decorated his cheeks along with the stubble, and a deep line between his eyebrows suggested he worried too much. Jen's posh London tone contrasted with his and left Molly intrigued by their differences.

'We've done quite a bit to the place since you were last here,' Elvar was saying to James.

'It's a constant work in progress,' Claudia added, 'but we feel we're nearly there.'

'Well, I love what I've seen so far.' James smiled. 'You should be proud of yourselves.' He turned back to Leifur and draped his arm across his shoulders. 'And we have much to catch up on.'

Jen pulled an iPhone from her pocket. Its swirly pink cover matched the colour of her jumper perfectly. 'Do you have WiFi?' She looked between Claudia and Elvar.

'Yes, of course. The details are in your room. How about I

show you there now?' Claudia gestured towards the walkway. 'Let the boys catch up, then everyone's meeting in the guest lounge for drinks at six.'

Molly left them to it and escaped back to her room. She needed to pace herself; she was out of the habit of socialising and it felt overwhelming meeting new people. Her first impression of James and Jen as a couple was interesting though. Even if Jen hadn't been amused by James's mishap in the snow, Molly liked how he'd laughed it off. Howard wouldn't have done that; he hated being made to look a fool and wouldn't have found the situation funny in the slightest – although he may well have sniggered while watching someone else crash into the snow. She wondered how she and Howard would fit in with such an eclectic group of guests.

7

Molly loved the magic of winter with the snow sparkling in the muted sunlight, but she still felt out of sorts, as if she was in limbo, waiting for something – or rather someone – before she could fully embrace being here. It was as if she couldn't give herself permission to relax and have fun, but she wasn't sure if it was because she was still overwhelmed by grief and sadness or because she wanted Howard to be here so they could begin to put things right between them.

Dinner the evening before had been a jolly affair, fuelled by Kat and Lils's happy chatter and dominated by Leifur and James reminiscing over their uni days, a strange mix of partying and climbing mountains – not at the same time, they'd stressed with booming laughter. Once again, Molly had been content to sit back and listen while tucking into fried salmon with barley and blue cheese, charred leeks and a red wine sauce – a dish she was definitely going to make for Howard when they were back home. She wasn't the only one happy to blend into the background; Jen was quiet too, although she seemed happier in the warm with a glass of wine in her hand.

Having spent the first couple of days relaxing and spending time with Alda, Molly jumped at the chance of a morning out with everyone. As they drove from the lodge, all colour drained away to a landscape of predominately white, grey and black with an occasional spruce contrasting against the snow. In summer, the same landscape popped with fresh greens, but this was the Iceland she'd longed for, the mystical, adventurous side. Jagged rocks jutted through the white, and the wind swirled snow across the road as they drove at a steady speed, encased in the solidness of the ten-seater 4x4.

Molly had been to Raufarhólshellir lava tunnel once before, but it had been a while ago. She soaked up the palpable excitement of Kat and Lils as they attached crampons to their walking boots, while Graham helped Maggie adjust her helmet and Jen looked unamused at putting a helmet over her sleek and shiny hair. James looked right at home, the first to be kitted out, whipping out his phone to take a selfie.

Even with Claudia there, Molly wished Howard was with her so she didn't feel quite so alone. She was surrounded by couples – and she included Claudia and Elvar in that, even if he wasn't with them now. It frustrated her no end that Howard didn't feel the same way about Iceland being an opportunity to spend time together, instead prioritising work over their relationship. Once again, she reminded herself that he would be here tomorrow and this feeling of loneliness would dissipate. As she tightened the helmet strap beneath her chin, she tried to decipher the churning in her stomach; surely she wasn't nervous about heading into a lava tunnel she'd explored before, when in years gone by she'd gone ice climbing? It worried her why the nervousness manifested itself whenever she thought about Howard.

The comfort of the sheepskin rugs dotted on the benches was in stark contrast to the sound of the wind howling outside and an icy dampness permeating inside. Gloves were pulled back on as everyone readied themselves for the tunnel. Molly tried to empty her mind as she checked her helmet light worked before they stepped outside, Molly at the back and Claudia at the front with the guide.

The wind whipped at the hair that was poking out from beneath her helmet and it was hard to see anything through it beyond ghostly grey, the sun not long risen, the sky dominated by ashen clouds. All that was visible of the tunnel was a hole with steps cut into the snow.

The pace was slow as everyone navigated the icy entrance, the line briefly stopping for Jen to pocket her phone and steady herself by grasping the sides of the snow tunnel's walls. Kat missed her footing and shrieked, then giggled as she righted herself, before Molly heard the gasps as, one by one, they entered the tunnel.

Molly remembered the awe-inspiring feeling from the first time she'd been here, knowing she was walking somewhere that had been formed by the path of lava flowing from a powerful volcanic eruption over five thousand years before. Pillows of snow covered the rocks scattered across the ground and daylight flooded through the tunnel roof where it had collapsed, forming a 'skylight'. Below it, snow piled up like a mini mountain. Snowflakes drifted in, adding to the powdery heap of pristine snow.

They chatted in hushed whispers as if talking any louder would disturb the magic – or dislodge an icicle. They wound their way around snow-topped boulders, the powder beneath their feet muffling any sound. The guide stopped every so often, divulging titbits of information, before continuing further into the tunnel where the snow-coated ground changed to a metal walkway dotted with ice.

Molly had taken a picture of Alda when she was little with her gloved hands cupped around a smooth round lump of ice almost twice as big as her grinning face. Unexpected memories stole through her, once again the echoes of the past taking her by surprise. That had been on a holiday to Iceland with her parents, before she'd met Howard. Her mum never really did anything out of her comfort zone. Getting on a plane for her was fine; being kitted out with crampons and a safety helmet to explore a lava tunnel was not. Her mum was a real homebody; she'd never worked and had been happiest pottering in the garden or making cupcakes and entertaining friends and family. At least that's what it had always felt like. But with Elvar's gentle persuasion, her mum had embraced the experience. Deep down she'd had an adventurous side.

Kat and Lils were just in front of Molly, their usual chatter paused as they gazed around open-mouthed. James and Jen were a little further ahead, while Graham and Maggie were chatting to Claudia and the guide.

'It blows my mind,' Lils said, gesturing around the cavernous tunnel as they followed the others, 'just how long ago this was formed. And can you imagine the sheer power of the lava that created something this size. What I would give to travel back in time to witness a phenomenon like this.'

Kat glanced at Molly. 'Lils's a history buff.'

'I'm a manager of a multiplex cinema, but I would have loved to have done something that involved history – I get my fix volunteering at a National Trust property as a guide, but if I had the skills I'd be an archaeologist or I'd restore old paintings. Something that mixes creativity with history is my absolute dream.'

'I keep telling her it's never too late to retrain,' Kat said, keeping her eyes fixed on the metal walkway. 'Been there, done that. You only regret what you don't do.'

Beneath the shadow of her helmet, Lils rolled her eyes. 'It's not that easy – retraining takes time, money, energy. I work shifts, often weekends and evenings.'

'You could argue it's the perfect job because you have the time to take a course during the day—'

'I do need to sleep you know!' Lils laughed, but it sounded like bluster to Molly. 'Not to mention do the housework, shop, all the million other things that need to be done. Plus life has a habit of throwing some serious curveballs.'

Kat gently touched Lils's arm before she gave Molly a knowing smile. Lils wandered ahead, trailing her gloved fingers through powder-soft snow. The sound of their crampons knocking against the metal walkway echoed as they followed, leaving behind the feathery flakes of snow swirling down through the opening in the ceiling as the tunnel closed in.

'It's all too easy to put things off,' Kat said in a hushed tone to Molly. 'And trust me, I know more than anyone that Lils has valid reasons, but sometimes you just have to follow your dreams. I did. That's how I ended up being a dog groomer. Honestly, my dream job!' She laughed. 'Life's too short not to.' Molly hmmed in agreement, knowing how true Kat's words were, particularly when she'd put her own dreams on hold. The years had raced by and she was still stuck in the same job, not progressing, not feeling satisfied in any way. She'd always had an excuse for not changing her job, for not taking a chance and doing something different, something related to her true passions. Recently those reasons had been absolutely valid – there was no way she could have done anything other than survive while being a carer for her mum, but the truth was, she'd stopped herself from taking a chance long before.

They continued walking deeper into the tunnel. The lava walls glittered, the volcanic rock lit by red and mauve lights.

Despite having seen it before, Molly was struck by its breath-taking beauty as their helmet lights highlighted sparkling ice on the walls and the threads of bronze and amber colour within the rock.

'Well, this is quite something,' Kat said as they entered a cavernous part of the tunnel.

Hundreds of icy stalactites decorated the curved ceiling of the tunnel, while the metal walkway was littered with huge chunks of ice as if glass boulders had been haphazardly strewn about.

'So what do you do, Molly?' Kat turned to her after they'd all taken photos.

'Oh, I'm a bit like Lils with a job I do because it pays the bills rather than one I'm passionate about. I don't really feel as if I have a proper career. I like how you two have recognisable vocations: a cinema manager and a dog groomer. Mine's just a job, nothing special.'

'What's the job?' Lils asked. 'And more importantly, what's the dream?'

Huh, that was a question. 'The job bit is easy to answer – I'm an HR manager for an entertainment company. The dream...' Molly sighed; it was something she hadn't shared with anyone and it was hard to articulate, even to strangers. 'It's a difficult one. Cooking is my passion; I adore the creativity of developing new recipes and experimenting with flavours but I've never really wanted to work in a restaurant kitchen. It might be a bit too much to ask for, but I want the freedom to do my own thing. I've often thought about kitting out a van and touring festivals but that doesn't really work with our life.'

'You and your husband?' Lils asked.

'Boyfriend. We're not married yet. I'm not sure he'd be too keen on me doing something like that.'

Lils frowned. 'Because you've talked to him about it?'

'No, not really. To be honest, I've not really talked to anyone about it, mainly because I'm not sure in my own head about the way forward. The truth is, my job is easy, it keeps life simple—'

'So you've stuck at it.' The line between Kat's eyebrows deepened, which made Molly assume she disapproved.

'I think I have to work it out in my own head before I say anything to my boyfriend. He thinks practically and plans everything in minute detail. It needs that level of thought and planning before I can begin to talk about it with him.'

'It sounds as if you're making an excuse to not do it,' Kat said softly.

Ahead of them, Lils spun round. 'Kat, you can't say that!'

'It's okay.' Molly smiled at Lils who was looking wide-eyed at her friend. 'Kat is probably right, but I've had lots of reasons over the last couple of years for putting things off. It's difficult when you're not 100 per cent sure about the direction to go in.'

'I'm lucky in that respect,' Kat said. 'I'd toyed with the idea of being a veterinary nurse but for reasons I won't bore you with, that never worked out. I ended up doing lots of different jobs in my twenties, from stacking shelves in Sainsbury's to being a sales rep for a cleaning company; you know, any old job that fitted in with the kids and paid the bills, but I knew I wanted to work with animals. So I started dog walking in my spare time and trained as a dog groomer, worked for someone else for a while then a few months after my marriage ended, I started my own dog grooming business.'

'It was like ripping a plaster off.' Lils smiled as she navigated her way around the clumps of ice decorating the walkway. 'She got divorced, quit her job and started her own business all within a year. Quick and painful and completely mental in many ways, but she totally rocked it and is so much happier.'

'Much happier without my waste-of-space ex too. And

although doing all that was ridiculously scary at the time, they were the best things I ever did. Apart from having my kids.'

'So now you spend your days doing what you love,' Molly said wistfully.

'Yep, grooming lots of lovely pooches. Not at all glamorous but so bloody rewarding. I absolutely love it.'

The conversation petered out as they watched their footing on the slippery rocks. The tunnel curved and the guide started to talk again. Molly tuned out of what she was saying, focusing instead on what Kat and Lils had been talking about. Other people had it hard too. Life was rarely straightforward and sometimes taking a chance and doing something scary could ultimately lead to a better life. She'd always put things off because life was comfortable. But comfortable had also led to monotony and boredom – at least where her job was concerned. Her relationship with Howard was stagnant too. A fading memory could be reversed; surely that initial spark and love could become their reality again. There was nothing stopping them now, beyond themselves. It was the same with her job. Maybe the new year was the perfect opportunity to push herself and take a chance, just like Kat had done. She could learn something from their friendship too; they were different in looks, jobs and personality, yet there was a true connection, an underlying friendship that had survived the good and bad times. Molly and Claudia were opposites too, yet they had a sisterly connection. It made her wonder if it was possible to become closer to her sister, to have the same sort of easy relationship that Kat and Lils had with each other.

They went down steep steps to a large metal platform surrounded by walls of solid lava. The tunnel did continue further, but it wasn't for the fainthearted – a four-hour hike, deep into the tunnel's depths. Molly, once up for an adventure, shivered at the thought.

Their group bunched together at the rear of the platform, their helmet lights flashing on to the sides of the tunnel where thousands of years before the lava had swept through, leaving behind a solid wall ridged with horizontal lines, a mix of coppery green, shimmering brown-pink and glittering bronze, smooth and damp in places, solid and rough in others. Although awe-inspiring, like much of the island, the rocky ceiling and domineering walls gave Molly the feeling of being trapped.

'No daylight reaches this far in.' Their guide gestured around the cathedral-like cavern. 'Do you want to experience how dark it is without the lights on?'

There were murmurs of yes, a couple of nos too, but a general excited consensus as the couples among them linked arms.

'Everyone turn off your helmet lights.' The guide glanced around. 'Ready?'

She switched off all the platform lights. The tunnel was plunged into darkness, an absolute blackest black, a darkness that Molly had never experienced before. Kat's and Lils's giggles turned into shrieks followed by nervous laughter that trickled around the group.

'I don't like it.'

Jen's voice.

A waft of aftershave. A hand brushed Molly's arm.

'Sorry.'

James.

In the velvet black, Molly suddenly felt overwhelmingly alone. Claudia was somewhere and other people surrounded her: Jen and James, Kat and Lils, Graham and Maggie. What she would give to have an arm held firm with hers right now. The comforting presence of another person, of someone she loved...

With a start she realised that she wasn't necessarily thinking of Howard.

Her other senses were heightened. Water dripped, a crampon clanged against the metal, a hushed whisper was surprisingly loud, James's breathing was gentle next to her. Even in the midst of winter in Iceland, it was never this dark, a darkness so absolute it almost felt as if she'd been swallowed whole.

'Ready for me to turn the lights back on?' the guide asked.

'Yes please.' Jen's voice was the loudest among the mutters of agreement.

Lights flickered into life and the cavern streamed back into focus. Molly blinked. James's face was inches away from hers. He met her eyes and laughed.

'Sorry! It's really disorientating in the dark.'

Molly shifted her gaze from him to the coppery colour of the volcanic walls.

'Time to head back.' The guide's voice cut across the chatter as she gestured back the way they'd come.

Molly, now at the front, set off, her crampons clanging on the metal steps as she started the climb up and back through the tunnel to what remained of the daylight, cross with herself for feeling so unnerved by the thought that it wasn't Howard's company she was craving.

8

After leaving the lava tunnel, they drove back to the lodge and Molly retrieved the new batch of rye bread that had been baking in the hot spring for hours. The round loaf was almost cake-like in consistency, and while she left it to cool, she boiled some eggs in the hot spring water before joining everyone inside for a communal lunch with salad and a smoked salmon pâté to go alongside the eggs and bread. She then enjoyed a relaxing afternoon playing board games with Finn and Alda up in their apartment, while Claudia, Elvar and Leifur dipped in and out.

The conversation with Kat and Lils stayed stubbornly fixed in her mind. She didn't hate her job, but she didn't love it either. Being in Iceland was always a reminder of what she was missing out on. If you wanted something badly enough, you just had to take a chance, as Kat had done, Claudia too. The sad truth was, Molly now had the money to invest in her dream; what she lacked was the guts to do anything about it.

The next day, Molly didn't join Elvar, Claudia, Alda, Finn and the guests on a trip to Reykjavík visiting the Christmas markets and ice skating at an outdoor rink. It would be a full day with them returning for dinner that evening, and Molly wanted to be here when Howard arrived at around 3 p.m. Claudia had offered to meet him in Reykjavík, but Howard had been adamant that he'd hire a car and drive from the airport. At least then they'd have the option of doing stuff by themselves if they wanted to. Perhaps a romantic night away at the Blue Lagoon would be the perfect way to inject some passion back into their relationship.

Once again, Molly found herself in the unusual position of having free time and nothing to do. She'd expected to be spending this time with Howard rather than knocking about on her own, but with only a few more hours until he arrived, that would soon change, although with moody clouds clustering and snow beginning to fall, she would be glad when he was safely here. To kill time, she could find a cosy spot and read or she could embrace the elements. She plumped for the second option.

Wearing a woolly hat, thermal socks, fleece-lined boots and a snuggly robe over her swimming costume, Molly swapped the delicious warmth of her room for the icy outside air. She gingerly made her way down the path that led to one of the hot tubs, but continued past, crunching though the snow to reach the edge of the river. The lodge had an outdoor pool too, naturally heated by the thermal water running beneath the surface, but there was something appealing about wild swimming.

Freezing air filtered beneath her robe and her thighs were already painfully cold. The sun was only just beginning to rise. Its weak rays didn't warm the air but they did allow a glimpse of the landscape that surrounded the lodge, a barren whiteness in every direction apart from the silver-grey river winding through. It was the perfect bathing spot, shallow and clear, and despite the below zero temperature, she could feel the heat rising from the thermal river.

Molly was just hidden from view from the restaurant and

although the guest suites overlooked where she was, everyone was out. Claudia and Elvar, along with the locals, were used to the delights of taking a dip in the thermal water in the depths of winter, yet it still felt a novelty to Molly. She imagined how crazy she must look slipping off her boots, shrugging off her robe and baring her skin.

The shock of the freezing air abated as she waded into the warm water and sank down with a sigh until she was submerged up to her neck, the flowing water rocking her gently. The river remained this temperature all year round but it was extra special when surrounded by snow. Everywhere was a pristine white apart from the pockets of darker areas studding the hill where the steam streamed into the air.

The creak of footsteps compacting the snow made her turn.

Leifur was striding towards her. So much for no one spotting her.

'You're braving the cold?' Kitted out in thermal trousers and a cream and dark grey patterned jumper, he stood on the snowy bank looking as if the cold didn't bother him one bit.

'I'm fine in here,' she said, releasing a stream of breath into the air. 'I'm just not sure I'll be brave enough to get out.' Leifur's intense gaze was making her feel rather exposed in just her swimming costume. 'You didn't go out with everyone then?'

'Not today, no. I'm not sure Jen would have welcomed me joining them.' He raised an eyebrow.

'Have you met her before?'

'No. Heard a lot about her though.' He scrunched his lips as if he wanted to say more but felt he shouldn't. 'I'm just doing some jobs before my daughter gets here.'

'How old's your daughter now?'

'Six. She's just started school so I don't see her as much, but she'll be here for a couple of days.'

'That'll be nice. What about over Christmas? Will you get to see her?'

He stuffed his hands into the pockets of his trousers and shook his head. 'She's spending it with her mamma. She'll be here till Christmas Eve, so that's something.'

There was a sadness in his tone and Molly didn't know what to say. They used to have so much to talk about; admittedly it was difficult to hold a conversation with her bobbing in the river while he was braving the cold on the bank. He was obviously still working through heartbreak, while factoring his daughter into the equation; his life hadn't been easy either.

'We, um, haven't talked as much as I'd have liked to. It's great living here with Elvar and Claudia, but there are always people around.' He looked tense, his hands still rammed in his pockets, his cheeks red, she assumed from more than just the cold. 'And now your, er, boyfriend will be arriving?'

'He will indeed.' She kept her tone neutral, uncertain of his, and the possible meaning behind his words. She had fond memories of the time she'd spent with him and she wasn't sure how that made her feel.

He smoothed a hand down his beard. 'You know, I've, er, thought about you over the years.'

How to reply? She swallowed and dropped her gaze, relieved that the heat from the water would disguise the real reason she was flushing. The truth was, there had been times when she'd thought about him too, the what could have been if both of them had made different choices.

'After that summer, I hoped you'd come back again,' he said smoothly.

She met his eyes. 'I did, but you were with someone.'

'It didn't last.'

'And then I was with Howard and still am.'

'I know.' He shrugged. 'I'm teasing. I understand you have a boyfriend; doesn't stop my imagination though. I'll leave you to it.' He faltered before flashing her a cheeky smile. 'Unless you need help getting out?'

'I'll be fine, thank you.' A few years ago she'd have jumped at the chance of Leifur helping her out of the river, his warm, strong hands on her bare skin. The memory of them during that summer snuggled in a sleeping bag kissing flashed into her head as clear as if it was yesterday rather than a decade ago. But he was a confused contradiction, switching from thoughtful reflection to suggestive teasing. He walked away, cutting through the deep drifts of snow up towards the outdoor pool. Memories tugged at her of a time that had been so simple and perfect, adventurous and passionate.

The lush warmth of the river had gone a long way to soothing her, but her thoughts returned to Howard. Once he was here she'd have to make an effort to talk to him, to figure out a way they could move forward from a challenging couple of years when all she wanted to do was hide away. Hibernate. Wouldn't that be blissful, to disappear for the rest of the winter and not have to deal with messy emotions.

Molly gasped as she emerged from the water, the icy air like tiny knives stabbing at her wet, goose-bumped skin. Even wrapped in a robe, by the time she'd navigated her way along the path to her room, she was shivering uncontrollably. She slowly thawed out as she dried herself in front of the wood burner.

Intending to not venture outside again at least until Howard arrived, she dressed in a skirt, jumper, tights and boots and made her way to the lounge. With most people out, it was empty, but the crackling fire was welcome so she curled up on the sofa closest to it. She was contemplating nipping to the apartment kitchen to grab some lunch when her phone rang and Howard's name popped up.

She frowned and answered. 'Hey there, I wasn't expecting you to call yet. Aren't you on the plane? Don't tell me you're delayed?'

'Not exactly.'

The icy wildness visible through the window seemed to seep in as a chill swept over her, swiftly followed by the all-too-familiar feeling that Howard was about to let her down. She pulled a throw over her lap.

'What's happened?' She wasn't sure she wanted to hear the answer.

'I missed the flight.'

'What?' Molly shook her head, not quite comprehending his words. 'How on earth did that happen?'

'Oh, it's been one of those days.' His voice was tense, echoing the way she was feeling inside. 'A friend let me down at the last minute with a lift to the airport. I'd overslept too, then by the time I managed to get an Uber, I had to get them to drive me home again because I'd forgotten my passport. There was so much traffic on the M5. Everything that could have gone wrong did.'

Molly clenched her teeth; he was making no sense. She had so many questions. *Which friend? When have you ever overslept? When have you ever not planned everything to the tiniest last detail? How on earth did you manage to forget your passport?*

He was lying, she knew he was. Her boyfriend of seven years who was fastidious about the way he looked, about keeping the house neat and tidy, who was always early wherever they went, who planned journeys and going away with military precision, was lying through his teeth. Molly was the one who usually risked making them late. The same way she liked the uniqueness of old buildings with their imperfections, Howard preferred a clean modern look. It was the same with their personalities;

Molly was more laid back – at least she had been when they'd met – while Howard was particular and organised. They complemented each other with their different strengths, or so she'd thought. Howard always had a backup plan, so there was no way he could have missed his flight – at least not by accident.

'Surely you can get another flight?' She could hear her voice rising, the tension coiling in her stomach.

She was comfortable sitting by the fire and didn't want to move, but she was aware she was somewhere public where anyone could walk in at any moment. Howard's silence in answer to her question spoke volumes.

Gripping her phone, she left the lounge, swapping the warmth for the cool air of the glass walkway as she listened to Howard's explanation that there weren't any available flights, so he'd hired a car and had driven to his parents' house.

'You're at your parents' already?' Molly screwed up her face. For him to have been at Bristol Airport earlier that morning, missed the flight and now be all the way up in Shropshire before he'd even phoned to let her know what had happened didn't make sense.

'Yeah, I'm here and I just think we make the best of it. At least you're with Claudia and your family. It'll do you good to spend proper time with them and I won't be on my own here either.'

'What are you saying?' Molly fumbled with the key card to her room. 'That you're not going to try and get another flight even after Christmas? There must be something available before the New Year. From Heathrow, Birmingham, Bristol. Anywhere. I'm here for two weeks.'

'Molly.' There was a heartbeat of a pause. 'Please try and understand.'

'Understand what?' She closed the door of her room a little too hard.

Except she did understand. Somehow she'd known for months that there was a problem, years even. Perhaps even from before her mum's diagnosis there were niggling issues. Everything had been pushed to the back of her mind as she'd focused on her parents rather than her relationship with Howard.

'We need to talk when you get back.' His voice was resolute, as if he'd rehearsed the line.

'What's really going on, Howard?'

'I'm going to spend Christmas with my parents. You're with your sister. It's all good; you're where you should be. And I'm where I want to be.'

Where I want to be.

That was all he needed to say.

'You didn't even go to the airport this morning, did you?' Molly sat on the bed with a thump. 'You just went straight to your parents. That's the real reason you delayed flying out here, because you never intended to come. Why on earth didn't you talk to me when I was home?'

'You'd just sold your parents' house. Honestly, Molly, your emotions were all over the place, it didn't seem like the right time to say—'

'And this does! When I'm miles away in Iceland, waiting for you to get here so we can have a Christmas together that's finally filled with...' What? Joy? Laughter? Hope? Jolly festive vibes? All the things that had been missing for the last few years. Was she really in the right mental state to embrace the holidays and rediscover the joy she'd once had? It was no wonder Howard had chosen his family over her.

Molly smoothed out a crease in her skirt. 'I know these past couple of years have been unbelievably hard – on both of us. I've not been there for you and I know I can't have been easy to live with. But I thought being here was the chance for us to spend time together.'

Silence. Where was he? Tucked away in his old room in his parents' five-bed Shropshire home: architect designed and modern with underfloor heating, all white walls and clean lines, no creaky floorboards in the place. It was what he was used to and what he liked. Had he fled there because it was easier than dealing with her and her messed up emotions? What sort of relationship did they really have?

'I'm sorry, Molly,' he finally said.

Through the window, the daylight made the white snow blindingly bright against the ash-grey clouds that had rolled in. Snow was falling thickly, and to think she'd been worried about him driving from the airport. Now it made sense why he'd been adamant about hiring a car; he hadn't wanted Claudia or Elvar making the journey to pick him up when he'd never intended to come.

Molly prepared herself for the truth.

'What are you really trying to say?' She let her words hang and the silence grow. The only sound was his breathing in her ear and the wind swirling snow flurries against the window. She wasn't going to wait until they were back home together for an answer. 'Are you breaking up with me?'

'Molly...'

'Just answer me, Howard! Are you breaking up with me?'

A beat of silence that seemed to last forever.

'Yes,' he finally said. 'I'm sorry, Molly. I've been feeling this way for a while, there's just never been a good time. You've been so upset and when we are together you don't talk to me. We live together, but we're not really together, are we? We haven't been for a long time.'

'I've not talked to you because when I do I'm conscious of not unloading on you, and as for the other stuff...' She trailed off. She didn't know what to say. It was impossible to put into words how much she wanted him to just hold her, to show her he loved her in any other way than trying to instigate sex, but he never did. His focus had always been on the physical side of things, although even that was a distant memory. What she'd needed was for him to actually be there for her, to hold her with no expectation of it leading to anything more than a cuddle. She'd desperately needed love – gentle and heartfelt, someone to care and look out for her without her having to ask.

'I think we'll be better off going our separate ways—'

'You coward.' Spits of ice hitting the window mirrored her heart battering her chest. All her anger, sadness, loneliness, uncertainty and stress smashed together making her want to scream, to rage, to shake him, but he hadn't even allowed her that. 'How could you do this? After everything I've been through.'

'I thought if we talked at home you wouldn't go to Iceland at all.'

'And that would have messed up your Christmas plans, wouldn't it? You total bastard.'

'You've hardly been easy to talk to, Moll. You're constantly upset—'

'With good reason! You have no idea. In one breath you're complaining I haven't talked to you, the next I'm not easy to talk to. Which is it?'

Yet more silence.

'Actually you've just answered my question by not talking to me about any of this till now. I don't remember you once really asking how I am or allowing me the opportunity to talk to you, because I've known all along you don't want to hear it. These last two years I've dealt with everything on my own because you've not been there for me.'

'I'm sorry you feel like this.'

'Is there someone else?'

'Let's not talk about this now. We will when you get home.'

'That's nearly two weeks away. You're assuming I can carry on as if nothing's happened. You've changed everything, yet you're refusing to talk about it. I deserve to know the truth.'

'Molly, you're angry and upset, so we're going to stop this conversation now,' he said firmly.

She barely heard anything else. He might have said something about being home when she got back, that they would talk properly then. He'd taken control and by doing what he'd done when she was miles away in Iceland, he'd removed himself from the situation.

He'd been intent and calculating; she wondered how long he'd been planning this. How long had he not wanted to be with her? A wave of nausea rushed up her throat. Her hands were sweaty, her chest tight, her eyes stinging with tears. Beyond the sound of the swirling wind outside, there was silence. Heartbreak added to her unresolved grief. Even somewhere as incredible as this, she couldn't escape the feelings. Everything felt like a lie. She was in one of the guest suites because Claudia had wanted to treat her and Howard to a proper holiday. Saying they deserved it. It was a room for couples; it should have been her and Howard repairing their relationship. Apparently, it needed more than just patching.

The truth was out. The unsettled feeling and her uncertainty over the past few months hadn't been a figment of her imagination. No, in Howard's mind they'd been over for a while, he just hadn't had the guts to talk to her, to tell her the truth face to face. He'd taken the coward's way out, free of conflict so he could head to his parents' for a perfect family Christmas.

Much like the way her past kept echoing around her, the

threads of her future disintegrated. Everything she'd envisaged drifted away, like the steam spiralling and dispersing into the icy air on the riverbank opposite. Not that she'd really been certain of what she'd wanted, particularly when there'd been such a strain between her and Howard, but she hadn't been ready to throw away seven years together without even trying to make things work. What on earth was she supposed to do now?

9

Molly went through the rest of the day in a daze, hiding away in her room, not wanting to face anyone, least of all her sister. 'I told you so' was the last thing she needed to hear. She lay on the sofa in front of the wood burner feeling too numb to even cry.

It was only when Alda came knocking after everyone had returned that she realised she couldn't hide away however much she wanted to. If she did, questions would definitely be asked. She promised Alda she'd join her in the lounge, then she washed away her tears and reapplied her make-up. She told herself she would continue with the lie that Howard had spun her – that he'd missed his flight and as it was so close to Christmas he'd gone to his parents' house instead. Of course she knew how lame it sounded, but she could sell it as the truth.

Still in their outdoor gear, Kat and Lils passed her in the glass walkway, laughing together about Kat's impressive tumble while ice skating. They smiled and said they'd see her at dinner. The questions about Howard would be inevitable, so she decided to find Claudia first and explain so she at least wouldn't bring up the subject at the table; perhaps then no one else would comment on his absence.

Claudia, lighting the candles on the restaurant tables, spotted Molly the second she entered.

'Where's Howard?' She frowned as she held a match to a candle in a glass holder. 'Shouldn't he have arrived by now?'

'He missed his flight,' Molly said as calmly as she could.

Claudia's head shot up, her eyebrows furrowed. 'He what?'

'Missed his flight. He's going to stay with his parents for Christmas. He'll sort something out for the New Year.' And now her own lie had accidently popped out. 'I'm so sorry if this has messed things up for you.'

Claudia appraised her coolly. 'It's no problem for me, it's you I'm worried about. You must be upset.'

'It's fine; these things happen.'

Claudia's disbelieving look suggested the opposite but she didn't push it further as the guests started to arrive for dinner. The restaurant was about to open too, so Claudia welcomed everyone, bustling about, opening wine and being a good host, asking if everyone had enjoyed the day in Reykjavík. The conversation around the table was focused on that, and Molly could quietly listen.

Claudia had cleared away the extra plate setting for Howard, so at least it wasn't obvious that he was missing. Molly had also noticed her whisper something to Elvar. No one else said anything and Leifur was the only other person who would be likely to notice, but he arrived late with his daughter Birta. Wearing a festive party dress with her hair in bunches and a shy smile, she stole all the attention, much to Molly's relief. Only Elvar, after the main course was served, acknowledged Howard's absence with a comforting hand on her shoulder and a hushed, 'Are you okay?'

'I'm fine, thanks,' Molly mumbled, desperate to hold it together as she focused on her plate of pork fillet with creamy mash and wilted kale.

James engaged Birta with stories of her dad when he was younger, slowly bringing her out of her shell. There were big personalities around the table: Kat and Lils chatted with ease, the conversation free-flowing between them and James, Leifur and Claudia. Graham, Maggie, and even Jen chipped in every so often.

The happiness that flowed around her accentuated Molly's sadness. If she'd been feeling lonely before, being dumped on the cusp of Christmas multiplied that feeling tenfold. She toyed with her food, chewing small mouthfuls of the tender pork that was doing nothing to settle the churning in her stomach. She'd lost everything; first her parents and now Howard. She'd been languishing in a pedestrian job she wasn't passionate about and putting up with a relationship that had become stagnant, long before outside forces pushed them further apart. Had they just bumbled along because it had felt easy and was what was expected? She was nearly thirty-five and yet any talk of the next step of getting married or having kids had been dismissed by both of them for various reasons, neither of them wanting to rock the boat, yet neither of them actually being happy.

It didn't help that Claudia and Elvar had the strongest relationship of anyone Molly knew and that included her parents. They worked together and raised their kids in a true partnership filled with love and support. Claudia wasn't one for romantic gestures, so the occasional touch, a look or a smile between them meant so much and was noticeable. Celebrating thirty years of marriage, Graham and Maggie seemed pretty content too, while James and Jen and even Leifur being here with his daughter accentuated how alone she was. Perhaps she needed to spend

more time with Kat and Lils, but then again, there was a solid
relationship there, their friendship having survived all the ups
and downs of life.

As their plates were cleared away and rye bread ice cream
with rhubarb syrup was brought out, Molly politely chatted to
Graham before their attention was diverted to a raucous conversation between James and Leifur about the first time they'd gone
snowboarding together. James had been brave – or stupid –
enough to attempt a red slope at the end of his first day, resulting
in bruised knees, a sore bottom and his pride dented.

Other people's happiness only increased the heaviness in her
heart, so as soon as dinner was over, Molly feigned tiredness,
saying no to a drink and escaping to her room instead.

Standing by the window gazing out at the suffocating darkness, she felt detached from her emotions, as if the iciness
outside had penetrated her very being, leaving only numbness
and an ache in her chest.

She wasn't surprised when there was a knock on her door a
little while later. With a sigh she padded over and opened it.

Claudia was standing in the chilly hallway with a frown.

'Are you okay?'

'I'm fine,' Molly said tightly.

Claudia folded her arms. 'You can talk to me, you know.'

'I know.' Molly shrugged, yet she stopped herself from saying
anything else.

'You can't continue to keep everything bottled up.' Claudia
gave her a weak smile and left.

Molly sat on the end of her bed. It wasn't just being with her
happily married sister or the presence of other people in solid
relationships that was getting to her, but it was also this place. Its
peace and beauty were almost otherworldly, the picture windows
looking out on a view that would have remained unchanged for

centuries. The snow pure and untainted, the river wild yet somehow soothing. She should have been sharing the experience with Howard. That's how things were supposed to be. She and Howard should be out there now in the hot tub, sipping wine, relishing the warm bubbling water while an icy breeze chilled their faces.

It wasn't helpful to dwell on the 'what ifs'. There were a lot surrounding the last year. What if her mum hadn't got ill; what if her dad had coped better; what if they hadn't gone through the trauma of him suffering a catastrophic heart attack; what if she'd actually shared her pain and sadness with her sister; what if she'd paid more attention to Howard; what if he'd helped her more...

What if, what if, what if, WHAT IF!

Molly grabbed a pillow, buried her head in it and screamed.

It didn't change a thing. But, as she loosened her grip and let the pillow fall to her lap, she had released a little of her pent-up anger. Claudia had been completely right about her bottling everything up. In order to feel in control, she'd constantly tried to supress her feelings and now, after what Howard had done, it was as if the cork had popped. Not in a celebratory bottle of champagne sort of way, but in a grief-stricken one, which was accentuated by being somewhere she'd once felt happy and carefree.

Her coping mechanism when she was around other people had been to keep her emotions in check by not talking about things, not with Howard, her friends, not even her sister, and when she did, her matter-of-fact way of speaking didn't betray how she was really feeling.

She scrunched the corner of the pillow. Perhaps it had been a mistake not talking to Howard, because her true feelings had tainted their life with sadness and a hopelessness that had permeated their relationship and home. He'd given up on her, that was the truth of it. And yet, hadn't she given up on him too?

If she'd truly been invested in their relationship and believed they had a future together with the possibility of marriage and perhaps children, wouldn't she have let him in, shared her heartache and talked to him? The same way he should have been there for her. They'd both been pushing each other away.

Molly threw the pillow onto the bed and wandered over to the window. The weather had improved from earlier. She could see along the curve of the river to one of the hot tubs perched on the bank. James and Jen were submerged together for a post-dinner dip, looking relaxed as they gazed up at the clear, star-dusted night. Perhaps there would be a chance of seeing the sky dance with the northern lights tonight.

She turned away, aware that she was spying on their private time. There was every chance of seeing the northern lights from the hot tub, but there was something even more special about driving out into the night. Elvar loved doing that, bumping along snowy tracks into the wilderness, giving a handful of guests a true adventure, only stopping when the darkness was absolute.

Despite feeling emotionally battered, she wasn't sure she'd be able to sleep, not while constantly mulling over where it had gone wrong with Howard, wondering what he was doing, how he'd explained the situation to his parents, whether he felt any remorse after discarding her.

What she needed was a distraction.

Molly felt bad about not opening up to her sister before; Claudia was owed an explanation about what had happened with Howard, particularly when she'd treated them to a romantic suite that could have gone to paying guests. She couldn't keep shutting Claudia out, even if it felt too hard to tell her the truth. No good would come out of lying; it would only delay the process of beginning to heal and move on.

Molly made herself leave her room and came across Claudia

in the entrance hall holding a tray with two mugs of hot chocolate.

'I'm taking this out to James and Jen,' Claudia said. 'Grab the door, could you.'

Molly opened it and followed her out. The short walk to the hot tub was bracing. Claudia was hardened to this lifestyle, but Molly's teeth were chattering just a few paces along the path. Wondering why she'd even come out, she didn't continue all the way, but at least the chill blast had gone some way to clearing her head.

Claudia paced back up the path with the empty tray.

'What on earth's going on, Molly?' A fog of white puffed into the dark as she strode past her and pushed open the door to the lodge.

'Nothing.'

Everything.

Once again, her initial reaction was to avoid telling Claudia the truth. But to what end? How long was she going to keep her feelings to herself, unwilling to open up and share the burden with her family who loved her? She couldn't carry on like this; she didn't need to.

Claudia tutted as she made her way to the stairs that led to her apartment. 'Don't talk rubbish. It's not like Howard to miss his flight. If that's what really happened.' She paused. 'Besides, if that was the case, why hasn't he just booked another one? There must have been a later flight or ones available at another airport?'

Molly sighed and followed her upstairs and into the living room, which was a smaller and even cosier version of the downstairs guest lounge. Claudia flopped onto the sofa in front of the fire and patted the space next to her. 'Finn and Alda are in their rooms; Elvar's outside and Leifur's with Birta. We can talk. *If* you want to.'

Molly sighed again, but sat down. She'd come to find her sister to talk to her, so what was she waiting for?

'He didn't miss his flight,' she said quietly.

'I didn't think so.'

Molly still felt like a child around Claudia, the difference in their ages always giving Claudia the authority.

'What was his reason?' Claudia asked.

'He thought if he told me when I was back home that he wanted to spend Christmas with his parents, I'd refuse to come out here.'

Claudia gripped the edge of a cushion. 'So what you're saying is, it's not just that he wanted to have Christmas with his parents, but he didn't want to have Christmas with you?'

'Shit, Claudia! You don't need to spell it out!'

'Sorry, I didn't mean it to come out quite like that.'

Hot tears pricked at Molly's eyes. The numbness that had been present since the phone call was slowly morphing into anger and sorrow. 'It's the truth though, not just about not wanting to spend Christmas together, but that he doesn't want to be with me any longer.'

'He broke up with you?'

Molly nodded but couldn't look at her sister, still wanting to hold it together.

'He broke up with you,' Claudia repeated in disbelief. 'Over the phone, just before Christmas and your birthday.'

'I honestly don't think he intended to; it's just I pushed him. I wanted to understand why he hadn't talked to me and why he let me believe that he was going to join me out here.'

'Stop making excuses for him.' Claudia's words flared with anger. 'He was calculating; of course he would have expected you to question him. When has he ever been late in his life? He's completely anal about being on time, fastidiously neat. So don't you dare think that you pushed him into breaking up; what else do you think he was doing?'

Molly was losing the battle with her emotions. It hurt so badly, that ache in her heart that had consumed her since her mum's diagnosis. Now it was burning hot and angry like the thermal water bubbling beneath the snow-covered landscape.

'Is there someone else?' Claudia asked more gently.

'Apparently not.' Although, when Molly thought about it, through the fuzzy haze of shock, she wasn't even sure if he'd answered her question. He often worked late and had been away a lot since his promotion; he'd had plenty of opportunities to have an affair.

'You know, I've got a right mind to ring him and give him hell.'

'You're not going to do that,' Molly said firmly.

'Of course I won't, but how dare he treat you like this after everything you've been through.' Molly heard the wobble in Claudia's voice. Was she feeling even more protective now they'd lost their mum? The whole dynamic of their family had changed since losing their parents in quick succession. All of them were still adjusting.

'It's not been easy for anyone,' Molly said quietly. 'We've all been through hell; Howard included.'

'There you go again, making excuses. He hasn't been there for you when you needed him. He didn't step up and that's unforgivable.'

'It's been a challenging time for everyone.'

'Yes! Yes it has, but even so, that's never an excuse to not support your partner through a crappy time. Especially through a crappy time. Through sickness and health, remember.'

'We're not married.'

'Doesn't matter; if he loved you, he'd have been there for you regardless of how difficult it was and is.'

Molly heard the truth in Claudia's words. She stared at the flames flaring amber and claret in the grate, sending light flickering over the evergreen boughs that were decorated with gold pinecones and deep red berries strung along the mantel. 'There were cracks in our relationship before – he was stressed with work, with his new role, leading a massive team. He's been working loads and away a lot. I've not been around either.'

'You're too nice, Moll.' Claudia tentatively squeezed her knee. 'And, you may not see it now, but he's done you a favour.'

Anger sparked again. 'You've never liked him, so of course you'd say that.'

'It's not that I dislike him, it's just I've seen him for what he is. He's held you back, just like Dad held Mum back.'

'That's utter rubbish and you know it!'

'No, it's you who doesn't know what Dad was like when he was younger. When you were growing up he behaved completely differently to when I was a child.'

Molly shook her head, not wanting to accept what her sister was saying. Claudia had always been hard on their dad and they'd always jarred, probably because they were too similar – not that either of them would ever have admitted that.

'He was hellbent on making a success of his business and had little time for anything else,' Claudia ploughed on. 'He wasn't easy to live with. And as for Mum. She had such ambition but she felt pressured into staying home, being a mum and looking after Dad and us. Gardening and baking were her passions, but if she'd been born at a different time or if Dad had been different, more amenable, more forward thinking, less bloody restrictive and downright sexist, she'd have been able to turn her hobby into a career. I've witnessed Howard do the same with you—'

'You're wrong. I have a job.'

'A job, yes, not a career, not a true vocation, despite having a passion you'd love to turn into your livelihood.'

Molly launched herself from the sofa as if she'd been struck by a hot poker. 'This isn't fair turning my upset at what Howard's done back onto me. Yes, I have dreams and ambition that I haven't yet fulfilled, but you can hardly place all the blame on Howard – how the hell do you think I could have done anything for myself over the last couple of years? You have no right to talk about this because you weren't there.'

Claudia's face crumpled at Molly's words. They stared at each other for a moment, Molly's blood boiling hot as lava.

'No, you're right,' Claudia said quietly. 'I wasn't there. I just saw this coming and I'm sorry you're having to deal with this on top of everything else.'

Molly didn't want to be cross with her sister, but most of all she didn't want to continue to feel this broken. A sob caught in her throat. 'It's all too much to deal with. I knew things weren't right, but I didn't expect this. Everything that's familiar, everything I love, oh... It's all ending and I don't know how to carry on like this.'

'Hey, hey, it's okay, Moll.' Claudia looked startled, her nostrils flaring as if she was trying to dampen her own feelings. 'You're not on your own. You understand that, right? We can't change what he's done, but we can support you. *I* can support you.' She leaned forward to grasp Molly's hand and looked at her in a way she couldn't decipher. Firelight danced across her face, catching her angular cheekbones. It was the warmth of Claudia's hand, her presence and gentle, unexpected touch that meant the most. 'Tell you what. Elvar's decided to take the guests out in about half an hour. There should be a decent chance of seeing the northern lights. Go with them. Clear your head, have a think, have a cry. You'll feel better for it. Embrace being here and try to forget about Howard – for a while at least.'

10

The panic that had built up in Molly's chest was fleeting and for once she was grateful for Claudia's unsentimental, practical side, talking her out of a pit of despair and into doing something that would temporarily take her mind off things. So she took her advice and got ready to head out with Elvar, understanding that if she went to bed she'd only lie there tossing and turning, getting more and more upset. There was something in what Claudia had suggested, to try and forget about Howard and make the most of her time in Iceland, because right now, she felt so let down she didn't even want to think about him, which meant she needed to feign happiness or at least appear to be okay. Claudia knew the truth, which meant Elvar soon would, but beyond that it would be her secret. Wasn't pretending to be okay exactly what she'd been doing for months and months on end, keeping going even when she felt she was falling apart? Why would it be any different now?

At ten-thirty, Molly met the others in the lodge's entrance hall. Kat and Lils were wrapped up so much their faces were barely visible, while Graham and Maggie were wearing matching blue

Gortex coats. They seemed to be perfectly suited to one another and it made Molly wonder what the chances were of her finding that perfect person; someone who was a joy to be around, who she could talk to about anything, who was there for her without question through the good and bad times, who just got her. Being honest with herself, it wasn't Howard. It had never been Howard, however much she'd hoped he was 'the one'. She'd been living a lie for longer than she cared to admit.

'Jen's not joining us?' Elvar asked as James entered the hallway on his own.

'She is,' he said apologetically. 'She's just drying her hair.'

Elvar nodded and carried on explaining where they were going while they waited for Jen. Elvar was in his element and his enthusiasm for heading out in the freezing cold at night was infectious. Wrapped up in thermals, coats, boots, hats and gloves, as soon as Jen joined them, they all bundled outside and into the 4x4.

Unlike the day Molly had arrived when the cloudy sky had been heavy with snow, the night was dark and clear, much colder too, the wind chill dropping the temperature significantly, the conditions ideal for the night sky's true beauty to be revealed – if they were lucky.

Elvar didn't drive for too long, just far enough to an elevated area of snow-covered lava fields so the darkness wasn't polluted with light from the village in the valley. In daylight it was possible to see for miles to a backdrop of mountains with nothing but white in every direction, all the way down to the snarling grey ocean. Now nothing was visible apart from the dark sky swirled with stars.

The iciness hit Molly the moment she got out of the 4x4, the freezing wind whipping flurries of snow into her face. Elvar switched off the headlights, plunging them into darkness. It took a moment for Molly to get her bearings before Elvar led them a little way through the snow and pointed them north, to the wide open sky, its vastness speckled with stars that glinted like millions of silver lights.

'Now we wait,' he said.

Molly knew he was grinning. Even if he wasn't going to spend the whole time standing out with them, she understood how much he craved being out in the wild, encouraging guests – and his family and friends – to embrace the empty but beautiful landscape.

They all stood together. Occasional hushed chatter filtered through the group as they gazed up at the sky in wonder. They were high up and the wind whistled around them. An icy dampness stung Molly's cheeks and made her fogged breath puff into the night. Compacted snow creaked as every few minutes someone would pace about in an attempt to warm up. Snow coated a lonely tree, the barrenness compounded by the deep powder covering everything, adding to the silence.

Yes, it would be more comfortable back at the lodge looking out on the night while sitting beside a roaring fire, but Molly felt unexpectedly free standing out in the cold. It was a feeling she hadn't had in a long time and it wasn't just because of what had happened with Howard; she'd been trapped by responsibility and grief.

Molly admired Kat and Lils's sisterly friendship, something she felt she'd never really had with Claudia. They were standing together, their chatter indiscernible even in the quiet of the night, while Graham and Maggie had wandered off a little way, their arms linked as they gazed up together. Elvar was around, wandering between them and the 4x4, so she didn't feel like a third wheel with Jen and James, not that they were doing the loved-up couple thing. Jen was pacing about, looking at her phone as much as at the sky.

By the time they'd been standing out for nearly an hour, the cold had really set in. Even Kat and Lils's chatter had become sporadic. Molly was glad of her thermals beneath her outer layers, and her new hooded fleece kept the heat in, yet even so, the cold was seeping through. The tip of her nose was freezing, her fingers too, despite being encased in thermal gloves.

'Oh God,' Jen said through chattering teeth. 'I was expecting it to be cold but not this blooming cold.'

'It'll be worth it if the northern lights show,' Molly said. 'There's supposed to be a decent chance of seeing them tonight, although it's never guaranteed.'

It was hard to make out Jen's expression with a snood pulled up over her nose. Molly didn't like to mention there would be almost as much chance of catching sight of the northern lights from the comfort of the lodge.

'I can't use my phone with these damn gloves on.' Jen shoved her iPhone back in the pocket of her coat and stomped her feet; Molly wasn't sure if it was an attempt to keep warm or simply a childlike gesture.

Elvar's voice carried across from somewhere behind them. 'You are welcome to keep warm in the jeep. I'll bring over a hot chocolate in a moment too.'

'Oh, you're a lifesaver.' Jen spun around and set off through the deep snow. 'You don't mind do you, James?' she called back.

He waved a hand in reply. 'It's not her cup of tea,' he said under his breath, glancing back as if to check she'd gone. 'The cold, standing about not doing anything. It's all part of the experience but she gets bored easily. Not that she's particularly keen on adventure either...'

Molly raised an eyebrow, surprised that they'd come to Iceland if she didn't like any of those things.

Elvar timed handing out mugs of creamy hot chocolate perfectly, just before the bitter cold felt overwhelming. It smelt divine, the warmth welcome through her gloves as she cupped the mug, the steam snatched into the air by the wind.

'Adventure is kinda at the heart of what they do,' Molly said once Elvar had returned to the jeep with a hot chocolate for Jen.

'Yeah, that goes without saying and what I'm most excited about.'

'They've always chased adventure and that adrenalin rush. At least my sister has for as long as I can remember.'

'And Elvar's the same, right?' James said. 'Not that I know him well, but Leifur's an adrenalin junkie. Ever since I first met him, he's been dragging me off to climb some mountain or hike in the middle of nowhere.'

'Like that summer we all went wild camping.' Molly scrunched her nose at the memory and glanced at James, his cheeks red with cold. 'I think I was rather self-absorbed back then and yes, probably a bit focused on Leifur.'

'It's not surprising; he's a good guy.'

'I remember lots of group chats late into the night, but I don't think we ever got the chance to talk properly.'

'I was rather self-absorbed too. There'd been a lot going on in my life. I spent most of my twenties trying to figure things out. I loved being here though. It felt easy, out in the wild, with good friends, hiking all day and getting back to basics. I've missed all of this.' He sighed a breath of frozen air and looked around them. 'Leifur's been saying for years to come out and stay. But life has a habit of taking over. Me and Jen have both been working a lot this year and we hadn't been away together. We usually go some-where hot for a couple of weeks in the winter – Jen's choice I

should add – and she suggested we do what I wanted this time...'
He sounded reflective as he trailed off.

'But like you said, it's not her thing.' Molly had sensed that
from the moment she'd arrived. 'I'm sure she'll be happier once
she warms up.'

'I think she had this romantic notion that we'd stand out here
for fifteen minutes and ta da! The northern lights would appear
on cue and dance across the sky.' He gestured with a gloved hand
to the dark night. Stars were scattered across the endless space,
but no hint of the aurora borealis. The uncertainty was part of the
fun and then of course the surprise and wonder when they did
show made it all worthwhile.

A mouth-watering smell of hotdogs drifted towards them
from the jeep – Elvar's midnight treat whether the northern lights
showed or not. Molly had been worried about being on her own,
but everyone was friendly and now Jen had deserted James, he
seemed happy enough to keep her company.

James stamped his feet and pulled his coat sleeves over his
padded gloves. 'Unlike Jen, I knew it was going to be this cold, but
the reality is even colder than I remember.' He laughed frozen
breath into the night air.

Molly smiled as she sipped the hot chocolate, relishing the
warmth as she swallowed. 'I find standing out in the cold waiting
for the lights to show – if they show – is all part of the fun.'

'Nature's unpredictable.'

'It wouldn't be special if it wasn't.'

James glanced at her. 'You must struggle being so far away
from your sister?'

'It's kinda all I've known. It feels like Claudia and Elvar have
been together forever. They had a whirlwind romance and within
months she'd moved out here to live with him.'

'You've never been tempted to come and join her?'

'Oh, this is her life, not mine.'

'And where's yours? Remind me where you live?'

'Cheltenham.' She almost said *with Howard* then remembered she was trying not to think about him. 'A nice part of the world but not a patch on Iceland. How about you? I know you were at Liverpool Uni with Leifur, but have you always lived in Scotland?'

'For the most part. I was born there and only left Scotland to go to uni, and apart from travelling for a few months with Leifur after graduating, I headed home.'

'When did you meet Jen?'

'Three years ago. We got engaged in April last year.' She couldn't make out his expression but his voice sounded tight – although that might have had something to do with the cold. 'We met at a New Year's Eve party in Edinburgh. My opening line was "I'm James and I own a castle". I was drunk and showing off but it was rather misleading.'

'In that you don't own a castle?' Molly was confused. She may have been captivated by Leifur that summer, but she was certain she'd have remembered talk of James owning a castle.

'Oh, I do, but at the time I technically didn't, at least not all of it and I didn't live there most of the time either.'

Molly frowned. 'I have so many questions!'

'Most people do.'

'Go on then, tell me.' Molly gestured at the surrounding darkness. 'We have time.'

'It was my grandparents' castle in Perthshire – fourteen bedrooms, a great hall, formal garden plus forty acres of fields and woodland. It's idyllic but a monster of a place to look after, although it was their whole life. They lived and breathed it and worked damn hard, never going on holiday and giving up all sorts of things, ploughing everything they had into maintaining it. They ran it as a successful hotel for years and they never really retired but things got difficult when my grandad's health deteriorated. They transferred a large share of the castle to me so I wouldn't get hit with an obscene amount of inheritance tax and be forced to sell it. They retained a share and were still able to remain living there.'

'It was passed to you and not your parents?'

'Oh, aye.' He looked from her to the night sky. 'I never knew my father and my mother died when I was in my early twenties; not that she was around for much of my life anyway.'

'I'm so sorry.'

He shrugged. 'My grandparents raised me. They loved the place. It had been bought by Grandad's grandfather, so in the family for a while.'

'Not an easy place to give up, I imagine.'

'Aye, not easy at all. And then when Grandad died, my granny just gave up. She passed away only six months later, I believe of a broken heart.'

His openness caught her unawares.

'I'm so sorry, that must have been incredibly hard to deal with.' *I know how hard that must have been.* She had a strong desire to spill her heart to him too, but she stopped herself.

'She was a real romantic, my granny. She was overjoyed when I got engaged to Jen. For a time it brought a bit of a spark back into her life, the idea of planning a wedding. But of course, it couldn't erase her loss.'

The bitter cold heightened the sorrow inside Molly's chest. She found her voice. 'So you kept the castle?'

'I managed to, mainly because my grandparents had been pretty savvy, like I said, transferring part of the equity of the castle to me. They'd always been careful with their money and had a good financial advisor, so it meant I was able to keep it, which is what they wanted.'

'Is it what you wanted though?'

'Oh aye, I love it. For the most part, it was my childhood home, somewhere I'd be devastated to give up.'

'Do you live there now?'

He finished his hot chocolate, placed the mug on the snow and shoved his gloved hands into his coat pockets. 'I wish. I spend as much time there as I can. I work part time for Forestry and Land Scotland – I cut my hours to help my grandparents more. But our life is in Edinburgh – that's where Jen works, although I travel about a lot for my work and then spend the rest of my time focusing on the castle. I rent out some of the land and have secured a grant to renovate the oldest part of the castle. It's a juggle.'

'Would you want to turn it back into a hotel like your grandparents had?'

He shrugged. 'It needs a lot of thought. Jen likes the idea of running it as a boutique hotel, but the reality is hard work. I think it would be better to Airbnb the rooms or to hold creative retreats there. Lots of the castle needs renovating but there's so much potential. Alistair, the groundskeeper, and his wife, who was my grandparents' housekeeper, still live in the gatehouse cottage and keep the place ticking over, plus there are another two cottages on the grounds that are rented to holidaymakers all year round already. I want to do lots of the work myself but Jen doesn't have the patience. She's a successful solicitor with a serious work ethic and is desperate to stay in Edinburgh. If it was down to her, she'd sell it and invest some of the money in an Edinburgh townhouse.'

'I take it that's the last thing you want?'

'Absolutely. It belongs to my family. The first few years of my life were er, haphazard and rather challenging. I was four when I went to live with my grandparents; they and the castle were my one constant and the only stability in my life. I loved them and I love the place. It's old and a good chunk of it where my grandparents lived is dated, but it's in pretty decent condition and the sense of history is extraordinary. It needs commitment, hard work and a huge dose of passion to breathe life back into it, but it's the only place I've ever thought of as home and I won't give it up without a fight. It would break my heart to end up having to sell it.'

'I know how that feels, at least on a smaller scale, through selling my parents' house – it was Grade I listed but certainly not a castle.' She said it matter-of-factly, not wanting him to pick up on any emotion.

'Was that recently?'

Molly nodded, a plume of white releasing into the still dark night as she sighed. 'Not long ago and it was a necessity after losing both of my parents. I know something of your loss.'

'I'm so sorry you've been through heartache too.'

They were both quiet for a moment as they gazed upwards. Molly moved the conversation on to the history of James's castle, then told him what little she'd known about Ashford House. Elvar brought over some hotdogs and they greedily munched on them while the sky remained stubbornly dark.

Far from being bored or annoyed, she enjoyed standing out in the cold. After endless months feeling trapped and stressed with the house sale and paperwork issues, her mind constantly focused on things she didn't want to be thinking about, she felt free. Out here, she could pretend that everything was fine. Even without the northern lights making an appearance, there was wild beauty in the endless sky.

'I think we will have to call it a night.' Elvar's voice rang out across the barren landscape as he gestured to the sky that had failed to show them even a hint of its magic. 'There will be other chances.'

No one argued as they trudged back to the 4x4, the snow creaking beneath their boots.

'That's it?' Jen asked as they all clambered in and did up their seatbelts.

'Nature's unpredictable,' James said, repeating the words he'd said to Molly earlier. He glanced back, caught her eye and gave her a knowing look.

Molly settled on the back seat next to Graham and Maggie, and Elvar started the engine.

'Well, that was a huge waste of time,' Jen muttered as they left behind the cold and unforgiving landscape and headed back towards the lodge and the promise of warmth and comfy beds.

11

Although Molly was glad to climb into bed and sink beneath the covers, she'd been sorry to cut short her conversation with James. First impressions were funny – he'd been friendly and up for a laugh when she first met him ten years ago, although it was the attractively single Leifur she'd fancied. But being back together now, it was interesting how quickly she'd felt drawn to him. Perhaps it was from years spent working in HR, sitting in on disciplinary meetings and interviews, that she'd got good at sensing who a person was in a short space of time.

Molly couldn't understand how the beauty of Iceland's snow-covered landscape had been lost on Jen. Perhaps the land of fire and ice would begin to work its charms and by the time Jen left, she'd be won over by dreamy winter nights and adventurous snow-filled days. Much like Claudia and Elvar's chalk and cheese personalities, James seemed completely different to Jen, although Molly didn't know them well enough to understand if their differences complemented each other or if they had nothing in common. All she knew was that James was as friendly as Jen was downbeat. She appreciated how he was able to laugh at himself, a quality that had always been missing in Howard.

Despite the late-night stargazing, Molly woke early, worries swirling around her head and the wind whistling outside. Conscious of the empty bed next to her, she was unable to get back to sleep. She'd been left reeling from Howard's callousness. While yesterday she'd felt numb, now a fire flared in the pit of her stomach along with a desire to rage at him. Except he was hundreds of miles away in the warm embrace of his family. While she'd lost her parents, he'd escaped to his, not allowing her the chance to confront him, nor having the decency to be honest to her face.

She grabbed her phone from the bedside table. Without thinking it through, she called him. It rang and rang then went to answerphone. His familiar voice asked her to leave a message. She didn't. She chucked the phone on the bed. Of course he wasn't going to answer. The reason he'd done what he'd done was to avoid an awkward confrontation.

Claudia's words about him having done her a favour played over and over as she showered and got dressed. It had always been obvious to Molly that Claudia had never believed she and Howard were a good fit, and now he'd proved her right. Shouldn't she be more upset than she was? Yes, she was angry at his timing, at his cowardice, but wasn't there a small part of her that was relieved to not have to share all of this with him or to have to make the effort to try to fix their relationship?

Tomorrow, Christmas Eve, she was turning thirty-five. It felt like a milestone age, one where she ought to be settled and happy, whereas she was anything but. She knew she shouldn't compare herself to other people, but at the same age, Claudia had been married and living in Iceland for over ten years. So many of her friends were married or in long-term relationships, with kids and careers they were passionate about. Comparing herself to other people was futile and wasn't going to make her feel any better, but she couldn't help it. Howard had pulled the rug from under her, removing himself from her life and leaving her scrabbling about wondering how the hell she was going to fix things. First she needed time to heal. Perhaps that was how she should use what remained of her time in Iceland, to figure out her life so she had a solid plan for when she confronted Howard.

Molly breathed deeply, knowing if she didn't keep a firm grip on all of her sadness and uncertainty, she'd fall to pieces. She'd put on her make-up and face the world; she was relieved to have other things to focus on and the company of her family.

Before leaving the room, she paused in front of the mirror. In thermal waterproof trousers and her fleece hoody, she looked set for a day out exploring the south coast. Her chestnut hair was wavy and looked glossy in the glow of the lights. She breathed deeply and studied herself, the lines on her forehead showing the stress, her choice of berry-pink lipstick a warpaint.

I can do this, she told herself.

She would take things day by day and use the unexpected time alone to fix herself. She would work out what to do next and how to approach the New Year as a thirty-five-year-old newly single woman.

The drive along the south coast would be the last day out until after Christmas. Molly knew that Claudia would have insisted that the festivities be centred around the lodge – spending time as a family with the guests, eating, drinking, soaking in one of the hot tubs and having a swim in the naturally heated swimming pool. Christmas traditions were a mix of Icelandic and British, but for a brief time, they would focus on home rather than adventure.

Despite Molly offering to help, Claudia insisted that Molly went out for the day, while she stayed home with Alda to focus on preparing for Christmas. Finn rode in the front of the ten-seater 4x4 with Elvar, while Molly found herself at the back by the window with Leifur next to her and Birta on his other side.

Kat winked as she and Lils slid onto the seats in front with James and Jen in front of them.

They set off in darkness, the lodge's lights glowing, while iron-grey clouds swamped the moon and stars, the promise of daylight distant. Elvar had been keeping a close eye on the weather, checking forecasts to ensure they were safe to head out along the south coast towards the village of Vík. It would be a long drive and a long day.

Cosy in her hooded fleece, Molly was content to sit quietly and gaze out as they left the lodge behind in the valley, following the river for a short while as it wound its way through the icy wilderness.

Craggy snow-covered mountains towered over the road outside Hveragerði. They raced along the clear road to Selfoss, crossing the bridge over the churning ocean-green river and through a village of new houses built in the old traditional style. They continued across a desolate, flat landscape that would be moss green in the warmer months, Elvar commenting that they were driving over 'the largest lava field in the world'.

'Your boyfriend didn't come?' Leifur's voice was hushed as he leaned closer, his shoulder just touching hers.

Molly continued looking out of the window, not wanting to meet his eyes. 'No, he didn't.'

'Claudia said, he um, let you down.'

'If you mean broke up with me, then yes,' Molly said through gritted teeth, livid that Claudia had blabbed. Heat rose up her chest. She didn't want to have this conversation with Leifur of all people or risk anyone overhearing. She glanced ahead; they all seemed to be listening to Elvar, while Birta had headphones on and was watching something on an iPad.

'I've been where you are, in a failed relationship. Sometimes it's for the best. It was for me, even with Birta. You don't have children; it will be easier.'

A failed relationship. She didn't know how to take that, or Leifur's assumption that her breakup with Howard would somehow be easy. The stark reality was that life was passing by in a blur, and what did she have to show for her thirty-five years apart from heartache and disappointment? She knew that it was her grief talking, but the time when she'd been truly happy felt like a distant memory.

She sighed. 'Sometimes I wish I could rewind my life ten years or so, to when everything seemed so simple.'

'Like that summer?' Leifur leaned even closer and looked at her intently; familiar brown eyes that pooled with memories, of her gazing into them, of them kissing. 'Me and you... We had some good times; it was just too short.'

Had that been what she meant? A carefree summer in Iceland, full of adventure, hiking, exploring and camping out in the wild, the possibility and excitement of the beginning of romance, of snatched kisses and passionate fumbles beneath the midnight sun.

'We had fun, but it was a long time ago, Leifur,' she said, aware that he was mentioning it now straight after she'd admitted to breaking up with Howard.

His cheeky look spoke volumes. However, the what-could-have-been was futile; their lives had diverged and they'd met other people. It wasn't as if she'd fallen in love with him. They'd not been serious, they'd not fallen out, they'd not even slept together. She considered him to be a friend, and that was exactly what she needed right now, someone far removed from all the crap back home.

Birta started talking to Leifur and he turned his attention to her, allowing Molly to return to her contemplation as she watched the landscape zip by – a few sporadic evergreens dotted about like snow-covered Christmas trees; Icelandic horses, their coats and manes obvious to spot against the white; and a couple of small tin-roofed houses perched on the edge of a hill over-looking a winding stream. She'd seen it all before, in the different seasons, but she marvelled at just how unique and special it was.

Beyond Urriðafoss, a large glacial river which was a dirty moss-green colour, the relatively flat landscape became more mountainous. Leifur laughed as phones began to ping.

Kat snorted. 'Oh my God! We really know we're in Iceland now!' She held up her phone and read the text message. 'From Civil Protection: You are close to Hekla, an active volcano that can erupt without warning. Take care.'

'Take care. Are they serious?' Jen said in disbelief.

'Don't worry,' Leifur said reassuringly, although Molly could hear the amusement in his voice. 'It hasn't erupted since 2000 and they monitor the volcano, so it's only a real problem if you're actually on the mountain as there's only a thirty-minute warning. It's a three to four-hour hike up the mountain and then the same to get back down again, so you do the maths.'

'Have you hiked it?' Kat asked, wide-eyed.

'Once,' Leifur said, gazing past Molly at the majestic moun-tain on the horizon, its white peak bold against the smoky-grey sky. 'My heart was thumping the whole time. It's one to tell the grandchildren,' he laughed, 'and warn them to not be so foolish and go up it themselves. The same goes for Birta.' He gently nudged his daughter who was oblivious to the conversation.

'There's absolutely no way you'd get me anywhere near it.' Jen shook her head. 'It's a death wish.'

'It's a challenge and an adventure.' James peered past her towards the mountain, set within the bleak and unforgiving landscape.

'You wouldn't seriously want to go up there, would you?' Jen asked.

'Probably not, but I can see the appeal – the adrenalin rush would be insane. It's right up Leifur's street.' James turned in his seat and grinned at his friend. 'Probably safer than climbing Everest or K2.'

'I wouldn't want to climb any of them.' Jen shuddered.

'I'd like to climb a mountain,' Lils said, looking at Leifur. 'But not one that can explode with little warning or where the chances of not making it back down are stacked against you. Somewhere like Mount Kilimanjaro would do me – a proper challenge but it feels doable.'

'You're a bit of an adrenalin junkie?' Leifur raised his eyebrows.

'Oh, I wouldn't say that!' Lils laughed. 'I just believe if there's something you want to do, you shouldn't put it off. You should absolutely go for it, even if it's a little scary. Life's too short to put your dreams off till tomorrow,' she said wistfully.

'I agree with you 100 per cent. What about you, Molly?' Leifur turned to her. 'Would you hike Hekla?'

'Not a chance, although like James I understand the appeal. Perhaps I would have said yes in my twenties.'

'Just as well none of us suggested it back then!' Elvar called from the front.

Kat nodded emphatically. 'That's the thing, isn't it. Most of us were fearless in our twenties. I'm sure I would have been if I hadn't been juggling kids, a failing marriage and paying the bills!'

'I'm only thirty and you still wouldn't get me up there,' Jen said firmly, turning back to the window.

James caught Molly's and Leifur's eyes and mouthed, 'I would have done.'

Molly smiled, enjoying being part of the banter and camaraderie of the group.

As if sensing Jen's horror at the idea of climbing anything deemed dangerous, the grey sky ahead darkened, clusters of moody, pitch-black clouds rolling in erasing the small patches of blue sky. Molly noticed that Elvar didn't make a comment about Katla, an incredibly dangerous caldera volcano that had made a hole in the earth ten kilometres in diameter not far from the town of Vík. Molly may have lost her spark and spontaneity in recent years, but as she gazed longingly at the mountainous landscape that was as dangerous as it was beautiful, she realised she hadn't fully lost her sense of adventure; it just needed to be teased out. Iceland was certainly the place to rediscover it.

12

As quickly as the weather had closed in, within a few minutes of them arriving at Reynisfjara black sand beach, it had cleared again. Inland, the pale blue sky had returned with the glimpse of sunshine between swirls of high white cloud, while over the ocean clouds the colour of a ripe bruise clustered.

Elvar pulled up in the parking area filled with other vehicles before warning them about the unpredictability of the ocean with its sneaker waves that could surge unexpectedly up the beach.

'Don't get too close to the ocean and don't turn your back.'

After the long drive, everyone tumbled out, eager to stretch their legs and be blasted awake by the cold.

Groups of people were dotted all over the beach, but it wasn't crowded. The sheer power of the ocean was evident in its constant rumble then roar as wave after wave broke in slow motion like rolling, foam-tipped beasts snarling onto the black sand. Narrow rays of sun strained through the murky clouds, catching the spray and highlighting the rock stacks emerging from the ocean.

Molly strolled with everyone across the snow and onto the beach where the powdery whiteness mixed with the fine black grains. Closer to the ocean the beach glistened a sparkly black, the waves constantly washing away any snow that tried to settle.

Leifur remained with his daughter towards the back of the beach, laughing as she played. Digging with her gloved hands to reach the sand, she shrieked with delight as she mixed the snow with the dark grains, a rosy-cheeked six-year-old entranced by the snow rather than the majestic scenery.

Molly stood beyond the snowline and gazed out in wonder. Even though she'd been here a few times before, it was mesmerising. The constant roar of the waves smashing onto the sand drowned out the voices. With no one directly in front of her, it was easy to imagine she was the only person witnessing the raw beauty and power of the ocean which continuously churned the shore, pulling whatever was in its way back into its depths.

What would she and Howard have talked about if he'd been here? Would they have behaved like a loving couple, a younger version of Graham and Maggie, or would they have come across as unsuited to each other as James and Jen seemed to be? Of course she was making assumptions; she imagined people may well have said the same about her and Howard over the years. She had no clue what difficulties they might be facing. She hadn't been able to see the problems in her own relationship let alone someone else's.

On her left at the end of the beach, grey pillars of rock reached up to the sky – they were the inspiration for the Hallgrímskirkja church in Reykjavík. The cliffs behind them were studded with snow and ice. Birds swirled above, white specks against the blue sky, wheeling out over the ocean, dodging the churning waves and circling the foamy tips as though they were playing a game of dare.

Kat and Lils were taking pictures of each other a little way from her, the ocean backdrop wild and daring. Molly imagined their social media would be sprinkled with photos of their Icelandic adventure. Elvar offered to take a photo of them together.

Cutting across her view, James and Jen strolled over the ebony sand. Jen paused to adjust her woolly hat then grabbed at her ear. Molly could hardly see her face, she was so wrapped up, but she heard her cry above the thundering waves.

'My earring!' Jen dropped to her knees and scrabbled around in the sand. She pulled off a glove and traced a manicured finger across the cold grains.

'What does it look like?' James asked.

Jen glared at him as if it was his fault. 'It's my diamond one.'

James didn't say it, but Molly was certain everyone who overheard was thinking it. Why on earth would anyone wear diamond earrings somewhere like this?

Jen frantically resumed her search. The sand mixed with the snow made everywhere sparkle, making it impossible to find a tiny diamond earring among the glittering black.

James stood over her, his arms folded. 'You're never going to find it, Jen.'

'Well I won't if you don't help,' she snapped back.

Kat and Lils had begun to slink away; Molly's immediate thought had been to go over and help, but...

With her shoulders hunched, Jen rested her hands on her thighs. 'It was a stupid idea to come somewhere so bloody freezing when we could have gone to Dubai or the Maldives. Anywhere else.'

'You know why we came here,' James hissed. 'Not even attempting to enjoy yourself isn't helping.'

Molly decided to follow Kat and Lils's lead and leave them to it. There was no way she was going to involve herself in a domestic. She was about to walk away when Elvar rushed forward, his eyes wide and nostrils flaring.

'Sneaker wave!' he yelled.

Molly whirled back round.

Instead of folding on to the sand in slow motion, a wave broke away and speeded up, an arrow of water sneaking up the beach sending people racing in the opposite direction. James grabbed Jen and tugged her out of the way, both of them scrambling frantically before landing with a thump on the snow-covered sand just out of the wave's hungry grasp. Water swamped the area where Jen had been looking before streaming back, dragging sand and, presumably, the diamond earring with it.

Jen shrugged out of James's arms and stomped away, brushing off snow and sand while muttering, 'Now it's gone forever.'

Elvar paced over, held out his hand to James and pulled him up. 'Nasty things, sneaker waves coming this far up the beach. That's why I never turn my back.' He nodded and left James alone.

James looked as upset as Jen, but presumably for a different reason. There was an underlying tension between them and it was evident just how different they were. Not that a relationship couldn't be successful when clashing personalities were involved.

James met her eyes and she realised she'd been staring. Instead of dropping her gaze and leaving him to his thoughts, she wandered over.

'Are you okay?'

'My heart's racing.'

'I bet, my heart was, just watching that.'

It was a reminder of Iceland's danger as much as its wild beauty, almost as if the ocean had known something had been lost, wanting to retrieve it and keep it for itself.

'Jen would have been happier soaking up the winter sun somewhere hot with a pool. I take it you heard that.' He glanced after Jen, a small figure stalking across the snow to the parking area. 'Without a doubt I'd prefer to be here, but I do wonder if I'm punishing her by making her come here.' His demeanour suddenly changed and he laughed. 'But we're here and need to make the most of it. And it's Christmas Eve tomorrow.' He waved his hand around the vast beach, almost empty all the way to distant snow-covered cliffs on their right, while in the other direction tourists scuttled, posing for photos on the basalt rock stacks before jumping off again. Occasional shrieks cut through the air when a wave suddenly snuck up, scattering people who had dared get too close. The danger was real; Elvar's warning was wise and she knew he never relaxed here, he and Finn always keeping a close eye on their guests, keeping them safe. James nudged her arm. 'At least it brought a bit of excitement into the day after our earlier talk about climbing Hekla.'

Molly was pretty sure it was excitement Jen could have done without. And she wondered what James had meant by him 'punishing' her. It was a strange thing to say.

'It's certainly an unpredictable landscape,' she said instead. Her heart was still thumping, yet she felt alive. The adrenalin rush, the biting cold, the windswept beach and the unpredictability had all been sorely missed.

James nodded his agreement then gestured up the beach. 'I'd better go see how she is.'

* * *

With limited daylight, they didn't spend too much at Reynisfjara, just enough to take in the ferocious ocean, snap selfies and wander along the beach to the basalt stacks. Once they were back in the jeep, their chilled hands and faces slowly thawed on the drive back to Seljalandsfoss, one of the south coast's most famous waterfalls. Elvar wanted them to get there before the light faded and it felt very much like they were chasing the sun, the darkness desperate to take over.

Many others seemed to have had the same idea and the car park was busy with cars and coaches on day trips from Reykjavík.

'We'll stop for forty-five minutes,' Elvar said, 'then back to the lodge for dinner.'

Their earlier packed lunch of grilled chicken with salad and chilli mayonnaise had filled Molly up, but as she left the jeep and stepped into the icy air, she realised she was longing for a roaring fire and a hot meal. *Adventure is all well and good*, she thought wryly, *as long as there's comfort and warmth at the end of it*.

Molly set off from the jeep on her own, forgoing the queue for the loos that Kat, Lils and Maggie had joined and not wanting to wait around to get a coffee. Leifur was leaning against the side of the jeep pouring a hot chocolate for his daughter. She liked the contrast in him; the adventurous appealing side that had drawn her to him in her twenties, and the softer, more mature side.

After witnessing a young woman lose her footing and crash bottom first on to the ground, Molly gingerly picked her way along the slippery path towards the waterfall, passing other people making their way back. Lots of footfall had compacted the powdery snow into an ice sheet and she was glad of her faithful walking boots, although a solid arm tucked in hers would have been more comforting.

A spray of fine mist poured off the graceful waterfall which fell between overhanging chunks of ice and huge dagger-like icicles. The sky was now a clear watercolour blue, and the sun was beginning to set behind her, casting a soft golden light over the snow. Molly's breath caught at the sight of a rainbow shimmering within the cascading water. She stopped on the bridge that crossed the stream flowing from the base of the waterfall, the dark water cutting through the banks of snow, its cold beauty making her shiver. An icy wind whistled across the flat landscape from the ocean. The blue sky and retreating sun were not enough to take the edge off the chill.

'It's something else, isn't it.' James joined her and gazed along the dark, bubbling stream to the waterfall.

Molly glanced behind him. 'Jen didn't want to see it?'

James shook his head. 'She's in the jeep with a coffee still thawing out after black sand beach.' He gave her a weak smile. 'She's properly cross with me after losing her earring.'

Buffeted by the wind, they turned back to the waterfall. Birds circled the craggy cliffs which were decorated with jagged icicles. Despite dozens of other people further along the path taking photos and talking together, the only sound was the rushing water and the swirling wind. Molly couldn't see anyone else; perhaps they'd followed Jen's lead and stayed close to the jeep, opting for the comforting warmth of a hot drink.

'Can I ask you a question?' Molly said, feeling it was rather too personal but deciding she was going to ask it anyway, particularly after his earlier comment. 'If this kind of holiday is Jen's idea of hell, why come?'

There was a pause as if he was weighing up how to answer. If he'd answer at all. He pushed up his glasses and gazed into the distance.

'She owed me,' James said with little emotion. 'She said it was my choice. Leifur has been telling me for years to come and stay and I've kept putting it off for various reasons. Elvar and Claudia had a booking fall through and offered us the room at a huge discount – I jumped at the chance.'

Molly had so many questions but she acknowledged how

rude it would be to ask the most pertinent one about his relationship with Jen. They left the bridge and walked on towards the smaller falls further along the cliff. While the continual thunder of water behind them faded slightly, the screeching wind was constant, biting at their exposed cheeks. Molly considered that perhaps Jen had been wise to remain in the jeep.

'I was supposed to be here with my boyfriend,' Molly said to fill their silence. 'But he missed his flight and is staying with his parents for Christmas instead.'

The fib felt easier than the truth. Despite his jovial demeanour there was also a sadness about James, as if he was struggling with a great weight, which made her want to share something of herself with him, to show him that her life was far from perfect and things hadn't worked out the way she'd wanted them to either.

'He's missing out.'

'He is indeed.' Although she was sure Howard wasn't thinking that in the slightest, but James wasn't to know.

'I was hoping that once we were here, Jen would embrace the experience.'

'Maybe she'll like going back to Reykjavík. I think the plan is to visit again sometime after Christmas.'

'Oh, she's definitely one for city living.'

They'd walked as far as they could in the time they had, so they retraced their steps back towards the waterfall, which glowed golden in the fading light. Their boots crunched the slick snow as they crossed the bridge, the stream below winding through the snowy landscape towards the setting sun. It was so low on the horizon that Molly imagined they'd be plunged into darkness at any moment. She suddenly felt desperate to be back in the jeep, cocooned and safe on their way to the lodge. With the wind whipping up flurries of snow and fewer people around the waterfall, the sheer expanse of the icy landscape made Molly glad of James's company.

'I love the wild remoteness,' James said as they passed the towering waterfall, its constant flow of water grey against the white snow and brown rock. 'It's what I love most about Scotland – the landscape, fewer people, wild open space. I can happily spend days outdoors and I'm lucky I get to work in the country-side. No two days are the same. I don't think I could cope with having a permanent office job.'

'I do and I hate it. Not the people, not even the actual job, it's fine even if it's not what I want to do, but it feels restrictive.'

'Do you have a dream job?'

'Yes, but I've always found excuses to not go for it.'

'I understand that completely. The ease of what's familiar and comfortable is often what holds me back.'

Reluctantly, they turned their backs on the waterfall and followed the slippery, well-used path back towards the car park. Molly took in the flat landscape ahead. Only the vehicles and the stream were visible against the white.

'There are more trees in Scotland,' Molly commented.

'Ha, yes, there are indeed. I work to preserve them, the forests and habitats, and that's my passion. We have Jen's flat in Edinburgh, but it's not where I'd choose to be.' His words were threaded with melancholy. 'Jen and I have differing ideas about a few things. Nothing was too apparent when we first met, but you must understand how that can change as you get to know someone, not that being different isn't necessarily a good thing. I'm not sure I'm making much sense!'

'You are, completely. It's the same as me and my boyfriend; over the years I've discovered we have a lot more differences than similarities.' Molly slowed her pace, steadying herself on the ice and pushing down the urge to grab James's arm. 'Maybe I didn't see it in the beginning, you know, when we were head over heels in love.'

'Aye, yes, the rosy glow of a new relationship when everything seems perfect.'

They reached the jeep and their conversation trailed off. They were the last back. Everyone else, apart from Elvar, was already inside. James gestured for Molly to go in first. Warmth hit her as she opened the door and slid on to the back seat next to Leifur. James joined Jen but she barely glanced up from her phone. It was hard to believe they were engaged; his sadness made her wish that she'd asked the difficult question – why he felt that Jen owed him. It was an odd thing to say, at least for a supposedly loving couple.

13

Darkness descended not long after they left Seljalandsfoss, and although it wasn't late, it felt it by the time they'd driven back to the lodge. Molly offered to prepare that evening's communal dinner, her take on an Icelandic favourite of hot dogs with mustard, crispy onions, thinly sliced raw onions and mayo with gherkins and capers. They all ate together before she headed to her room for a hot bath and an early night.

Despite sleeping well, she woke early with a feeling of dread. There was never any warning about which days would be good, which would be bad, but the combination of Christmas Eve and her birthday were bound to make her feel weepy.

Even the twinkling lights decorating the outside deck did little to cheer her up. The darkness and leaden clouds filled with snow suited her mood. Not wanting to face the day or breakfast with everyone else, she snuggled back down beneath the covers.

She'd enjoyed herself yesterday, heading out along the south coast, taking in the sights that still felt fresh and new. She'd enjoyed the company too. She'd also believed she'd got a hold on her emotions and had managed to put Howard to the back of her mind. Yet this morning she felt drastically different about it all.

By the time she woke for a second time, it was mid-morning. Even though it was her birthday, her phone remained message-free from Howard. She had birthday messages from a handful of friends and a plethora of 'happy birthday' posts on Facebook. It warmed her heart that friends took the time to send her birthday wishes on a day that was busy with family festivities. Howard was organised and lived by his online planner; there was no way he wouldn't realise it was her birthday. His silence was as if he'd erased her from his life; at least temporarily. Once they were back home, he'd have to face her.

Molly got a hold on her disappointment about Howard's radio silence by forcing down her emotions, something she'd had plenty of practice at. After getting dressed, she decided to go and find Claudia. It would be a day filled with Christmas cheer whether she felt that way or not. She took a few deep breaths and opened the suite door. Outside was a basket and a card with her name on it tucked among some breakfast goodies.

With a lump in her throat, Molly picked it up and returned inside. She sat on the sofa that looked out over the river and popped the basket next to her. It contained a covered bowl of Skyr yogurt with a berry compote and granola, fresh sourdough bread with butter and little pots of jam and a flask of coffee, along with a box of chocolates, a bottle of Icelandic Eagle Gin and a couple of cans of tonic water. Molly pulled out the handwritten card.

Happy birthday, Moll. I thought you might fancy a lie-in and a bit of peace this morning. Enjoy the breakfast. Claudia x

It was uncharacteristically sensitive of her sister, not that Claudia wasn't thoughtful, because she was, always striving to make her guests' stay the best it could possibly be, but she'd never been sentimental or gushy over birthdays. The unexpected gesture meant even more to Molly that morning.

She tucked in, relishing the smooth yogurt with the sweetness of the berry compote. Through the window, more and more of the landscape was revealed as the winter sun began to rise. For a moment she forgot her worries, until the thought struck her that she was alone, on her birthday. Gulping back a wave of distress along with a mouthful of coffee, she grabbed her phone and opened WhatsApp. Her thumb hovered over Howard's name as she considered sending him a message, but she didn't know what to say. And, more importantly, why did she want to say anything? She craved the love and companionship of another person, and her loneliness was tricking her into believing she needed him. But he didn't care for her or love her, so why should she feel anything for him?

After devouring the breakfast and snuggling up on the sofa to read while she finished her coffee, Molly went in search of Claudia, but discovered from the housekeeper that she and Alda had gone shopping. She spotted Elvar and Finn outside busy doing jobs and she remembered that Leifur was taking his daughter to her mum's so he wouldn't be around till later either. Kat, Lils, Graham and Maggie were nowhere to be seen. Only James and Jen were in the lounge and she didn't fancy joining them. She was at a loss for what to do when she spied the swimming pool through the restaurant window, glowing an enticing cornflower blue, bright and welcoming among the snow-covered branches of the surrounding trees.

Back in her room, Molly changed into her swimming costume, shoved her feet into fur-lined boots and, wrapped in a robe, braved the minus seven temperature by the outside pool. Shuddering with cold, she disrobed, kicked off her boots and sank into the warm water, a blissful contrast to the icy breeze billowing around her face.

Steam rose from the milky, blue-lit pool, spiralling into the grey morning. Molly always thought it resembled a much smaller version of the famous Blue Lagoon. The ability to soak in the warm, naturally heated water, while surrounded by ice and snow in every direction, was the perfect way to see in her thirty-fifth birthday.

As a child, having a birthday on Christmas Eve was always a little strange. There was so much anticipation for Christmas that the specialness of it being her birthday too was lost. She was never able to have a birthday party with friends as they were either away or busy with their own families, so nothing got organised. Her family had their own traditions which they'd continued with even after Molly was born. She hadn't thought much about it then, as it had been normal, but looking back she realised it had made a difference to never have a special day of her own. While her dad was usually working, her mum had always been preoccupied, busy preparing food, putting the finishing touches to the decorations, doing last-minute shopping and furiously cleaning, leaving little time for Molly.

Claudia emerged from the lodge in just snow boots and a woolly hat, a black sports swimsuit clinging to her toned frame. She whipped off her hat, glanced at Molly and dived into the pool, her pale, lithe arms slicing through the rippling water as she swam over.

She bobbed up next to her. 'Happy birthday, Moll.'

'Thank you. And thank you so much for breakfast and the goodies; that was really thoughtful.' Molly fought back tears. Claudia's gesture this morning was something their mum would have done. The connection caught her unawares. 'I can't believe this is already my second birthday since losing Mum.'

Claudia pursed her thin lips. 'I know it is.'

'I don't exactly feel like celebrating.'

'I understand that, and don't worry, there's no surprise party planned,' Claudia said with a wry smile. 'It doesn't mean you can't enjoy yourself though. You're allowed to celebrate the good things in life; Mum would want you to.'

Molly glanced away. Tears pricked her eyes as snowflakes drifted by, instantly dissolving in the warm water. One side of the restaurant overlooked the pool as well as where the river curved and they could be seen through the branches of the trees. Molly could just make out Kat and Lils having lunch at a table next to the floor-to-ceiling window.

Molly turned back to her sister. The rising steam and her foggy breath distorted her features. 'It doesn't feel like there's much to celebrate.'

'Oh you can't think like that.' Claudia slicked a damp hand through her short hair and swam closer.

'Why can't I? It's how I feel. It's how I've felt for months, but somehow it's worse now. I don't know, maybe it's because I'm here. The expectation to celebrate and to be happy when all I feel is sadness.'

'I know today's difficult—'

'It's not just today,' Molly said forcefully.

'The situation with Howard can't have helped.'

'No, it hasn't but on the flip side it's been freeing to not have to put any effort into making things work with him. However much

I was longing for us to have time together, part of me was dreading having to try and fix us. And the awful thing is, if he hadn't done what he did, I would have carried on limping along trying to patch up our relationship because the alternative of breaking up with him would have been too hard.'

'You'd considered it?'

'No, not at all, but somehow it's actually made sense. We'd drifted apart so badly and we've hardly talked – at least not properly – for I don't know how long.'

'That's no way for a relationship to be,' Claudia said softly. 'Not what you deserve at all.'

Beyond a snow-decorated pine tree, Molly could now make out James and Jen sitting at the corner table, the best spot, which looked out over the bend in the river.

She could see some of herself and Howard in James and Jen; the lack of communication and the differences between them. Howard had given up on them, but not all problems in relationships were insurmountable.

Molly felt Claudia's eyes on her and turned back. 'Howard is just one thing and actually the simplest to deal with; it's been everything else I've struggled with. I have no idea how to drag myself out of so much heartache. How I can possibly turn my life around, into something positive?'

'But the funeral, selling the house, it's all over now, Moll. Mum certainly wouldn't want you wallowing in—'

'That's what you think I've been doing? *Wallowing*? You have no idea.'

'I didn't mean it quite like that.'

'Then what did you mean?'

Her silence said it all.

'You weren't there, Claudia!'

'It wasn't from the lack of trying, Moll. Don't you dare think that I didn't want to be there.' Her cheeks flushed, whether from the heat of the water or anger, Molly wasn't sure. 'You've closed yourself off from everyone.'

'Because it was the only way I could cope!'

'Well, you're here now and so am I, so talk to me about Mum and Dad, about Howard too if it helps. Hell, all of them, instead of bottling everything up and letting it fester.'

'You think I want to feel like this?' A burst of anger flamed. It was one thing her sister thinking it, quite another her talking about Molly's behaviour out loud. 'You don't understand what I had to deal with. *Your* life was uninterrupted.'

Claudia looked as if she'd been slapped in the face.

Molly blinked back tears. 'I'm so sorry. That was unfair.' All the anger, upset, heartache, bewilderment, anxiety and sorrow that Claudia had described as festering rose to the surface on days like today, a special day that reminded her of the past and all that had been lost, bubbling hot and angry, twisting and turning her words into misdirected anger at her sister. 'The last two years must have been tough for you as well.'

Claudia took a deep breath and wiped a wet hand across her flushed face. 'If I could have physically been there more, I would have, believe me. We have our business, guests, the kids. They may be older now but I couldn't just up and leave for more than a week or two at a time, or leave Elvar to deal with everything on his own.'

'I know you've been hurting too. I'm so sorry. It's just...' Even being submerged in the warm, soothing water didn't help to temper her heartache. 'It's more than losing Mum and Dad and Howard leaving me. The truth is, I don't even know who I am any longer.'

'What are you talking about?'

Without warning, tears streamed down Molly's face, plopping into the warm water. She shook her head, distraught at herself. How to put what she was feeling into words? 'I'm not sure I can explain it or that you'd even understand.'

Through the rising steam, Claudia held her gaze. 'Try me.'

14

―――――――

'Have you ever felt as if you didn't belong?' Molly wiped away tears as she stared at her sister, then shook her head. 'No, of course you haven't.'

'Hey, wait a minute.' Claudia dripped water as she raised a hand. 'Don't be so hasty to decide things about my life. I belong in Iceland, but it didn't feel that way when I first moved here. And I can't begin to tell you how many times growing up Dad made me feel like I didn't fit in to his vision for our family. I was too much of a tomboy but not the son he wanted. I was never good enough and then I was too rebellious – in his eyes at least. Compared to other teens, I really wasn't. It was only after leaving home and experiencing life away from his influence that I began to understand who I was and what I wanted.'

'It's been the opposite for me,' Molly said. 'I felt like I did fit in when I was growing up; that was never the problem. It's more recently. I don't know, time seems to have raced by and I've got nothing to show for it. I feel a stranger in my own house, that there's nothing to look forward to. I'm disengaged from everything and everyone, even friends, Howard especially.'

'It's been an incredibly tough time; don't you think this is your grief talking? What I said before about wallowing wasn't right. But I do mean it will take *you* to change your outlook, to try and look at things positively even if you don't feel that way.'

'You mean fake it?'

'Yes, if necessary. I do that quite often. I'm not constantly happy, particularly over the last couple of years.' She gave Molly a knowing look. 'So I put on a brave face for guests and fake being happy and upbeat. Sometimes it's exhausting and there are plenty of times when I just want to hide away and not face anyone. It's more straightforward for me because I don't have a choice, whereas you do and that probably makes it harder to force yourself to do something or act a certain way when you know you don't have to. I'm not saying it will be easy, but maybe it's necessary?'

'But you have support. You have Elvar and the kids, a home, a business that you work hard at that you love.' Molly flung her arms around, splashing water into the icy air. 'I have none of that.'

'You have so much more than you realise. You're only talking like this because you've hit rock bottom.' Claudia looked at her firmly. 'I'm sorry if this sounds harsh, but if you want things to change and you want to stop feeling like this, *you* have to do something about it. You can't rely on anyone else, least of all Howard; he's made that abundantly clear. And however much it hurts that we don't have our parents around any more, we have to hold on to the good memories. We have each other, we have so much. You just can't see it at the moment through the upset. You're only thirty-five; still a baby.' Claudia faltered then surged through the water and hugged her, something she rarely did. All the sadness Molly had been battling since first thing that morning spilled over, hot tears trickling down her chilled face and dripping into the water. Claudia pulled away and held her at arm's length. 'Feeling better?'

Molly nodded. Even though Claudia looked more like their dad, there was an awful lot of their mum in her. Her tough exterior hid a much softer side that Molly had only occasionally glimpsed, but right now she appreciated it more than she could say.

Needing to get back to the guests, Claudia left Molly in the pool. She bobbed about in the water a little longer, mulling over what her sister had said. Normally she wouldn't give much sway to sisterly advice, not when their lives were so different, but Claudia understood something of her heartache, more than Molly had given her credit for.

Molly had needed a cry. After Howard's bombshell phone call, numbness had spread through her, and bit by bit the emotions had built back up. How could someone she'd built her life with discard her so easily? Whatever he was feeling – embarrassment, resentment, confusion – Claudia had been right about him not being worthy. Respect, love and openness was the least she deserved.

* * *

During a late lunch, Claudia surprised Molly with a birthday cake she and Alda had made the day before while Molly had been on the day out to black sand beach. Everyone sang 'Happy Birthday', Molly blew out the candles, cut the cake and, as generous slices of the vanilla sponge were passed around, she opened presents – a gorgeously snuggly scarf from Claudia and family, and a lino print of Skógafoss waterfall from Alda that she'd made herself. Molly was overwhelmed by the kindness and she was fully drawn in to the festivities that continued long into the afternoon. Kat and Lils in particular were full of Christmas cheer – and a fair bit of booze. Both of them had hinted at heartache in their past, certainly when it came to love, and yet here they were, living life to the full. She should take inspiration from them. Nothing would get better unless she tried. As Claudia had suggested, wasn't faking happiness better than wallowing in disappointment and despair?

Leifur returned late in the afternoon after dropping off his daughter, and Molly was sure he was suffering. His usual unflappable enthusiasm had dampened enough to be noticeable. The lodge, however, was the epitome of a perfect Christmas: snowy and cold outside, glinting lights and roaring fires inside.

Not only was Christmas Eve her birthday, but over the years it had also grown to be one of Molly's favourite days of the year. After a childhood learning to balance her birthday with the expectations and traditions of her family, as an adult she'd discovered a newfound love of a Christmas Eve birthday with all the festive anticipation that went with it. Once Claudia had moved to Iceland with Elvar, there was the delight in the Icelandic tradition of Jólabókaflóð, the joy of giving and receiving books, then snuggling up to read by the fire with a mug of hot chocolate and snow falling outside.

Claudia included guests in their Christmas Eve tradition and after a dinner of smoked lamb with fennel, celeriac and creamy mashed potato, and once everyone was settled in the lounge, she passed out packages wrapped in brown paper, tied with string and decorated with dried berries, pinecones and evergreen fronds.

For a few minutes there was just the sound of rustling paper to accompany the spit and crackle of the fire.

Molly held the book in her lap. Raynor Winn's *The Salt Path*.

Claudia leaned across from the armchair next to hers and

touched Molly's arm. 'A true story of the healing powers of the natural world. I thought it might be a book that helps you to process things.'

There were moments when Claudia just got her and understood what she needed. Three times in a day, her sensitivity had taken Molly by surprise.

Molly ran her fingers over the muted colours of the illustrated coast path, birds and the swirling sea on the cover. She glanced back at Claudia with a genuinely thankful smile, and as she gazed around at the guests, friends and family snuggled up with their books on armchairs and sofas, she realised in this moment of contentedness, she didn't need to pretend.

'Thank you.' She opened the book and flicked through to the first page of the prologue.

She was soon emersed, the rich language conjuring arresting images that roused familiar emotions within her. She lost track of time as the evening ticked by. Something as simple as a yearly tradition, the comfort of a book, of someone else's story and experience, while surrounded by the people she loved and a handful of people she was beginning to get to know, was such a tonic.

Molly stifled a yawn, put the book down and untucked her foot from beneath her, wiggling it about to get rid of the pins and needles. Elvar was stoking the fire and Graham had nodded off in the armchair opposite, his mouth wide open. She could just make out the faint glow from a phone tucked within the open pages of Jen's book. James, on the other end of the sofa, had a glimmer of a smile as he read, looking content and relaxed as he embraced Claudia's favourite Icelandic tradition. Leifur was focused on reading an Icelandic-set psychological thriller and Molly couldn't work out if his furrowed brow was from sadness or concentration. She could only imagine his heartache at not being able to spend

Christmas with his daughter. *I'm not the only one suffering*, she reminded herself.

What Molly loved the most was the peace. Even Kat and Lils weren't chatting, both of them happily reading. There was only the spit of the fire, an occasional creak of a door, the sound of the wind tunnelling past the lodge and the rhythmic tick tock tick tock of a clock on the bookshelf.

By ten-thirty, people began to drift away; Graham and Maggie first after he'd started snoring and she'd woken him with a nudge to the ribs, then Alda and Finn disappeared upstairs with their books. Elvar and Claudia gave hushed calls of goodnight, while James and Jen followed not long after. Although it was traditional in Iceland to open presents on Christmas Eve, Claudia had held on to their Bliss family tradition of opening them on Christmas morning.

Molly was too warm and comfy to want to move, plus the book had gripped her and she was relishing being immersed in someone else's life and adventure that was threaded with heartache. Claudia had chosen well; she always did.

Leifur broke her concentration, sitting on the armchair where Claudia had been and handing her a glass filled with a pale golden liquid. 'Sorry if I said the wrong thing yesterday, bringing up your, um, boyfriend,' he said quietly. 'I don't always think through if I should say something or not.'

Molly swirled the liquid around the glass and nodded. 'And I'm overly sensitive about everything at the moment.'

'You've had a tough time.'

Molly frowned.

'And now I've probably said too much again.' He shrugged his broad shoulders but his eyes twinkled. 'I know what you've been through with your parents, with everything you had to deal with back home. Claudia and Elvar talk about you often; they're worried about you.'

Molly fought against a wave of emotion and covered it by sipping her drink. 'My goodness, that's delicious.'

'A local Icelandic gin. Made from wild arctic thyme and honey.'

She took another sip and nodded. 'It's good.'

Lounging in the armchair in a woollen jumper and jeans with one leg resting on the other, he looked comfortable and happier than he had done earlier.

'Did you get Birta to her mum's okay?' Molly asked to fill the brief silence.

Leifur nodded, the sadness returning with a strained look.

'That must have been hard,' Molly said gently. 'But you'll be here tomorrow?'

'Elvar... All of them, they're like family, you know. They are family. Since I lost my parents, since my marriage ended, apart from my daughter, they're everything to me. They've treated me so well.'

Molly felt a niggle of guilt jabbing at her insides after the cross words she'd had with Claudia in the pool. Leifur had hit rock bottom and they'd been there for him, because they were close by and could. Even though she'd apologised, she shouldn't have taken her frustration and anger out on her sister, but she'd felt the need to channel it somewhere. Really it needed to be aimed at Howard, but he wasn't here.

'Don't you have an older brother? Or have I not remembered correctly?'

'You remember fine. He lives in the north with his family but we're not close. He wasn't close to our parents either after a big falling out with our father. Nothing has been easy with my family.'

The sorrow in Leifur's words made Molly realise how good she really had it with Claudia. They may be different and Molly may have struggled shouldering the bulk of the responsibility and organisation after losing their parents, but at least they'd talked and worked things out together. There'd been no arguments or animosity over the will or when clearing out the house.

'This is not what I hoped for.' He gestured absently with his hand. 'Not that I mind spending Christmas with Elvar – I cannot tell you how grateful I am and how much I consider them to be family,' he stressed again, 'but it's not what I imagined after getting married and having our daughter. It broke me when things didn't work out.'

Molly smoothed her fingers over the book resting in her lap. That was the challenge of life, dealing with the fallout when things didn't happen the way you wanted them to. She was experiencing a similar thing. 'Sometimes it sucks being an adult.'

Leifur laughed. 'I get that. I often look at Birta and find it hard to remember a time when I was that happy and free. I only ever feel that way when I'm outside exploring. I like taking guests out but I'm happier on my own. Not too sure what that says about me!'

Molly shrugged. 'It says you're happy in your own company. As I've got older, I've liked my own company more too. It might also be the aftereffect of the last couple of years when the constant intensity of looking after Mum just built and built till it felt as if I was going to explode. And then to lose her. I've craved time on my own, but I don't think it's actually helped me.' She sipped the warming gin, tucked her feet beneath her and rested her chin in her hand. Leifur was watching her intently, his dark eyes boring into her, not in an unlikeable way. Things had become stale with Howard; she'd been lying to herself about her feelings towards him, everything a confused muddle, grief and anxiety twisting around each other. 'Even being around Howard felt suffocating. I believed we were going to use this time to fix all that was wrong with our relationship, but it turned out it was too damaged to be fixed.'

'Sounds like it's time to rediscover who you are.'

'You're right, but it's hard. I don't particularly want to analyse my life, although it feels necessary to figure out a way forward and what I want to do next. But it's Christmas so I'm going to hold off for a couple of days at least.' Molly raised her glass. 'Thank you for the drink.'

'Anytime. And happy birthday.' He drained the remainder of his. His hand brushed hers as he stood. 'I'm going to head upstairs.' He stifled a yawn and laughed. 'It's been one of those days. *Góða nótt.*'

'Night.' Molly watched him until he was out of sight. Deciding it was time for bed too, it was her turn to stifle a yawn.

Only Kat and Lils remained, lounging on either end of the sofa nearest the fire.

'Nice chat with Leifur?' Kat said cheekily as Molly walked by. 'I really wouldn't mind him disturbing my reading time either.' She giggled and winked. 'I have to say though, this idea of giving books on Christmas Eve and spending the evening reading is wonderful. A tradition I might have to steal.'

Molly tucked her book beneath her arm. 'It's lovely, isn't it, and one that's been in our family since Claudia moved here.'

'This is my first ever Christmas abroad,' Lils said. 'So it's all a new experience for me.'

'This is my first Christmas where I won't see my kids for any of the festive period.' Kat looked up at Molly. 'They're both grown up and spending tomorrow with their partners' families, but not seeing them is the only sad thing about being far away.'

'You'll Zoom though,' Lils said reassuringly.

'And Christmas here is really special. There's nowhere quite like it.' Molly swept her hand towards the towering Christmas tree decked out in lights and the dark snowy landscape framed in the window beyond. 'I'll see you in the morning.'

The chill of the glass walkway was a shock after the sleepy warmth of the lounge and she was shivering by the time she reached her room. The king-size bed was welcoming and the flashing lights on the mini Christmas tree threw patterns across the walls.

As she got washed and changed into her pyjamas, Molly couldn't help but wonder how Howard's evening had been. She got on with his parents well enough, his sister too, but their traditions were different to her family's. Although Claudia would have gifted a book to Howard, she'd packed one for him along with a bottle of bourbon as a Christmas present that he could have enjoyed in the hot tub. Both remained unopened in her suitcase.

She slipped into bed; she had intended to continue reading and have a screen-free evening, but she took a sneaky scroll through Facebook to see what her friends had been up to. Once again she thought about messaging Howard but it was late and his parents' annual Christmas Eve party would still be in full swing. Besides, she didn't have the energy to even begin to think about what she would actually say, or how she would reveal her upset at him not even attempting to contact her on her birthday. She was curious though. Howard rarely posted anything on Facebook but his sister did.

Molly didn't have to scroll far through his sister's feed. The first post was a selfie of her clutching a glass of prosecco in front of a towering fake Christmas tree decorated in red and gold. The next post gushed about how wonderful the Christmas Eve party was and she'd added a dozen photos – the familiar faces of Howard's family. Lots of beaming smiles and raised glasses, yet Howard seemed to be absent, until she zoomed in on one.

Howard was a blurry shape in the background but visible enough for Molly to make out that he was standing with someone, his hand on the small of their back, leaning in close as if going in for a kiss. Perhaps it was a cousin and he was greeting them; she didn't know them very well but they were often at his parents' parties. She zoomed in more. The woman was sideways to the camera but it was the look on Howard's face that struck her. Even though it was grainy, she could see the happiness, make out the laughter on his lips and the look on his face. A look of what? Love? Desire? Whatever it was, it certainly wasn't the way he looked at Molly and she was certain it wasn't a relation. She scrolled through more photos posted earlier in the night and managed to pick out the brunette with Howard in the background of another. Her red dress was easy to spot. She looked familiar too. With her heart racing, Molly clicked on Howard's profile. He had over five hundred friends but she was determined to scroll through every bloody one if she had to. Luckily, she came across her quickly: Emma Hastings, account manager at Birkenhead Logistics. His work colleague.

The knot of stress in her stomach moved to her chest, causing a tight ache to spread. She dropped her phone on the bed, rested her hands on her thighs and breathed long and deep. Apart from sporadic moments when she'd been distracted by the beauty of the black sand beach and soaking in the thermal river or standing out in the cold chatting to James and listening to Kat and Lils's amusing anecdotes, she'd moped about, wasting precious time feeling sorry for herself. Claudia had been right – dammit, she always was, her older, wiser sister – she deserved to be happy and her chance of happiness was in her own hands. Instead of wishing that life was different, that the awful things that had happened could be erased, she needed to face up to things and deal with them, however hard that would be.

Molly saw the whole of the last two years so clearly. As she'd retreated inside herself, her time, energy and love taken up by the aftermath of losing her dad then looking after her mum, Howard had pulled away too. The late nights at work and the weekends away weren't just a coping mechanism as she'd assumed, but his way of escaping, and there was someone with their arms wide open to comfort him – she wondered how long he'd been unfaithful for. Had he never intended to come with her to Iceland for Christmas? Did he think he was letting her down gently by not being truthful? Disappointment after disappointment had crashed through her life, leaving her heartbroken, but at least the truth of it was plain for her to see. Howard had obviously moved on emotionally and physically; it was about time she did too. Tomorrow, the start of her thirty-sixth year, was going to be different. There was nothing stopping her now.

Molly took a screenshot of the image, clicked on Howard's name on WhatsApp and attached it. She thumbed a quick message and sent it before she lost her nerve.

You really are an arse.

She smiled grimly. It wasn't much, but somehow it made her feel better.

15

'You're an arse. That's what you wanted to tell me on Christmas Day?'

In a state of tired confusion, Molly had answered when Howard's name had flashed up on her phone. She was rapidly regretting it. How dare he sound livid. What right did he have? Her heart pounded from being rudely awoken, while anger coiled in her stomach.

'And you think this was how I envisaged Christmas to be? Abandoned and dumped, while you hide away at your parents'?'

'I'm not hiding away.' He sounded like a spoilt brat having just had a telling off. Good, she hoped he was squirming, she hoped his perfect family Christmas without her was being rudely interrupted. Even if she had good reason, she knew how bitter she sounded.

The adrenalin coursing through her was dissolving her tiredness. Even in the quiet darkness of her room, she suddenly felt incredibly awake. 'What about the photo? You getting cosy with that brunette?'

'It's really not what you think it is.'

'And what exactly do I think it is? Because you obviously feel the need to deny that it is something.'

'There were loads of people there last night; lots of Mum and Dad's friends.'

'Yes, I saw your sister's Facebook profile. Lots of family photos but at least a couple of you with Emma Hastings. That's her name, isn't it? I know you work with her. How long have you been having an affair?'

'What the hell are you talking about?'

'Honestly Howard, what's the point in denying it? You've already broken up with me. You've dumped me at Christmas, made it perfectly clear we have no future. There's not really any way you could hurt me more.'

A heartbeat of a pause. In the gentle glow of the fairy lights decorating the outside deck, snow drifted down. A proper white Christmas; it should have been perfect. There was so much wrong with her life and, she was beginning to realise, Howard was a massive part of that.

Molly sat up and switched on the bedside lamp, banishing the darkness to the corners of the room – the room she was actually grateful that she didn't have to share with a lying, cheating boyfriend. 'You phoned to berate me for calling you an arse. Well I'm sorry, you really are. You lied to me about coming to Iceland, your lack of support during the hardest time in my life speaks volumes about how little you care about me and now you're lying again about last night.' She decided to channel Claudia's direct-ness. 'Grow some bloody balls and tell me the real reason you stayed. Tell me the truth.'

Silence. Just his breath on the other end of the phone. For a moment she thought he was going to hang up.

'Yes, I work with her and yes, I'm seeing her.' His voice was unwavering, emotionless even.

'You're having sex with her?'

'Well, it's not like we've been.'

His words cut deep. How often had she longed to be held and to be loved over the last year or so? But there'd been little warmth or comfort from Howard, at least not the kind she was craving. Sex hadn't been top of her priorities but it obviously had been for him and he'd found it with someone else. Gentle intimacy, a cuddle where there was no expectation of anything else had been sorely missed and, if he'd comforted her in that way, who knew where it might have led. She was constantly being made to feel as if it was her who had been putting up barriers between them, but he'd never once tried to understand how to take them down, how to simply be there for her during the worst time in her life.

She didn't want to give him the satisfaction of revealing how upset she was, so she attempted to keep her tone neutral. 'It was my birthday yesterday.'

'I know.'

'You partied with the woman you're having an affair with on my birthday. You really are despicable.' That was all she needed to know. Claudia was right; he didn't deserve her. She could do so much better. She didn't need anyone to make her feel worse about herself than she already did. 'Do you know, it's actually helpful to understand how little you care about me.'

'Molly...'

'No, let me finish. What you've done is helped me to accept the situation.' She wiped a tear from her cheek. 'You go and enjoy your bit on the side. Enjoy your Christmas, because that's what I'm going to do. I didn't think I'd be able to without you, but I can and I will.'

She ended the call. Her hands were shaking, her heart battering her chest. Tucked up in bed, she felt safe, cocooned in her own little haven. Perhaps now she could embrace being away from reality for a short time.

Last Christmas had been a blur, wading through grief. Was it her fault that Howard had wandered? Could she have done more to heal their strained relationship, paid him more attention, opened up to him? What if she could have kept the spark between them alive so he hadn't felt the need to go off chasing another woman? But why should it have been just down to her to make things work? If she had the ability to go back and change the past couple of years, for her parents to still be with them happy and healthy, she would in a heartbeat. Yet changing things to still be with Howard, she was now certain that she wouldn't.

Molly showered, put on make-up and a new blue-and-red long-sleeved maxi dress and emerged from her room determined to not let Howard upset her any more. *I'm feigning happiness,* she told herself. It had been a family tradition to dress their best on Christmas Day, no slouching around in joggers and a jumper. Everyone always made an effort to look smart and their mum had taken pride in making each Christmas the best yet, until she couldn't any more. Taking pride in herself and their house had been one similarity between her and Howard at least. He always looked smart; the only time he'd be seen in casual wear was if he was going to the gym. He was all pressed shirts and smart trousers; clean cut and professional, meticulous in everything he did, way more of a clean freak than Molly was; definitely a touch of OCD there. Although she'd embraced and continued the tradition of getting dressed up at Christmas, secretly she'd always longed for the evening when it had been acceptable to change into something with an elasticated waist to ease the strain after copious amounts of turkey and trifle.

Christmas Day at The Fire Lodge was a joyful, communal affair. Molly had always admired how Claudia, Elvar, Finn and Alda lived, embracing sharing their home with guests, particularly at times when the focus should be on family. There were many reasons why people wanted to be away from home at Christmas and to have a place as incredible as this to escape to. Even though she had joyful memories of Christmas at her parents' house, Molly couldn't think of anywhere better to celebrate.

The day started with a leisurely breakfast of smoked salmon on freshly baked rye bread and Molly was in charge of retrieving it from the hot spring. Claudia had married the best of a traditional English Christmas with an Icelandic one, and despite alcohol being expensive, there was Bucks Fizz as well as coffee to go with their otherwise Icelandic breakfast.

The lively banter was a good distraction after her conversation with Howard, and she was grateful for Kat and Lils injecting much needed humour into the conversation, so she found it easier to pretend to be okay.

When everyone had finished, Claudia stood and raised her nearly empty glass of Bucks Fizz. 'Right, who's up for the Christmas Day post-breakfast, pre-lunch dip in the pool!'

Wide-eyed, Lils nearly splurted a mouthful of coffee.

All dressed up, Molly had completely forgotten about Claudia's Icelandic Christmas tradition, but she knew she wasn't going to get away with chickening out. Much like Elvar, Claudia had a way of persuading people to give anything a go.

'Any takers?' Claudia smiled manically.

'Go on then,' Kat said with glee. 'I didn't imagine I'd be in my swimming togs on Christmas Day, but there we go!'

Lils jumped to her feet. 'Sign me up too!'

'Molly, Alda, Finn – you know the drill!'

Nope, Molly thought. *No escape.* Not that she actually wanted to; her sister's enthusiasm was infectious.

Elvar guffawed. 'Swim suits optional!'

'You're kidding, right?' Jen looked shocked.

Claudia whacked Elvar. 'Of course he is. Swim suits are most definitely mandatory.'

'Unless we're on our own,' Elvar said under his breath, although from the titters that swept around the breakfast table, almost everyone had heard. Alda shook her head in dismay.

Jen scraped her chair back. 'I think I might give it a miss.'

'Oh, come on Jen,' James said, dropping his napkin and following after her. 'It'll be an experience. It was fun in the hot tub the other night...'

'For anyone who wants to,' Claudia announced to everyone else, 'see you in the pool!'

* * *

Molly returned to her room and swapped her dress and tights for her swimming costume. Throwing a robe over the top and shoving her bare feet into boots, she headed outside. Grey clouds threatened snow, and there was no hint of the blue sky or the sunshine they'd enjoyed on the day they'd been to black sand beach.

'Beat you to it, just!' Ever competitive, Claudia was on the other side of the pool, already stripped off. She kicked off her boots and dived in, her body streamlined beneath the milky-blue water.

With a sigh and already shivering, Molly removed her own

robe and boots and slid into the pool, the heat of the water a shock on her goose-bumped skin.

Kat and Lils emerged soon after, their squeals and laughter infectious as they turned the freezing air blue with their swearing.

'Don't look at my wobbly bits!' Kat yelled as she submerged herself in the water with a satisfied sigh.

Elvar, Finn, Alda and Graham were next, swiftly followed by Leifur and James, strolling out in bare feet.

Kat and Lils whooped with laughter.

'You're both bonkers!' Kat shook her head.

Wearing a confident smile and only a towel wrapped around his waist, Leifur looked as if he was thoroughly enjoying himself and it was no colder than a spring day. Molly's eyes drifted to his bare chest ridged with muscles hard-earned from a physically demanding, outdoorsy way of life. In a white robe and picking his way across the snow with a pained expression that made it seem as if he was walking on tiny daggers of ice, James looked less sure.

'The cold does us men no favours.' Leifur laughed and nudged James before whipping off his own towel. Molly was sure she wasn't the only one whose eyes were drawn to his rather snug-fitting swim shorts. He liked the attention, he always had. She also knew he had nothing to worry about in that department. Her eyes snapped back up and met his. He winked and dived in, barely breaking the surface of the water, his muscled arms slicing effortlessly as he swam the length of the pool. The delicious heat of the thermal water did nothing to dispel the heat rushing through her body at the direction her thoughts had taken.

'Wahey! Go on, James!' Lils yelled as, with a deep breath, James dropped his robe on the snow, took off his glasses and placed them on top.

Kat's wolf whistle made everyone laugh. James's cheeks flushed as he stepped to the edge of the pool. He didn't have Leifur's bravado, but he was surprisingly muscled. His defined chest and smattering of hair had been kept well-hidden beneath chunky jumpers.

'I can't see a bloody thing without my glasses,' he said through chattering teeth.

'I'd get in quick!' Leifur flicked water in his direction. 'Remember the effect the cold has...'

Once again, Molly's eyes dropped lower; her inner heat intensified. She tore her eyes away and floated on her back, gazing up at the smoke-grey sky, only hearing the result of James's dive ending in an almighty splash and laughter.

For a good twenty minutes, all ten of them bobbed about, their chatter spiralling with the steam into the freezing air. Leifur and Kat teased James about his impressive belly flop and Molly found herself enjoying being around people with a zest for life, while soaking up the beauty of the surroundings as drifting snow added to the festive magic.

Kat and Lils were the first to leave the pool, emerging with squeals and shrieks, steam rising off them. Grabbing their robes, they crunched along the path with raucous laughter. Molly couldn't help but smile as they disappeared inside. Her eyes flicked to the restaurant and Jen and Maggie sitting at a table together.

Leaving the others chatting, Molly swam over to Claudia.

'That was really sweet of Maggie to stay inside so Jen's not on her own.'

'It was.' Claudia nodded. 'Although I have no idea what we can possibly do to ensure she actually begins to enjoy herself.'

Molly dipped beneath the water until her chin was half submerged in an attempt to stay as warm as possible. 'You're doing all you can, Claudia. If she hasn't warmed to Iceland by now, I'm not sure she ever will. I mean, what's not to like?' She gestured at the pool surrounded by snow and glinting Christmas lights, the others distorted by the rising steam and plumes of foggy breath. 'James is fully embracing it.'

'James has been here before and is friends with Leifur. They both love this way of life.' Claudia swam closer and lowered her voice. 'I'm not sure a woman like Jen would ever be pleased with anything to be honest. Too high maintenance,' she mouthed. 'I'm surprised someone like James is with someone like her.'

Molly frowned. 'What do you mean?'

'You know what I mean. James is as outdoorsy as Leifur, happiest on an adventure, out in the wild. I don't really get that vibe from Jen, do you?'

Molly shook her head; that had been evident from the moment she'd met her.

'The vibe I do get though, from Leifur,' Claudia practically whispered, 'is how much he likes you. I see the way he looks at you.'

Molly ducked further beneath the warm water and ran a wet hand over her chilled face.

Claudia seemingly took Molly's silence as her needing further encouragement. 'Perhaps you should see where things lead. It's Christmas, once again you're both single, you're both lonely...'

'The little that happened between me and Leifur was a long time ago,' Molly said quietly. 'And to be honest, after what's happened with Howard, the last thing I want is a man.'

She caught Claudia's disbelieving look and realised how false that sounded even to her own ears. After all, hadn't her thoughts betrayed her at the sight of Leifur and, to be fair, James too when they'd stripped off to dive into the pool?

Nothing wrong with looking, she thought. But that was all her intention was.

16

———————

Once everyone had got dried and dressed, they met in the lounge to exchange presents. It had been hard to find gifts that would fit in her suitcase, so Molly had done what she did best and made iced snowflake biscuits and vanilla pecan fudge for her family. She'd made extra too, so she was able to give a little present each to Kat and Lils, Jen and James, Graham and Maggie, and Leifur. Afterwards, Molly joined Claudia, Elvar and Finn in the empty restaurant kitchen to start cooking. With Claudia in charge, Molly was tasked with preparing the trifle and was given free rein to get creative, while Claudia and Elvar focused on the Christmas dinner, and Finn made the stuffing and prepared drinks. With Christmas music blasting out and a fully equipped professional kitchen at her disposal, as well as a huge array of ingredients, Molly was in her element, laughing with her family as they cooked and chatted together, the upset of the last few days pushed firmly to the back of her mind. Once she'd finished the trifle, Claudia insisted she joined the others in the lounge where everyone, bar Jen, were still gathered in front of the fire either chatting or reading.

Molly plonked herself on the sofa next to Alda who immediately rested her feet on her lap. Quiet contentment eased through Molly as she relaxed back. Alda was reading the novel Claudia had given her for Jólabókaflóð and Molly admired how studious she was, so unlike Claudia at the same age. As a young child, her memory of a teenage Claudia was her rebellious streak and the raised voices between her and their dad. Molly couldn't remember a time when there wasn't a strained relationship between the two of them. They only ever argued, never talked. Molly had been too young to understand Claudia's reasoning for rebelling. Their dad's restrictions had been more to do with her being a girl than simple teenage angst.

'I miss Grandma and Grandad.' Although hushed, Alda's delicate voice startled Molly.

In the armchair next to them, James looked up from his book.

Molly met his eyes then turned back to Alda. 'I know you do.' She rested her hand on Alda's knee. 'I miss them too.'

Alda wrinkled her pale lips. 'It's strange to think we won't ever go back to their house. It's where I remember them the most. My memories of Christmas when I was younger are all there.'

'It was the perfect house to have Christmas in.' Molly stroked Alda's knee. 'But here will be our new place to create memories.'

'It wasn't the same last year, knowing Grandma wasn't around.' Alda didn't have to say more for Molly to see the sorrow etched on her face. 'Mamma was really sad. Nothing was the same.'

'The last two Christmases have been the strangest and saddest I've ever had.' It broke her heart to see Alda's sadness mirroring her own; she didn't want her niece to dwell on it. 'But you know what, we just need to take all the good bits from before and hold onto those. Enjoy the present and look to the future.'

'I lost my grandparents a little while ago too,' James said

quietly, closing the book he was reading and turning his attention to Alda. 'I know I'm older and was fortunate to have more time with them than you did with yours, but I've found it helpful to think of them often, however much it hurts. That way you're keeping their spirit alive. And I agree with Molly, sometimes focusing on the present and realising how lucky we are to be here enjoying each other's company, making different but new happy memories can be helpful. I often tell myself to be grateful for what I do have.'

Hearing about the heartache James was dealing with made Molly feel less alone, to know she wasn't the only one to be shouldering such feelings. It eased the tension in her chest to have his support while talking about this with Alda.

'Change is always hard,' Molly said gently. 'Particularly when it's tied up in grief. Selling Grandma and Grandad's house was incredibly emotional, yet on the day we completed, I felt this weird relief that it was over. I hope it means we can look back on our time there with fond memories rather than being constantly reminded that it's not the same without them.'

Alda's brow was still furrowed but she nodded in agreement.

'How's Finn been dealing with it all?' Molly asked.

'Finn has a girlfriend.' Alda scrunched up her nose. 'So he's fine. All happy and in love.' She giggled and stuck her tongue out. 'She's in Reykjavík, so he spends all his time on the phone to her.'

'Ah, that explains why he's holed up in his room so much of the time.'

James laughed. 'That's teenage boys for you.'

'That's why he doesn't care about going to university. One of the reasons anyway.' Alda shrugged. 'I think he'll miss out.'

'So you do want to go to university?' James asked.

'I want to travel and experience more of life than just what I know in Iceland.'

'Leifur did just that.' James put his book on the coffee table and leaned forward, resting his elbows on his knees. 'He was desperate to leave Iceland, to experience university and life in the UK. He came back though.'

'I might too.' Alda giggled. 'But I have to leave first.'

'All in good time,' Molly said, feeling very much like the wise aunt, not wanting Alda to wish away what remained of her childhood. Like Alda, she was lucky to have had a happy childhood – something she'd only really appreciated as an adult. 'You're on track though to do whatever you want,' she continued, wanting to build her confidence and give her hope. The one thing she'd missed from an otherwise perfect childhood was her dad never taking her dreams seriously. That was the last thing she wanted for Alda. She squeezed her arm. 'Your mum says you're doing really well in school – I'd love you to go to university in the UK. I'd get to see lots more of you that way.'

'Thanks, Molly.' Alda shuffled over and hugged her tight. A wave of love hit Molly. It was so needed, and so joyful to be embraced by her family. Alda pulled away and smiled, her eyes searching her face. 'It must have been hard for you.' She batted her hand as if trying to express what she meant when words couldn't. 'I hope you're okay, you know, after everything. And I'm really glad you're here.' She scooped up her phone from the coffee table. 'I'm going to phone my friends. Wish them a happy Christmas.'

With a lump in her throat, Molly watched Alda cross the lounge. She'd grown up so much since the last time she'd seen her, and back then at the funeral, Molly had been distracted and overwhelmed. What time they'd had together had been dominated by sadness. After a horrible time, this finally felt like the start of a new chapter, time with her family that was filled with something other than constant tears. Not that everything was completely fine; she still had a lot to work through: anger and discontentment, annoyance and heartache, unresolved feelings over so many things.

'She's a really lovely girl.' James pulled Molly from her thoughts. 'It's hard losing a grandparent at any age, but I think for a teen it must feel particularly difficult. It's long enough for them to really be a part of their lives but they lose out on their grandparents seeing them on the cusp of adulthood.'

Molly bit her lip and nodded. That was one of the things she found the hardest to deal with too, knowing what her parents were missing out on, not being able to see their grandchildren thrive and turn into the most brilliant young people. They would have been so proud. They *had* been proud. She wondered what her parents would make of the situation with Howard, the future they believed she'd have, snatched from under her. With Claudia in Iceland, it had been just her parents back home and now, without them, without Howard, she was truly on her own.

Fighting to control her emotions, she turned her focus to James. 'Are you doing okay? I know it can be strange being away at Christmas, particularly after a loss of your own.'

'Being somewhere completely different is actually helping. We went to Jen's parents last Christmas. It was the first without my grandparents, so it would have been strange anyway, but it was also the first with Jen's family and I felt very much like an outsider. I put not fitting in down to the way I was feeling, not wanting to celebrate.' He shrugged and leaned closer. 'Don't tell Jen, but I'm much happier spending Christmas here. The place, the company...' He laughed but somehow it sounded sad.

'And Jen, how's she finding it?' Molly asked, although she was pretty sure of the answer.

'Och, she'd much rather be at her parents'. Actually, anywhere else really.' His cheeks clenched and he breathed deeply as he gazed into the embers of the fire. 'She's in our room Zooming with them, some friends too I think.' He stood abruptly. 'We should really put more wood on the fire.'

The melancholy within his words and his demeanour saddened Molly. She wanted to reach out and hug him, the way Alda had done with her. After a loss, love and hugs were so needed. Even though he was here with his fiancée, Molly got the sense that it was something he was missing out on.

* * *

At three, everyone convened in the dining room for a three-course feast served by Claudia and Elvar. Back home, Molly would have been sitting with Howard watching the King's Speech, stuffed full of Christmas dinner, and she knew that was what he'd be doing with his family – and the brunette – right now. Claudia had amended the traditions they'd had with their parents with Christmas lunch taking place mid-afternoon to allow time in the morning for opening presents, getting outdoors for either a snowy hike or like this morning a dip in the thermally heated pool, then heading to the kitchen to cook. The evening would then be spent drinking, chatting and relaxing, watching a Christmas movie or playing a game.

Molly glanced around the table at the eclectic mix of people, which included her family and friends old and new. The hard truth was no one had it easy. Embracing change and adapting was a part of life. There were many stories of heartache around the table, she was sure.

As they tucked into perfectly cooked grouse with berry sauce and spiced red cabbage served with traditional crispy roast pota-toes, bread sauce and Finn's incredible sour cherry and bacon stuffing, Molly acknowledged her own heartache and disappoint-

ment didn't have to define her. She'd had pockets of fun in the
last few days and had actually managed to briefly put aside her
sorrow and live in the moment, just as she'd talked about with
James. Whatever was going on with Jen, he seemed to be buoyed
by Leifur, the long-time friends evidently enjoying each other's
company. Perhaps it was a comfort for both of them, to be
reminded of a time gone by when they'd had little responsibility
and life was just one big party.

With snow drifting past the picture windows and Christmas
music playing in the background, the chatter around the table
focused on past Christmases, the good, the bad and the funny,
accompanied by the scrape of knives and forks on plates.

After second helpings had been demolished and everyone
was looking decidedly rosy-cheeked and full, Lils stood up and
raised her glass. She waited until the conversation petered out
and all eyes turned to her.

'I just wanted to say, to Claudia, Elvar, Finn and Alda, thank
you for welcoming us into your home and for allowing us to
experience the joy of your life in such a magical location. The
food, the place. It's just...' She brought her fingers to her lips and
blew a kiss. 'There are no words!

'For various reasons, I wanted to get away this year.' She met
Kat's eyes and she encouraged her with a nod. 'There have been
times over the last four years where I wasn't certain I'd get to see
another Christmas.' She took a deep breath. 'When faced with a
scary cancer diagnosis, there's no guarantee of anything.' The
hush that settled was as quiet as a snowflake landing. Molly
sensed everyone was holding their breath, waiting for Lils to
continue in the hope that there would be a happy ever after, or a
happy for now at the very least. 'But I did make it to that first
Christmas and then I made it to another, then another. This
Christmas is very special for many reasons and we wanted to

celebrate that. I hoped Iceland would be magical, but it's exceeded all my expectations and we've met some incredible people.' Her eyes rested briefly on everyone around the table, landing last of all on Claudia and Elvar. She gave them a warm smile. 'You are both wonderful and I can't thank you enough. To Claudia and Elvar and all you've created at The Fire Lodge.'

Everyone raised their glasses to toast them.

Molly was certain she wasn't the only one moved by Lils's words and struck by what was left unsaid.

Kat squeezed Lils's hand, a brief look communicating so much between them.

'You hinted at it, so I'm daring to ask,' Claudia said gently. 'I assume you've come out the other side?'

'I have, thank you. I got the all-clear earlier this year. The cancer has gone.' Lils's hand shook as she picked up her glass. 'It's made me change my whole outlook – life's for living; we should never put things off. If there's something you want to do, go for it, challenge yourself and don't regret a thing. We just don't know what tomorrow holds.' She glanced between Claudia, Kat, Graham, James and Molly at her end of the table. 'I believe we all know something of heartache and how important it is to make the most of what we have, because life is fleeting and nothing's guaranteed. Oof, I'm not sure this is the right thing to talk about on Christmas Day!'

'I think it might be the perfect topic.' Claudia scooped a last forkful of red cabbage. 'Full of food, wine and surrounded by good company, I think Christmas is the ideal time to share our innermost feelings.' She didn't make eye contact but Molly sensed the comment was aimed at her.

'Then I should also toast Kat.' Lils gripped her wine glass tighter. 'Because without her support, I'm not sure I'd be here.'

'Don't be ridiculous.' Kat shook her head vehemently. 'You

absolutely kicked cancer's arse. That was all your doing along with the bloody wonderful NHS doctors and nurses. I may have supported you, but your strength and positivity are what got you through it.'

Lils's eyes glistened in the candlelight as she looked at the others. 'We may not share the same parents, but she's as close to a sister as I'll ever have. She was there for me when I got my diagnosis. She was there throughout treatment, a shoulder to cry on, bringing me lasagne and homemade curries, taking me to appointments and sitting with me, talking me out of a dark hole when I'd had enough. But she was also there for me at the end of treatment when I rang that bell after getting my all-clear. She kept me going by making plans for the future – like going to Iceland. She made me believe I'd get through it and actually have a future. I couldn't ask for a better friend.'

'Bloody hell, Lils!' James scrunched his napkin in his hand, his smile betraying his true feelings as he wiped away a tear.

'And now I've made a grown man cry!' Lils laughed. 'See, Claudia, I told you it wasn't talk for Christmas Day.'

'I think it's perfect and James can handle it. He's a big boy in tune with his emotions.' Claudia looked decidedly teary too, which moved Molly almost as much as Lils's words had.

Graham had remained quiet throughout, but he raised his glass and nodded at Claudia. 'I agree with you that this is the perfect conversation for today. Maggie and I made a bucket list for our twenty-fifth wedding anniversary and approaching our thirtieth we realised we hadn't crossed off one thing.' Graham glanced down the table at his wife now chatting to Elvar. 'Over the last two years alone we've lost two family members and three close friends. In the summer, a young work colleague of mine was given just a year to live. It makes you think, doesn't it. It puts everything in perspective and it certainly made us question what on earth we were waiting for. So I wholeheartedly echo what Lils put so beautifully. Life's short. It's full of unknowns too. Why put things off until tomorrow, when tomorrow's never guaranteed? I know Maggie and I are in a fortunate position – we have our health, we have time and money, so we're doing something about it. We're making memories and Iceland's the first to be ticked off.'

Lils beamed at him. 'What's next?'

'We have plenty more places we want to visit, but I've bought Maggie pottery lessons so she can tick that off in the new year, while I'm going to join an extras agency because I've always wanted to be in a film.'

The conversation that had been threaded with emotion was turned around with Graham's bucket list revelations, which soon got everyone else talking about the destinations they'd most like to travel to.

Molly had no desperate ambition to learn to throw pottery or act in a film, but she did have a strong desire to do something meaningful with her life, something she was passionate about and could be proud of. She made a mental note to stop putting things off.

Christmas Day afternoon ticked by and while the surrounding landscape was plunged into darkness, candles flickered warmth across the table and wood was added to the fire. Cheers went up as Claudia brought out Molly's Icelandic inspired trifle with frosted berries, sweet rhubarb and a custard infused with cardamon. Feeling full with food, tipsy on wine, gin and then a glass of Elvar and Leifur's homemade brennivin, a ridiculously strong liquor dubbed Black Death, Molly ended the day comatose on the sofa, yet somehow feeling very much alive.

17

While the weather was good, rather than spending the day at the lodge on Boxing Day, Claudia broke with tradition and decided to move the trip to Perlan in Reykjavík forward. After Christmas Day's indulgence, everyone jumped at the chance to get out and discover the delights of the famous landmark that overlooked the city with its high-tech nature exhibition.

Without Birta and encouraged by James, Leifur joined them, although Molly got a sense from Jen that she wasn't too keen on him crashing their couple time. Everyone seemed to enjoy themselves though, and it was a new experience for Molly too. They shivered in the 100-metre-long ice cave, took in the magical Arora show about the northern lights, then were nearly blown off the outside observation deck with its 360° view of Reykjavík, before warming up with hot chocolate and open sandwiches in the glass-domed restaurant.

They returned to the lodge after a long and joyful day and everyone, apart from Finn and Alda who had friends over and Graham and Maggie who had retired to their room, settled around the fire in the lounge, nursing festive drinks. The conversation was dominated by the day's experiences as they laughed and drank. Molly was grateful to be far from home, surrounded by new people. Even after Lils's emotional revelation from the day before, she and Kat had the ability to talk about anything, which, along with Claudia's input, kept the conversation flowing, while their easy friendship and bubbly personalities rubbed off on everyone. Well, almost everyone.

Jen was quiet, more so than usual. James tried his best to involve her but with little luck. He laughed and joked, but his smile didn't seem to reach his eyes. Claudia, Kat and Lils made up for it though.

'Honestly,' Lils said, raising her glass of mulled wine to Claudia and Elvar. 'As I said yesterday, this has, hands down, been one of the best Christmases I've ever had.' She shook her head. 'Christmas has never been the same as an adult. I remember the wonder as a child and I've never been able to recapture that, probably because I've never had children. I don't know, it's always felt as if something was missing.'

'Even with children, it's not always magical,' Kat stressed. 'Don't get me wrong, Christmas was special when my kids were young but it wasn't always easy. Because being an adult is shit-hard.' She laughed. 'I'm not being funny, but being a single parent trying to hold down a job, doing everything on my own and giving my kids a "Christmas to remember" was bloody tough.'

'There's always too much pressure to make everything perfect at Christmas,' Claudia said.

Kat snorted and waved her hand around.

'Yeah, I know how that sounds when we live somewhere like this.' Claudia tucked her feet beneath her on the sofa. 'Iceland does make it easy to nail the festive vibe when we're pretty much guaranteed a white Christmas, but this place hasn't always looked

like this. We used to run a tour business from our flat in Reykjavík and then when we bought this land, what, fifteen years ago,
there were just ramshackle buildings here. We had to start from
scratch. There's been a lot of grafting.'

'Oh, I imagine it takes a huge amount of work to make something so effortlessly luxurious and welcoming.' Lils dipped her
glass of ruby-red wine in Claudia's direction. 'Do you ever take a
day off?'

'Not often, but then we love what we do.' She stole a glance at
Elvar. 'Yes, we're looking after guests most of the time, but we get
to spend our time having an adventure in the outdoors, inviting
people into our home and hopefully giving them a holiday of a
lifetime. Plus, I get to do it all with my best friend.' She reached
for Elvar's hand.

'Oh, there's something wonderful about that.' Kat pressed her
hand to her heart.

Elvar and Claudia complemented each other perfectly, their
understated love and quiet respect for each other evident in the
little things and the gentlest of moments. Molly and Claudia's
parents may have loved each other but they never had the closeness, respect and understanding that Claudia had for Elvar and
vice versa. A lump found its way into Molly's throat. Seeing them
together highlighted everything Molly had been missing out on
with Howard. Why had she settled for someone who wasn't right
for her? Was it through a fear of being alone? Or was Claudia
right about their parents and what she'd said about the way their
dad had treated their mum? Had their unequal relationship
rubbed off on Molly without her even realising? She'd always
glossed over the cracks that had formed between her and
Howard, believing they weren't insurmountable, that they'd get
through them, that those challenges and difficulties were just

part of being committed to someone. Perhaps she should have paid more attention to what was really going on.

'Is it honestly worth it though, sharing your life with so many other people?' Jen piped up, surprising Molly and, by the looks of it, everyone else.

James turned to her and frowned.

'What?' she snapped. 'I'm interested, that's all.'

'It's fine,' Claudia replied with a smile. 'It's a perfectly reasonable question. And I guess the answer is, it's a choice, but one we made together that's enabled us to live where we do. It's turned our hobbies and lifestyle into our livelihood. Our family life is a huge part of that.' Claudia's tone was smooth and controlled. Molly was sure that no one else, other than Elvar and possibly Leifur, would notice the slight tightening of her lips. There was a definite undercurrent of annoyance, Molly was certain.

'I don't know how you cope spending so much of the year in the freezing cold and dark.'

'Jen,' James warned.

Her nostrils flared as she shot him a look. 'It's just my opinion.'

'Which is absolutely fine.' Claudia didn't miss a beat. 'It's not for everyone, I agree. Personally, we embrace the cold.'

'It's definitely not for everyone,' Elvar said. 'And it takes getting used to. If you've never been somewhere with temperatures like this or where it's dark for so much of the day, then it can be a shock. We make up for it with the midnight sun in summer.'

Jen looked unconvinced.

'My ex-wife doesn't like this time of the year either and she's Icelandic,' Leifur chipped in. 'Then again, there's quite a lot she's not too keen on.' He caught Kat's amused look and winked.

Claudia smoothed out a crease in her trousers. 'It does help that Elvar and I love this lifestyle. It has its challenges but we work through them together.'

'That's because you're a team,' Kat said with a stab of her finger. She was beginning to look rather merry with flushed cheeks and sleepy eyes. 'Not every marriage is like that. Trust me. I've got the divorce papers, the grey hairs and an arsehole of an ex to show for it.'

'Playing devil's advocate here because I'm interested.' Claudia waggled her glass in Kat's direction. 'But it must be easier to make a clean break if you're with someone who's obviously no good and a bit of a you-know-what. It's the relationships that are just bumbling along that must be hardest to move on from, surely?'

Elvar snorted. 'What are you trying to say, Claudia?'

Claudia beamed at him. 'Ha ha! I'm talking about other people. I know we're good.'

The look that passed between them somehow conveyed love and strength with a good dose of passion in a fleeting meeting of the eyes. Molly sighed inwardly, knowing she'd never had that with anyone; bumbling along was the perfect way to describe her and Howard. She also sensed she wasn't the only person feeling a little uncomfortable at Claudia's words. Leifur was nursing his drink and James suddenly seemed captivated by a speck of something on his jeans. Jen was curled up in the corner of the sofa, silent again, her eyes firmly fixed on her phone.

'You can't be with someone just because you fear being alone.' Lils joined the conversation. 'Even if you're with someone you quite like. I know it's easy for me to say – been there, done that, got the T-shirt. My ex-husband was a nice, pretty decent bloke. I look back and think of us as a vanilla couple, bumbling along exactly as you just suggested, Claudia. The passion had faded, we took each other for granted and honestly, we preferred to spend time apart rather than doing things together. I was scared shitless making that break, but I just wasn't prepared to waste any more of my life being miserable. Taking a chance and making a big scary decision was needed for my sanity. Easier, I know, without kids.'

'That was the problem for me.' Leifur's deep voice cut over the crackle of the fire. He'd been listening intently, only occasionally voicing his opinion, so his words now hushed everyone. 'Things hadn't been right between me and my wife for a long time, but Birta kept us together for longer because I was worried about her.'

'That's so sweet that you were thinking of her.' Kat sipped her drink and watched him carefully.

'In the end I had to think about myself, because how I was feeling and behaving was affecting her. Not being able to see her every day is the saddest thing as she lives with her mamma most of the time, so it's hard. Really hard.'

'Oh I get that, I really do.' Kat's face creased with concern. 'There's no love lost between me and my ex, but he's a good father and I know he missed the kids like crazy when they were younger. The same for me too. There were Christmas Days and occasional birthdays that I missed out on because they were with their dad. I completely get the heartache of being a single parent. It's not just about the mum.'

Kat's words tugged at Molly's emotions and evoked a reaction in Leifur. He smoothed his hand down his beard, his damp eyes glinting in the firelight. Molly wanted to hug him. Leifur was the rock-hard adventurous man she'd fallen for that summer in her twenties. His outlook on life had been 'go big or go home' and he was always up for an adventure, a free spirit who was now showing his vulnerable side, craving time with his little girl above everything else. Life had a habit of grinding people down, testing them to see what they were truly made of and how much shit they could take. Molly's heart ached for him and the memory of that summer together stirred uninvited feelings. Her eyes subtly traced his jumper-clad torso, up to his beard and defined cheekbones. Not all of those feelings were completely unwanted. Everything with Howard was fresh and hurtful, while lingering memories with Leifur were faded and confusing.

Everything was amplified at this time of year, particularly when it came to families, because what was the festive season about, if not for spending it with loved ones? For Leifur to be here with his friend's family and their guests instead of spending it with his daughter was heart-breaking. So many families would be going through a similar thing. Kat had said so herself. Even on the flip side, when Leifur spent time with his daughter, her mother would be missing out. There was no perfect answer.

'Once again this has turned into a bit of a communal therapy session!' Lils said.

Reserved laughter peppered the lounge.

'It's a positive thing, though, to open up and talk,' Claudia said frankly. 'Sometimes sharing our innermost thoughts and concerns can be hugely liberating.'

She didn't look at anyone in particular, but Molly sensed the comment was aimed at her. Perhaps Leifur too. Actually, a few of them could potentially take Claudia's comment to heart.

There was a noticeable gap between James and Jen, as if they'd had an argument and hadn't yet made up. Jen was clutching her iPhone like it was a comfort blanket. Everyone else looked relaxed, and although Elvar was quiet, apart from throwing in an occasional wise comment, he seemed to be enjoying himself. It was good to see him with friends, and Molly was glad that Leifur had Elvar and James's support during a challenging time. And she had Claudia's. Her eyes flicked to her sister. It was exhausting trying to keep her own feelings in check.

Among family and newfound friends, a desire to be open and honest swept through Molly. She'd been encouraged by Kat and Lils's openness and floored by Leifur's emotion. It was hugely appealing to see the freedom of being truthful and owning the hurt. If she wasn't able to speak the truth, how was she supposed to accept the situation and be able to move on from Howard? Because that was what she wanted to do. She wanted to carve out a new, happier path for herself, but first she had to accept that her life was far from perfect and she needed to be okay with that.

'My boyfriend broke up with me.' It felt as if she was looking down on herself and someone else had uttered the words.

Everyone turned to her. Kat raised an eyebrow, while Claudia leaned forward, her eyes wide as if silently willing her on.

'That's why he's not here. He didn't miss his flight; he never intended to get on it in the first place. Thought it would be a way of letting me down gently. He's also been having an affair. With a colleague. I'm pretty sure she's staying with him at his parents' for Christmas.'

The spit and crackle of the fire consuming the logs intensified as the silence grew.

'Wow, that was brave, Molly.' Kat was the first to speak.

Molly shrugged. 'You were all sharing, it felt right that I did too. I don't want to pretend any longer.'

'And you shouldn't have to.' Lils reached towards Molly and knocked her glass of mulled wine against hers. 'As someone who's had more failed relationships than I care to remember, it might not feel like it at the moment, but if his heart wasn't in it and he's been cheating and disrespecting you like that, then he's done you a huge favour by letting you go. Now you can embrace the freedom.'

Molly nodded, lifted by the heartfelt words of two women who seemingly had a hell of a lot of life experience between them. She knew how easily people could hide their true feelings, feign happiness when they were hurting inside, but Kat and Lils seemed genuinely content with their lives despite relationship breakdowns, heartache and trauma. They gave her hope and, right now, that was all she needed.

'It's definitely his loss.' Leifur caught her eye and held it long enough for her to feel her cheeks flush at his intensity.

She was the first to shift her gaze. Elvar was watching Leifur, a frown creasing his forehead. Elvar switched his attention to Molly and raised his glass. He smiled, not with pity, but somehow conveying the same feeling she'd got from Kat and Lils. 'You don't deserve to be treated like that, any time, but Christmas... Aah, you are here, with your family, with us all.'

'Yes, yes you are,' Claudia joined in, raising her glass too. 'So let's drink. To freedom and new beginnings.'

'Freedom and new beginnings!' echoed around the room.

'Out with the old this Christmas,' Claudia continued, 'and in with the new in the New Year! Iceland is the perfect place to embrace new experiences and opportunities, because, I believe, that's what you've been given. So cheers, little sis.'

Molly laughed, the sound unfamiliar, but it felt light and exhilarating to allow herself to be enveloped in the evening with a group of people who were supportive and comforting. Molly hadn't anticipated feeling uplifted by sharing a little of her heartache, but somehow she did. It hadn't changed anything, but it was a relief to not have to continue hiding the truth.

'Anyone want to share anything else!' Kat laughed and hiccupped at the same time.

Another ripple of laughter went around the lounge.

'I do.' Jen cleared her throat. 'I don't want to get married.'

18

'I beg your pardon?' Kat was the first to find her voice.

Jen turned to James. 'We shouldn't get married,' she repeated, firmer this time.

Apart from the flickering fire, the whole room stilled.

Wide-eyed, James looked at her in shock. 'Are you being serious?'

'Completely.' She tugged at her diamond engagement ring, pulling it off and dropping it on to the sofa between them, where it glinted in the firelight.

'I don't understand.' The colour drained from James, reflecting the snow-covered landscape. His brow furrowed. 'It was you who suggested we go away to work things out.'

'I didn't mean to bloody Iceland with your friends,' she hissed.

James visibly recoiled, Jen's words as much a slap in the face as if she'd physically assaulted him. 'Then why the hell go along with it?'

Molly was holding her breath. The tension in the room crackled. No one said a word, nor could anyone tear their eyes away from the scene playing out.

Claudia broke the quiet. 'Perhaps, er, we should give you some privacy.'

'No,' James said firmly. 'We're not going to disrupt your evening.' He turned back to Jen. 'Why don't you tell everyone *why* we were trying to work things out.'

'Oh, you'd love that, wouldn't you?' Jen's slender nostrils flared, her eyes flashing with anger beneath curled lashes. 'Showing me up in front of everyone.'

James looked as if he was doing everything he could to stop himself crying. 'No, you're right; it would be awful of me to do something like that, which is why *you* choosing to announce this in public rather than talking to me in private is so very wrong.'

Jen bristled and folded her arms.

No one moved, not even Claudia. Molly understood how intriguing other people's lives, could be, particularly when dirty laundry was being aired. It was human nature to be nosy, like slowing down to take a look when passing a road traffic accident. Despite Claudia's suggestion to leave them be, there was a morbid fascination in seeing how it played out.

Jen looked at James with contempt. '*You* lied to me from the beginning!' Her cheeks were reddening, her voice shrill.

'I never lied—'

'You made out you owned a castle, were wealthy—'

'I do own a castle.' James's voice was now steely. All the things he'd said and hinted at were beginning to make sense to Molly, and it wasn't hard to imagine that Jen may have behaved in a similar way to Howard. 'It was *your* assumption I had money, and I do, it's just tied up in the property and its potential.'

'*Its potential*,' Jen practically spat. 'You'll throw money you don't have at it and you want us to slum it for God knows how many years while you work on a project that's going to bleed us dry, doing all that work yourself. That's no way to live, so I'm not doing it.'

'It's been a lie from the beginning, hasn't it?' An undercurrent of rage threaded through James's words. 'You desperately hoped I was someone I'm not and when you realised that, you decided to keep your options open while testing the waters elsewhere. You want the best of bloody everything but don't give a crap about who you hurt in the process!'

Footsteps sounded and Alda appeared in the doorway of the lounge, a frown creasing her delicate features. Claudia stood and waved her away, turning back to the group still entranced by the real-life soap opera.

With tears in her eyes, Jen turned to Claudia. 'Do you know when the next available flight is?'

James shook his head. 'Are you serious?'

'I think this is enough for tonight.' Claudia's tone was kind but firm and Molly sensed she was desperate to get the evening back under control. 'James and Jen, we'll continue this conversation in just a moment. Everyone else, thank you for a memorable day, but I think it's time we called it a night.'

Along with mutters of agreement, Elvar sprang to his feet and wished everyone a good night. Kat and Lils followed, whispering together as they sloped away.

'James?' Concern filled Leifur's voice as he stood and looked intently at his friend.

James nodded. 'I'm okay.'

Leifur didn't look convinced but he headed off after Elvar.

Claudia turned to Jen. 'I can take a look but there's unlikely to be any flights for the next day or two, so there's nothing we can do tonight.'

'We're not sharing a room.' Jen's voice was as icy as the weather outside.

'My goodness, Jen. What on earth has got into you?' James's nostrils flared. 'It's him, isn't it? You're still seeing him, aren't you?'

'I'm not talking about this.'

'Oh, now you're worried about everyone knowing about our private life and your fucking affair!' James turned to the fire, his shoulders rigid and head bowed.

Claudia revealed her worry in knitted brows and scrunched lips. Molly sensed her internal battle of how she was going to manage the expectations of a couple who were breaking up under her roof at what should have been the happiest time of the year.

Molly cleared her throat. 'You can have my room. I'll move to the guest room upstairs.'

James swung round, his face contorting with emotion. 'We can't do that.'

She could imagine the confusion and devastation he was feeling. She'd faced a similar conversation just a few days before.

'It's where I usually stay when I'm here.' He was standing too far away to reach out and touch his shoulder, but she desperately wanted to convey how sorry she was and how much she felt for him. 'It was only because my boyfriend – my ex-boyfriend – was supposed to be coming with me that I'm even in one of the guest suites. Honestly, you can have it.'

James glanced at Claudia and she nodded, while Jen grunted an acknowledgement.

With tears in his eyes, he nodded at Molly. 'That's really, *really* kind of you.'

'That's settled then,' Claudia said as breezily as she could. 'Let's get things sorted.'

The drama had put paid to what had been a wonderful

Boxing Day evening. With the sleeping arrangements to sort out, Jen stalked ahead to their room, James following silently behind, Molly and Claudia trailing after him.

The second Claudia closed the door to Molly's room behind them, she turned to her open-mouthed. 'Oh my goodness. You couldn't have made that up.'

'I feel so sorry for him,' Molly said.

'I do too.' Claudia whipped back the duvet and started unbuttoning the cover. 'But he's well shot of her, just like you are with Howard. For two lovely people, how on earth did you both end up with nut jobs for partners?'

'You can't say that! Howard's lots of things, but not that.'

'Okay fine, but Jen' – Claudia lowered her voice despite it being impossible for anyone to overhear – 'is a piece of work. She's given off hating-being-here vibes from the moment she arrived. It was obvious how ill-suited they were to each other, but the affair thing.' She raised an eyebrow. 'I wasn't expecting that. And from Howard too. I'm so sorry, Moll.'

Molly nodded but was relieved when Claudia didn't continue talking about it. More than anything, she was grateful to be here, surrounded by her family.

As they stripped the bed and remade it with fresh sheets and a new duvet cover, Molly mulled over the idea that James had known about Jen's affair and had forgiven her – at least enough to try and make things work. She wasn't sure she'd have been as forgiving of Howard if she'd found out before he'd broken up with her.

While Claudia tidied the rest of the room and cleaned the en suite, Molly packed her suitcase. She took out the bottle of bourbon, the present that had been meant for Howard, and left it on the bedside table for James. The luxury of the guest suite had been a treat, but on her own, the romance was lost. In a weird way, perhaps it was for the best staying in Claudia's apartment where she usually did. Although it would put her closer to Leifur...

'I'll go and see how James and Jen are getting on.' With the used towels bundled in her arms, Claudia glanced around and gave a satisfied nod. 'Leave your suitcase in the hallway. I'll get Elvar to bring it up.'

Molly drew the curtains over the icescape outside. So far the northern lights had failed to show. The nights were stubbornly cloudy, hiding the lightshow that Molly was sure was playing out somewhere way above. Claudia had relit the wood burner, and amber light flickered over the reclaimed wood panelling and pale walls. She was about to drag her suitcase into the hallway when there was a knock at the door.

'Sorry,' James said as she opened it. 'I can come back if you're not ready.'

'No, it's okay, come on in.' She stood back and he wheeled his suitcase in.

Sadness was etched on his face. 'I really am sorry for this disruption.'

Molly waved her hand. 'You don't need to apologise. I'm just glad that I'm here and this is possible.' Molly could imagine Claudia's stress if she'd been a paying guest and James having this suite wasn't an option. 'I'm also sorry you're going through this too.' Molly saw a lot of herself in James, battered by the seemingly rapid disintegration of a relationship that obviously had been as damaged as her own.

'We're a right pair, aren't we.' James laughed. 'Both of us dumped at Christmas.'

He pushed his glasses up with his finger and smiled shyly. She'd felt at ease around him during the times they'd chatted together over the last few days, but there was a true connection now, both of them dealing with their own heartache and disappointed by love – or the lack of it.

'It's certainly not how I envisaged Christmas to be. But,' Molly said slowly, 'it could be worse. I'm determined to make the best of a shitty thing. I'm in a place I love and surrounded by fabulous people.'

James met her eyes. 'I should follow your example and try to look on the bright side. I've loved being here, which makes me realise how miserable I was last Christmas – you know what we were talking about yesterday. I'd put it down to grief, but er, after what's just happened, perhaps my gut instinct was correct.'

'It usually is, it's just we don't pay it any attention until something happens to force us to evaluate it. It's the same with me. I've ignored what my gut's been telling me for too long. I've pushed any negative feelings to the back of my mind, which is my way of coping, but then I've been juggling so much emotional crap maybe I just couldn't see what was really going on.' Molly brushed her hand against his. 'But whatever you're feeling and whatever you think about the whole situation, it's just happened, so go easy on yourself. It must be quite a shock.'

'Yes, and no. This is a truly horrible analogy but it feels as if I've been flogging a dead horse for a hell of a long time. Trying to make things work because, I don't know, I was afraid of the alternative, afraid of letting myself down, my grandparents in particular – which is just stupid because they're not here any longer and I shouldn't be thinking like that, not if it's something that will impact the rest of my life.'

'If your grandparents were anything like my parents, they'd only want what's best for you, and if that means moving on from a relationship that wasn't right, then it can only be a good thing.'

He nodded, but behind his glasses his eyes looked damp.

'Jen's determined to leave, but Claudia isn't hopeful about flights till at least the end of the week. She's going to have a look for her.'

'But you're staying, right?'

James nodded. 'There's nothing to go home to.'

Molly understood that completely.

19

'I'm sorry this isn't a patch on downstairs,' Claudia said, pushing open the door of the spare room. 'But Leifur's in the room you normally stay in.'

Molly put a hand on her sister's arm. 'Honestly, Claudia, it's perfect. I should have been up here with you all from the beginning.'

Claudia gave a nod that implied she agreed.

'I'll leave you to it and see you in the morning.' Her smile was full of pity as she slipped from the room.

Had her sister always believed Molly's relationship with Howard had been doomed from the start? Not everyone could be as happy and compatible as Claudia and Elvar. What was the magic ingredient? Luck? Lots of trial and error? Respect? Unconditional love? All of those things and more?

Molly's previous relationships had been relatively short, but they had been meaningful, not just flings. They'd fizzled out all the same. She often wondered if it was down to her social circle and where she'd ended up working. Instead of a creative degree, she'd been persuaded, by her dad, into doing business studies before ending up working in HR. The people she met and often socialised with, like Howard, were straight laced, serious, business and money minded, not at all creative. If she'd pursued a degree she'd been passionate about and was working in a more creative field, perhaps things would be different.

As her mum would have told her, 'You can't change the past, so there's no point dwelling on it. You have to make the best of what you've got.'

Molly agreed she couldn't change the past, but she could learn from it. She sighed and started unpacking.

The room was small and simply decorated, but it was cosy with a double bed piled with cushions and pillows. A lamp on the bedside table cast a soft glow over the cream walls, which were decorated with photos of her family's Icelandic adventures: Claudia hiking across a glacier that looked as if a gigantic chunk of a glacier mint had been dropped into the landscape; Elvar and Leifur with an erupting Fagradalsfjall volcano behind them, fiery lava spewing into the air. There was one of her mum and dad too, kitted out in their winter clothes, only their faces visible, enough to see her mum's smile contrasting with her dad's grimace. Claudia had taken the photo at Skógafoss, and Molly remembered their parents clinging to each other in front of the thundering waterfall, while a vicious wind buffeted them. Their dad had loathed the freezing temperatures and the icy dampness, while their mum had thrown herself into the experience, the waterfall completely stealing her heart. It had been her favourite place.

Nostalgia caught her unawares as it always did when she thought back on memories of her parents. She'd talk to Claudia about going there together, to retrace their footsteps; their mum would have liked that.

A knock on the door disrupted her thoughts.

'Come in.'

She turned to find Leifur silhouetted in the doorway, all broad-shouldered with unkempt hair. He looked manly and she couldn't help but compare him to Howard with his skincare regime and city clothes. Leifur was rugged and a little wild in personality and looks. Molly also knew how rugged he was underneath his clothes...

'Are you okay?' he asked.

'It's just a room.' Molly shrugged. 'A place to sleep.'

He met her eyes, his gaze drinking her in. It felt as if he was undressing her. She willed her thoughts about him in *that* way to dissolve.

'I've just come up from seeing James; he's pretty cut up.' Leifur shrugged. 'I didn't know what to say.'

'I don't think there really is anything to say.'

'He said you'd talked to him.'

Molly nodded. 'We're both going through a similar thing, although I didn't get quite such a public thrashing.'

'I didn't want him to get hurt, but he's better off without her.'

'It seems that way.' She met his gaze and it sent an unexpected thrill through her.

'Anyway.' He drummed his fingers on the door surround. 'I'm only in the next room if you need me.'

If you need me. Or did he mean want me...

He said goodnight and left her with a million thoughts fizzing: what Claudia had said the day before about Leifur liking her, followed by memories of that summer together. They'd been young and just as eager as each other. Was Leifur hinting at picking things up where they'd left off?

After a day filled with festivities that had ended with a surprising number of emotional truths, Molly was exhausted as she closed the curtains on the night. The spare room was at the back of the lodge, so she'd lost the river view, plus it didn't face north either. Not that it mattered with the night sky once again distorted by moody clouds.

Yes, Leifur was in the next room, but that didn't mean she had to take him up on his offer. And, the more she thought about it, the more she realised it really had sounded like an offer. She changed into nightclothes and slipped into bed, pulling the covers tight around her. It was fine for her thoughts to drift to memories though, of that summer camping trip in her twenties, Leifur's hands exploring her body. Surrounded by other people, it had felt naughty and adventurous, passionate and secretive. They had been unable to fully act on their desires, so the sexual tension had been at tipping point. Hushed fumbling, teasing fingers and explorative lips. Somehow that had been more exciting than if they'd ended up having full blown sex. There was nothing stopping her now. She snuggled further beneath the duvet that smelled deliciously fresh. Despite a desire to be loved, she didn't want to entertain being that vulnerable and exposed with someone. Just because Howard had dumped her, it didn't mean she was ready to move on; she'd barely got her head around his deceit. So she stayed snuggled, allowing the memories to pulse, acknowledging her body responding. It surprised her but not enough to do anything about it.

Her thoughts drifted, her mind in overdrive as she tried to sleep, thinking not just about Leifur but the last few days in Iceland. The moment her thoughts strayed to Howard, she shut them down. She focused instead on the memory of standing on Perlan's roof and the feeling of being on top of the world as Kat and Lils had linked their arms in hers and Elvar had taken a photo; of Kat's squeal as her glove had been snatched by the wind and James's booming laughter as he'd managed to catch it. She wondered how James was and whether he was lying awake in the bed she'd woken up in that morning, if he was thinking back on the series of events that had led to this point. She wondered if his heart was hurting or if, like her, he was slowly beginning to realise he'd been handed a gift.

'This is a nightmare,' Claudia said the next morning over breakfast in the apartment kitchen. With a piece of toast in one hand, she was scrolling on her laptop with her other. 'Tomorrow's flight is fully booked so the earliest Jen can fly back is Thursday. It hardly seems worth it, except...' She pulled a face.

From the little she'd gleaned about Jen, Molly could imagine what a difficult guest she would be to keep happy when this was the last place she'd wanted to be even *before* she'd broken up with James.

'We're going to have to keep them separate,' Elvar said. 'They were both going on our trip to The Star Lodge tomorrow, which doesn't make sense if Jen wants to go home. Plus I don't think she will actually like snowmobiling.'

Leifur snorted over his mug of coffee and Molly smiled.

'So maybe we suggest she does something else?' he added.

Claudia frowned. 'I didn't think the weather was going to be good enough to go?'

'It looks temperamental.' Elvar shrugged. 'We should be okay to get there and it's only for one night. If it closes in, we just stay an extra day. In the circumstances, it might not be such a bad idea to keep them apart.'

'Hmm.' Claudia huffed and Molly realised that while Elvar escaped on an adventure that would include James, Claudia would be left with Jen.

'I'm sure she'd like the Blue Lagoon,' Molly suggested as she buttered a piece of toast. 'Although I'd love to go there too.'

'You're coming with me,' Elvar said firmly with a twinkle in his eye. 'You have yet to see our new lodge or experience our star pods.'

'The Blue Lagoon is great,' Leifur said. 'But where we're going will be an adventure.'

Molly's heart did a little dance. 'You're going too?'

'Uh-huh,' he said through a mouthful of eggs and toast.

'That's decided then.' Elvar stood and stretched. He looked at Claudia. 'Sort out with Jen her return flight and suggest the Blue Lagoon as an alternative. Graham and Maggie weren't sure about going snowmobiling either, so suggest it to them as well. That way everyone is happy.'

Everyone except Claudia, Molly thought, watching her sister eat her toast with a scowl.

With nothing planned, everyone spent the day relaxing at the lodge, although after the events of the night before, there was an undercurrent of tension that Claudia and Elvar tried their hardest to dispel. Jen chose to eat breakfast and lunch in her room and it was to everyone's relief that she stayed there for the best part of the day. James was understandably downbeat but he had Leifur for company and the two friends escaped the lodge for a long walk. Molly knew how good it must be to have a friend to lean on. After all, she was going through something similar and she had Claudia, even if she hadn't been completely appreciative of her sister's companionship and support. Perhaps taking advice from her sister who had her life figured out would be a smart move.

In the end, it was just Molly, Kat, Lils, James, Leifur and Elvar who headed out on a whirlwind one-night adventure to The Star Lodge, leaving a disgruntled Claudia back home with Graham, Maggie and of course Jen. At least she had the support of Finn and Alda, but even so, Molly felt sorry for her, knowing how much she'd prefer to be joining them instead of babysitting an upset and, quite frankly, pain-in-the-arse grown woman.

Deep lines ridged James's forehead, erasing his usually cheerful demeanour as he exited The Fire Lodge, a rucksack slung over his back.

'Are you okay?' Molly asked as they crunched their way to the parking area.

He shrugged and sighed a plume of frozen breath into the air. 'I expect she won't be here when I get back. Not really sure how I feel.'

Leifur thumped his back. 'At least you can forget about her for a couple of days.'

James looked far from convinced as they scrambled into the 4x4. Molly knew forgetting about Jen would be the last thing James would be able to do; she'd been trying and failing to forget about Howard. When someone was so much a part of your life and had betrayed you, they were permanently etched in your thoughts.

They started out in fine, clear weather, but as they left the flatter area towards the south coast and cut inland, the terrain got steeper and wilder, the sky darkened and the wind picked up, lashing snow flurries at the windscreen. The 4x4 powered on, gripping the ice-slicked roads, and Molly knew they were in safe hands with Elvar.

As quickly as the weather had closed in, by the time they neared their destination, the sun had risen and the clouds had cleared enough to reveal patches of blue sky and a white land-scape bathed in the honey tones of the winter sun.

Molly had seen plenty of photos of The Star Lodge from inception plans, through the building work to the finished delights of a truly special place – a central dome with a wall of curved glass which housed the communal living space, plus a kitchen, three shower rooms and staff bedrooms at the rear. From the communal pod, glass and wood walkways snaked off on either side, leading through the woods to six private domed bedroom pods. It was Claudia and Elvar's pride and joy, a hub for snow sports and romance, and Molly couldn't wait to experience it.

Deep snow layered the roof of the unassuming wood-clad building surrounded by evergreens threaded with fairy lights. Bundled in their outdoor gear, they left the warmth of the vehicle and stepped into the powdery snow.

It was so incredibly quiet once the last car door had slammed shut. No birdsong, no traffic, not even a breath of wind. Just a calming white, the branches heavy with snow, and it delighted Molly, the sense of peace and space, a true wilderness.

'Right,' Elvar said, tugging on his gloves. 'The sun is out and the bad weather isn't forecast till later.' His wild curly hair poked beneath his hat and his eyes sparkled with enthusiasm. 'So, who's up for a snowmobile adventure!'

20

The tour of The Star Lodge would have to wait as Elvar, determined to take the window of opportunity with the weather, encouraged them to set out on a mini adventure. His spontaneity and enthusiasm rubbed off on everyone. Kat and Lils were up for anything, James and Leifur too, while Molly trusted her brother-in-law's judgement.

In the boot room of the lodge, he and Leifur kitted them all out in appropriate gear.

'Lils, you're with me,' Elvar said, handing her a helmet with a face shield. 'Kat, you're with Leifur.'

Molly couldn't help but smile as an almighty grin spread across Kat's face. She may have professed to be done with men, but her soft spot for Leifur was obvious.

'James, Molly, are you okay on your own or do you want to share a snowmobile?' Elvar looked between them.

'Er...' Molly was thrown by the suggestion.

James turned to her. 'I'm fine by myself as long as you are?'

'Yep, of course.' She feigned confidence. 'It's been a while, but it's just like riding a bike, right?'

The pristine snow looked too perfect to spoil. The silence was astounding. The snow blanketing everything had a way of dampening any noise; Molly could understand why it was often described as deafening. Their chatter, although hushed, filled the tree-covered valley, their boots compacting the deep powder, making it creak.

After a safety briefing from Leifur, and with helmets secured, they set off at a steady speed away from the lodge. Elvar led, following a trail through the woods that he obviously knew well, but it wasn't clear enough for Molly to want to lose sight of him and Lils. With James directly in front of her, it was comforting to know that Leifur and Kat were bringing up the rear.

She relaxed into it, gripping the handles as she focused on the way ahead, her confidence slowly returning as she remembered past winter holidays filled with adventure. She'd missed this freedom, of being able to say yes to things, but her heart ached at the reason why she felt this way now. The responsibility of caring for her mum as she'd battled an awful disease and then wading through the aftermath of losing her was over. Yet her grief was always there, rumbling into life when she least expected it, as well as at birthdays, anniversaries and family moments. She wasn't sure if she'd ever rid herself of the loss, but learning to manage those feelings while allowing herself to live life to the full was becoming easier as time passed.

Howard would have enjoyed this. The thought slipped into her head before she could censor it. She didn't want to be thinking about him, not now, not while she was relishing being far away and escaping everything. It was his loss.

It was hard to empty her mind when she was used to it being constantly filled with worry, but zipping along on a snowmobile, concentrating on winding her way between trees, was freeing and the adrenalin pumped as she got into the flow of shifting her body weight forward and back to manoeuvre smoothly. It was like riding a bike; those initial nerves were swiftly erased to the point that she felt as if she could keep going forever. She wished her other worries could be banished so easily. Although, she didn't actually want to keep going for too long, not with the promise of hot chocolate, comfy sofas and underfloor heating back at the lodge. The best bit, after an exhausting day out in the wild, was the joy of getting home.

It was early afternoon and the light reflected off the snow, making it sparkle, but the further they went, the gloomier it became, even when the trees began to thin out. Snow, whipped up by a tunnelling side wind, whistled through the gaps between the trunks. Up ahead, James was slowing so Molly made sure to keep her distance. Then they were out of the trees and the landscape opened up, wide, vast and white. Yet it was as if someone had dimmed the lights. Iron-grey clouds snarled across the sky, the possibility of a snow storm on the horizon.

Elvar slowed and raised his left arm in the air, bringing them to a halt. Even though he lifted up his face shield, it was hard to make out his expression, but she sensed his concern – the wind was ferocious, whipping around them, forceful and freezing.

Elvar and Leifur communicated without even having to utter a word. Leifur's wide eyes and definite nod of his head as Elvar pointed back the way they'd come said enough.

'We're going to head back now!' Elvar shouted to their small group. The four snowmobiles were gathered together, the view before them wild and windswept, the relative safety of the trees behind. 'We take the direct route, Leif!'

'Are you sure?' Leifur shouted back.

Elvar nodded. 'That's coming in fast.'

There was nothing more to say. In the same order, they followed Elvar with Lils gripping on tightly behind him. Tension pulsed through Molly; the earlier adrenalin twisted with a touch of fear. For Elvar to cut the trail short, he must be worried. And it did feel as if they were being chased. She didn't dare glance behind for fear of losing her concentration on the way ahead along the narrow, winding trail. Snow started to fall, not just light twirling flakes but thick and heavy.

Molly was uncertain how long they'd been riding before they'd turned back, but with the storm brewing behind them, the way back felt longer. She may have been relishing the adventure before, but she hadn't bargained for it being this adrenalin fuelled or terrifying.

Hard specks of ice attacked Molly's helmet. In a surprisingly short amount of time, visibility had dramatically decreased. Her heart pounded in her ears and the wind thundered through the trees as if a madman was chasing them. The desolate location and the disorientating whiteout seemed straight from a horror movie. Her eyes hurt from concentrating so hard on James and straining to make out Elvar and Lils's snowmobile further ahead, just a blur through the swirling white.

And then James glanced behind him. The front of his snow-mobile caught something, the knock jarring him. With his balance compromised, he swerved violently.

Molly squeezed her brake, praying James was doing the same with his. Hoping Leifur would see, she stuck her free hand in the air and waved madly.

James's snowmobile skidded off the track, sliding sideways into a tree.

Enclosed by her helmet, Molly's yell reached only her own ears. She ground to a halt, jumped off her snowmobile and threw up her face shield.

Her boots sunk into the snow as she waded over to James. 'You okay?'

He waved his hand and stuck up his thumb.

She was aware of Leifur skidding to a halt near them as, with a hand on James's shoulder, she steadied him as he clambered off the snowmobile.

He undid his helmet and removed it. 'Shit, my ankle hurts.' He leaned on her, hobbling a couple of steps away.

The wind roared along the snowy trail, making it hard for Molly to battle against it, even with her and James supporting each other.

Leaving Kat, Leifur heaved James's snowmobile from against the tree and pushed it back on to the trail.

Molly's heart pounded. They were within walking distance of the lodge; she could just make out the hint of a caramel-coloured glow through the white. As long as they didn't lose sight of that, they'd be able to ride or even stagger there if necessary.

'We need to get back!' Even though Leifur was shouting, his words were distorted by the wind. He turned to Molly. 'See Elvar and Lils? We head for them; the lodge is just beyond. Are you okay going ahead? I'll follow right behind you and James.'

Wide-eyed, Molly gave him a thumbs up, and, ensuring James got back onto his snowmobile safely, she set off towards Elvar. It wasn't far, but with her heart still pounding and the raging storm throwing itself at them, the sight of the lodge looming was welcome.

They stowed away the snowmobiles and their gear and tumbled into the safety of the lodge in a flurry of snow, howling wind and breathless chatter from Kat and Lils. Molly could see the fear in Elvar's eyes. The speed at which the weather had closed in had been scary. Elvar was responsible for them and it had been his decision to head out. The storm raging in hours early had taken them by surprise. Now they were safely back and out of harm's way, the two friends were taking the experience in their stride. Leifur took James away to get the medical kit and see to his ankle, while a still-shaken Elvar showed Kat, Lils and Molly around, leading them along one of the two glass walkways that led from the central dome and branched off to three separate bedroom pods, each of them completely private and hidden by trees.

Molly left Elvar talking through a few things with Kat and Lils and wandered back to the heart of the lodge. She sat on the sofa and gazed out through the curved wall of glass at the wind whipping up snow flurries. It was difficult to make out even the darker definition of the trees among the blur of white. They were insanely lucky to have been near the lodge when the weather closed in.

The underfloor heating felt blissful on her feet. She'd experienced the thrill of being out in the unpredictable wild, but there was no better feeling than being warm and safe now. It was something she greatly missed back home. Not that her home wasn't cosy, but her life was so sedentary. At work she sat in front of a computer for most of the day. Anything different involved meetings, which meant more sitting, and they were usually disciplinaries or listening to, and then evaluating, grievances. At what point had her life taken such a U-turn from what she'd intended? More importantly, how could she shake it up? How could she capture the feeling she had here and reinvent it back home?

Elvar joined her on the sofa and handed her a steaming mug of coffee. 'The forecast was wrong; it's wild out there.'

'You've let Claudia know we're safe?'

'*Ja.* Been talking to Kat too. She was shaken up watching James skid off like that.'

'I bet; my heart was in my mouth.' Molly shook her head. 'For a moment I thought he'd seriously hurt himself.'

'It was my fault. I was impulsive. We shouldn't have gone.'

Molly placed a hand on his arm. 'You just said it yourself, the forecast was wrong. You weren't to know the weather was going to change that quickly. And we're all fine and safe now, even if it sounds like the whole place is being torn apart.'

'I left Kat and Lils trying to decide if they're brave enough to have a star pod each or bunk together.'

'Claudia's coping okay, is she?'

Elvar raised an eyebrow and sipped his coffee. 'I know where she'd prefer to be. But, if the weather's okay tomorrow, she'll take them to Sky Lagoon in Reykjavík.'

'Ah, so not the Blue Lagoon. I still might get the chance to go.'

Elvar nodded. 'You should go with Claudia. It will be good for you two to spend time together.'

'We've been spending plenty of time together.'

Elvar stretched and rested his feet on the coffee table. 'I think there's a lot left unsaid between you, after all that's happened. Nothing's been easy, and you're both still struggling.'

For a rugged adventurer constantly on the go, he had a sensitive soul and Molly found it easy to open up to him. If only Howard had been more like Elvar, then she might have been able to talk to him too.

'I don't mean to hold things back from her, it's just hard to convey how I've been feeling. My coping mechanism has been to bottle everything up, which I know isn't healthy.' Already she could feel her insides constricting, her heart tightening, the pent-up emotion wrapping itself around her. It was accentuated because being in Iceland had briefly eased the feeling, even with the Howard situation. She looked at Elvar. 'I've been so consumed by my own grief, I selfishly didn't consider that Claudia was suffering just as much.'

Elvar's eyebrows knitted together as he cupped his mug. 'By not being close by, not being there for them or having that precious last time at the end with your mum, that hurt Claudia. You would both change things if you could. I know the loneliness of losing a parent when it's just *you*.' He pressed his fist to the centre of his chest. 'I understand what you both went through and had to deal with – you physically being there is a constant pressure, while Claudia often felt helpless being so far away.'

Molly took a shuddery breath. 'It's been hard because I missed you all. Howard... Howard was no comfort.'

'Oh Molly, I didn't mean to upset you.'

She shook her head. 'You haven't. This is all part of the healing process. Claudia's my sister and I love her, and it's helpful to get our pent-up feelings out in the open. I was so wrapped up in my own shitty trauma; it's been good to see things from Claudia's perspective. She must have felt helpless being far away and yet she did everything she could to support me. And I'm glad she had you supporting her.'

'The truth is, however you look at it, it sucks. But we're here for you too, Moll.'

'I know you are. You all are and I can't thank you enough.'

'And we're not the only ones who are, um, interested in your well-be—'

'We've decided!' Kat's foghorn of a voice broke through their quiet chat. 'We're going to have a star pod each and brave it tonight!'

Elvar patted Molly's knee and swung round to face them. 'You'll both be fine. I can assure you The Star Lodge is made of sturdy stuff. It won't blow away.'

'Oh!' Lils squeaked. 'To be honest, I wasn't imagining it would! I was thinking more along the lines of the pod cracking and me being buried by snow!'

'You watch too many scary movies,' Kat commented, flopping down on the other sofa.

'Have you seen James and Leifur?' Elvar asked.

'We're here,' Leifur said as he came into the communal area with James limping beside him. 'Pain relief and a heat pack will sort him out in no time.'

'Right.' Elvar finished his coffee and got to his feet. 'Let's get some food then hunker down for the night!'

21

After a simple and laughter-filled communal dinner, with the frenzied wind accompanying their chatter, everyone opted to go to bed early, all exhausted after the drama of being caught out in the storm.

The star pods were made for couples and oozed romance. The king-size bed with its luxurious feather duvet, pillows and snuggly throws didn't feel right to Molly now she was on her own. None of them fitted the profile of what this place was made for, with Kat and Lils having a pod each and her and James both unexpectedly without their partners.

The true beauty of the pods had been apparent when Molly had stored her bag away earlier. Apart from the door to the walkway that led back to the main part of the lodge, the whole of the circular pod was see-through. In a private glade, the bed faced the snow-covered trees and gave an uninterrupted view of the sky. Since then darkness had descended and angry clouds had rolled in.

Although there were two free star pods, Molly considered that

Elvar and Leifur had the better deal, tucked away in the staff bedrooms with their solid walls and small windows while the storm raged outside.

She imagined on a clear, dark night, when you could lie in bed and gaze up at the sky scattered with stars and alive with the northern lights, it would be utterly magical, not to mention romantic. But it was far from that tonight. Snow flurries whipped up by the wind smashed on to the pod, with an occasional thud too as if great chunks of ice had been dropped from a height. A jagged-sounding crunch made her jump. She wasn't sure how on earth she'd be able to sleep.

She felt on the edge of nothingness, even while snuggled beneath the covers in fleecy pyjamas with an extra throw wrapped around her shoulders. A blizzard of white whirled, the night sky beyond a dark grey; the only other thing visible was the ebony outline of trees edged with snow. It was just as well they'd managed to get back when they did; it could have been far worse. She wondered how James was after his tumble. He'd got off lightly with just bruising.

Loneliness flowed through her. Being somewhere like this reminded her that she was alone. Life was fleeting and could be lost in a moment. Yes, memories remained but to never again talk to the parents she loved, to no longer be able to share her hopes and dreams or her heartache and disappointment, for them to miss out on what came next. The dull ache in her chest was back. She'd lost too many people. Although she understood now that Howard wasn't right for her and she didn't love him the way she thought she had, she missed the companionship, the security and love of someone by her side. Love. Had she ever truly had that with Howard? Perhaps in the beginning, but those heady days of young love, laughter, of losing themselves in each other, were long gone. But she craved that. Love and all it entailed. Her mind drifted to Leifur and the memories of what could have been. The what might be...

So maybe she should move on. She'd already wasted seven years of her life on Howard. He'd utterly disrespected her by not caring and carrying on an affair behind her back. When she returned home, she'd face him, but now... What had everyone been talking about over Christmas? That life was too short. She'd had first-hand experience of that, so why did she continue to put things off when she used to be spontaneous and up for anything? What she needed to do was seize the moment and not dwell on the past. What came next was unknown, but that in itself was exciting.

With her head filled with possibilities and thoughts of the future, she flung off the covers, pulled on her fluffy socks and wrapped the blanket tighter around her shoulders. She padded along the half-glass half-wood curved walkway to the main communal area that linked all six star pods.

'Hey, Molly.'

A quiet voice from within the darkness made her jump. Her hand flew to her chest.

'Oh my God,' Molly said, her heart racing. 'I didn't think anyone would be in here.'

'Sorry, didn't mean to spook you.' James looked up at her from one of the sofas. 'I couldn't sleep.' He gestured to his foot resting on a cushion on the coffee table. 'Couldn't get comfortable. You weren't able to sleep either?'

'Too much going on in my head. Also, there's a storm raging out there.'

'I had noticed.'

'These pods are all well and good for gazing out at the night sky, but it honestly felt as if mine was going to take off.'

'It's not as bad in here.' He gestured to the space next to him on the sofa.

Molly faltered, uncertain whether she should join him or not, but she'd been craving company and with sleep evading her, a chat with James appealed.

She crossed the heated floor and sank into the comfy depths of the sofa.

'You were wise to bring a blanket,' he said.

'It's plenty big enough to share.'

'Oh that's okay, it's not cold in here.'

'Don't be silly.' She pulled the blanket from her shoulders and laid it over them before realising how surprisingly intimate it felt. 'It's nice to feel snuggly when the weather's so stormy.' She decided to bluster through the gesture. It was only a blanket and they were sitting on a sofa together, not in bed.

They turned their attention to the curved glass wall in front of them, which allowed a clear view of the snowy wilderness. Each bedroom pod was well-hidden in its own clearing; the surrounding trees made the privacy absolute and only the walk-ways disappearing into the wood were visible.

It did feel safer here, the space larger, the pod more solid. It somehow gave the sense of the storm being contained outside and unable to break through.

'It's funny how things work out,' James said. 'Jen would have hated this.'

'Yeah, I'm not sure Howard would have liked it either. It's supposed to be romantic and I'm sure without a storm outside it would be – if you were sharing it with the right person.'

James grunted. 'The right person. It's not just this that Jen would hate, it's been everything about Iceland in winter. She's not that keen on Scotland either, beyond Edinburgh. She likes her home comforts and having a bar and coffee shop within walking distance. Ideally a Selfridges too. It's easy enough to gloss over the differences when you believe you're in love.'

'Isn't it just.' Molly smoothed her hand down the blanket and watched the snow make patterns on the glass above. 'I quite like city living, but it does make me long for the countryside. I need regular doses to keep sane, if that makes sense?'

'Perfectly.'

'And I'm more than happy to embrace adventure and the wild, I just keep thinking it would have been nicer to share it with someone.' Molly shrugged and snuggled deeper into the sofa. 'I don't know, my mind's been all over the place these last few days. It's nice not being alone, though,' she said carefully, uncertain how he would take it. 'Rather scary on my own.'

'I completely agree, it's nice having the company.' He glanced at her, a shy smile forming. 'It's hard to sleep with a storm raging. But it's the one in my head I'm struggling with, rather than the one outside.'

'What have you been thinking about? Just Jen or is there other stuff?' Molly asked.

'Oh, there's plenty of other stuff, but things with Jen haven't been right for a long time; there's been constant firefighting – mainly on my part – and although I'm not surprised by what's happened, I was shocked at her timing and the way she did it. I don't know, maybe I've been too self-absorbed to be able to see what was really going on. Or I simply chose not to see and deal with any of it.'

'I can't tell you how much you sound like me. You've just explained how I've been feeling for months and months, failing to do anything about the problems I knew were there but chose to ignore. But I've been consumed by grief, as I'm sure you were, and that has a habit of taking over everything, making us behave and deal with things in a way that is purely to get through each day.'

A howl of wind echoed around them, whipping the falling snow into a frenzy and smashing it against the pod.

'Blimey,' James said with a visible shudder. 'I'm mighty glad we're not out there any longer.'

'Yeah, we were lucky to get back when we did.' Molly gestured to his foot, which was poking out from beneath the blanket. 'How is it?'

'A bit sore but I'll survive. That'll teach me for getting cocky thinking I could zoom around on a snowmobile at my age.'

'At your age!' Molly wrinkled her nose. 'You're the same age as Leifur, aren't you?'

'Yep, but he does this kind of stuff all the time. He's a seasoned pro.'

'You must be outdoorsy though with your job?'

'Well yes, but it mostly involves walking, some forestry maintenance, not zipping across the snow-covered wilderness at speed. I like to think I keep pretty fit, but I've not done anything like this for a while and certainly not in the sort of conditions we experienced earlier.'

Without meaning to, her memory flipped back to Christmas Day and the dip in the pool, James holding his own on the six-pack front next to Leifur – not quite as muscled and rugged but surprisingly fit.

'Well, I'm glad you're okay.' Molly turned her thoughts back to the present. 'But it did give us all a laugh – once we realised you weren't badly hurt and we were out of danger, mind!' Molly breathed deeply and let out a long sigh. 'It's been good to laugh.'

'You've really not been happy?' James asked.

'No, but then it's hard to be through the grief.'

'But I mean your relationship with Howard. It wasn't a happy one?'

'It was once but I can't pinpoint when things changed. All I know is it was before I lost my parents.'

'So it wasn't your grief that changed things?'

'Oh, it changed things; it changed everything, but it didn't change us not being right for each other in the first place.'

'It's funny, isn't it, to suddenly be so aware of a relationship after burying your head in the sand for so long.'

'It's the same for you, right?' Molly turned to him. His face was shadowed, his eyes half hidden by his glasses. 'You don't seem quite as upset as I imagined someone would be after their fiancée told them they no longer want to get married.'

James gave an empty laugh. 'That makes me sound heartless.'

'No, I didn't mean it like that. I just mean what you said about seeing it coming but not doing anything about it.'

'My sadness and the situation I'm now in is completely my fault, for giving her another chance after...' He trailed off but not before she heard the tremor in his voice. His breathing sounded ragged as if he was trying to stifle a sob. The wind battered the lodge and she felt a desire to reach out and hold him. Touch could be so powerful. The basic human need to love and be loved – right now they both just needed a hug. She shifted slightly closer, pulling the blanket up as she did. They weren't quite touching, but she could sense him, the rise and fall of his chest syncing with hers.

'You mentioned she had an affair?' Molly said it quietly, not wanting to upset him further but sensing he wanted to talk. Did Leifur know the difficulties James and Jen had been facing or had their blokey banter not strayed into that sort of emotional territory?

'Aye. It's been a tricky relationship to navigate because she works in Edinburgh and I travel a lot, plus I spend as much time as I can at Karthstone.'

'At the castle?'

'Aye, at the castle.' James sighed again and moved his foot, shuffling about to get more comfortable. His arm brushed against hers and remained there, their shoulders just touching. Molly tried to focus on his words, rather than the comforting warmth of another person. 'It's all so weird and messy. We met at a party in a whirlwind of happiness and then my life disintegrated when I lost my grandparents in quick succession. Add to that Jen's misunderstanding about the castle – it wasn't the fairy tale she believed it to be. It still isn't.' He gave a hollow laugh and his shoulder pressed firmer against hers. 'It might never be, but it belongs to my family. Anyway, the castle really has nothing to do with it. Jen's impulsive. She works hard and plays hard – a bit too much on both fronts. She's a flirt – I knew that, but I also have this old-fashioned view that even in this day and age when you're with someone, you focus on that person and give it your all. But Jen, alone in Edinburgh a lot of the time, liked the attention of a fellow solicitor a bit too much. A mutual friend of ours spotted her leaving his flat early in the morning. She could have denied it, but she admitted it, putting it down to a moment of stupidity and I er, gave her another chance.'

'Was this before or after you'd proposed?'

'Oh, after. Although maybe in hindsight, and considering what's just happened, I was too trusting that it was only a brief fling that meant nothing.'

'It never means nothing though,' Molly said gently. 'To be that intimate with someone, to lie and cheat because you're lonely or because you crave the attention, it always means something.

Although I think it says more about the person doing the cheating than anyone else. I just don't understand it; if you want to be with someone else, whether it's just for sex or to have a proper relationship, just do the decent thing and finish with the person you're with!'

'You think like that because you have morals and a good heart. I've never cheated on anyone and never would, but that's just me. Not everyone thinks like we do.'

'What I struggle to understand is, why give her another chance?'

'She pleaded loneliness and I was in love – I'd been drawn in by her. I know it's not really come across here, but she can be charming and she stroked my ego. Plus, my grandparents instilled in me to always keep trying, to not give up on something too easily.'

'Even a cheating fiancée?'

'Especially on a relationship.'

'Despite not being completely happy, which I've gathered you weren't?'

'No, I wasn't, but perhaps I didn't want to give up on the person I thought I was going to be spending the rest of my life with.'

Molly bit her lip. 'There's giving up and then there's a complete lack of trust. I'm not sure I could be as forgiving as you, considering I've just found out Howard's been cheating on me. Not that I could take him back even if I wanted to; he made the decision to break up with me.'

'I'm sorry you're going through this too. The truth is, I didn't want my grandparents to be disappointed in me.' He waved his hand towards the storm-ridden night. 'Wherever they are, looking down on me.'

Molly put her hand on his. 'Wouldn't they be more upset that you're unhappy and trying to make something work just because you think it's what they would have wanted for you?'

A tear rolling down his cheek made her catch her breath. It caught in his stubble. She had an overwhelming desire to wipe it away, but she stopped herself, the moment already feeling too intimate.

'Trying to honour my grandparents by following the morals they instilled in me has held me back from following my heart.'

'And it's not Jen?'

'No, it's not her,' he said quietly. He swiped away the tear and looked purposefully at her. 'How about you and your parents?'

'They didn't hold me back – at least not till the last couple of years and that was through no fault of their own.' Molly breathed deeply, catching the upset before it spilled over. 'I held myself back, never brave enough to take the plunge and do something for myself because it felt too scary.'

'You held yourself back or your boyfriend did?'

James could see right through her. She'd been lying to herself for long enough. 'Both. I've held myself back but he never encouraged me to follow my dreams.'

'That would have made a difference?'

'Yes, a huge difference, to have someone believe in me.'

Footsteps made them turn. A shadowy figure crossed the communal space behind them.

'Leif,' James said.

Leifur stopped in his tracks, next to the walkway that led to Molly's bedroom pod. His hand flew to his chest as he swung round. His expression was hard to make out in the darkness.

'Oh, you're both here,' he said with surprise.

'Yeah, neither of us could sleep,' James said. 'Come and join us.'

'Ah, that's okay.' He rubbed his eyes and yawned. 'Was off to the bathroom. Bit sleepy, got disorientated.' He turned abruptly and left the way he came.

James waited until Leifur's footsteps had retreated before turning back to Molly with an expression she couldn't quite make out. 'I think he was, um, coming to find you...'

22

Molly frowned. 'Don't be ridiculous.' Although her heart thudded, because wasn't the thought of Leifur and moving on one of the reasons she'd got out of bed?

'It's hardly ridiculous when I know he likes you.' James nudged his shoulder against hers. 'I just wondered if you were going to pick up where you left off?'

He was looking at her in a way she didn't quite understand. Somehow the question felt like a test or a challenge and she wasn't sure how to reply, mainly because she wasn't sure how she felt about Leifur. But this line of questioning while sitting so close to James was making her uncomfortable and she didn't know what to say.

'We're best mates,' James continued. 'I was there that summer, remember; I saw you two together. Plus me and Leif talk about stuff.' He nudged her arm. 'About women we've hooked up with.'

'Oh, we never properly hooked up, if you mean it in the way I think you mean.'

'That's not what he said.' James stared ahead at the still stormy night. Molly clenched her jaw, heat rushing through her.

She imagined the embellished version Leifur had given about what they'd got up to. 'He likes you, that's all. I think it was easier for him to confide in me rather than spilling the beans to your brother-in-law. Not that he went into detail!' James's obvious distress told Molly all she needed to know. Of course the two friends had talked, particularly if James believed they'd hooked up in an actually-had-sex kind of way.

She was glad of the darkness, but it made gazing out together at the wild night all the more intimate when they were discussing her relationship with Leifur, his best friend. She'd felt comfortable confiding in James and was drawn to him in a way she didn't understand. She wanted to put him straight about Leifur because she didn't want him to get the wrong idea.

'I'll remember that summer forever,' Molly said. 'You were there, you must know what I mean. We were young. I was single, relishing the adventure and the outdoors *and* snogging a fit Icelandic adventurer. But honestly, it wasn't much more than that.'

'Well, whatever did or didn't happen, I think he'd like more now.' James shifted as if he was suddenly uncomfortable too, the movement as he readjusted his ankle widening the gap between them.

Molly glanced at her watch; nearly eleven. 'I, er, I think I'm going to go back to bed and try to sleep. It seems a little calmer.' She gestured to the curved wall of glass. The wind seemed to have eased a little, the snow not swirling quite so ferociously. The sky had darkened and was clearer now the grey-white snow storm wasn't consuming everything.

James grunted an agreement. 'My ankle feels all right, I might try and snooze here.'

'Keep the blanket.' She slipped out from under it and left him there, looking cosy and content. 'Sleep well.'

She padded down the walkway, shivering at the hit of cooler air. She wondered how much of Leifur's happy-go-lucky adventurous side had rubbed off on James. Or had he always been like that too? He'd obviously grown up in a place surrounded by woodland with wilderness on the doorstep, but had Leifur's influence fuelled it even more? Throughout her teens and into her twenties, Claudia and Elvar's influence on her had been there, but it was her parents, her dad in particular, who had swayed her to opt for the sensible middle ground when it came to, well, everything: a sensible boring job, nice house, nice boyfriend, with only pockets of adventure sprinkled through it. The most memorable one was where Leifur had been the direct influence.

It was only a short walk, but she was shivering by the time she reached her pod. She slid beneath the heavy covers and snuggled down, aware of how peaceful it was now, even though a few clouds still clustered above. The drama of the day had finally crept up on her, leaving her exhausted, and this time sleep came easily.

* * *

'Molly.'

Through a haze of sleepiness she heard her name again.

'Molly.' Half whispered, familiar, but she couldn't quite work out who it was. Not Elvar, perhaps Leifur.

'The northern lights, Molly.'

James.

She opened her eyes and the beginnings of a moan about why he was waking her up morphed into a gasp.

The mattress sank on one side as James perched on the edge of the bed. 'I couldn't sleep for ages, then I think I nodded off for a bit, but woke up to this.'

The sky that had been streaked with dark clouds when Molly had finally fallen asleep was now alive with colour. Swirling wisps of green billowed across the sky, a hint of faint plum-pink joining in the dance. It was as if the aurora borealis had blown away the earlier storm that had rampaged across the sky. Mountains of snow had been dumped in a short time, pillowy piles resting against the sides of her pod, glowing under the sky's light show.

James grasped Molly's hand and she held her breath, wanting to desperately hold on to this moment, the magic in the sky combined with James's touch, his hand firm and warm in hers, gently tensing in time to the flickering movement of the northern lights.

'We should wake the others.' The intention was there, but she couldn't tear her eyes away from the expanse of vivid green framed by the ebony silhouettes of trees. The true majesty of The Star Lodge was revealed in all its glory, while they remained warm and cosy.

'Have you ever seen them before?' Molly whispered, her eyes fixed on the rippling luminous green.

'Once, a long time ago, but nothing like this.'

Considering how stubbornly cloudy the nights had been since getting to Iceland, and the ferociousness of the earlier storm, what they were seeing now was so unexpected that it made it all the more magical.

'How about you?' James asked.

'Oh, I've seen them a few times but this is something else.'

Spectacular was the only way Molly could describe it, the swirling luminance taking over the vastness of the clear night sky as she snapped a couple of pictures on her phone.

'Do you know what it feels like?' James said softly as he

continued to gaze. 'It's as if the heavens have opened and it's our loved ones up there dancing together.'

Molly's hand involuntarily tensed in his. 'Oh my goodness, you're going to make me cry.'

'Sorry, I don't want to upset you.' He rubbed his thumb along hers. 'It's a happy thought though, imagining my grandparents and your parents up there somewhere, shining down on us.'

It was a beautiful thought, but it failed to stop Molly's tears. James let go of her hand and shuffled further on the bed until his arms encircled her. She held on to him, his warm, strong body pressed against hers, comforting and so wanted in that moment. Molly sobbed into his chest, while his silent tears dampened the crook of her neck. The northern lights overhead were somehow both soothing and life affirming.

James let go of her and removed his glasses to wipe away his tears.

'Sometimes it's good to cry.' His gentle laugh filled the pod and made her smile. Her damp cheeks were tight with tears as she met his eyes.

She plucked a tissue from the box on the bedside table and dabbed her face. 'I assume it wasn't just your ankle that kept you awake?'

'No. After you left I kept thinking about what we talked about, how I'm still trying to make my grandparents happy even though they're no longer here. It's not actually making *me* happy. Jen wants me to be someone I'm not, and not being true to yourself is just miserable. It's no way to live.'

Molly understood that sentiment because it was everything she'd been feeling with Howard. Actually it was everything she'd felt her whole adult life, pleasing other people, doing what was expected of her, not rocking the boat, not being daring or spontaneous, not pursuing her passions for fear of failure and what other people would think.

'I craved the attention from Jen,' James continued. He cleaned his glasses with the edge of his top and put them back on. 'She was different to the women I used to date, younger too, although that shouldn't have been an issue. It's just she seemed too good to be true – too unpredictable, too likely to break my heart. She proved me right.'

'Why did you take things so far with her? You seem like someone who knows what they want. Someone who's happy to take their time to make things right, like the way you've been talking about the castle and your plans for it. It's a long-term dream, yet it sounds as if you rushed into everything with Jen.'

'The honest truth?' He twisted his lips. 'She reminded me of my mum with her free spirit and determination.'

'I did wonder why you lived with your grandparents from a young age. Your mum wasn't around?'

'She tried to look after me. "Tried" being the important word there.' His fist tensed round the edge of the duvet. 'I was too young to really remember living with my mum and there aren't many photos either. She lived in a shared house in Edinburgh and three or four times a year she'd drop me off at my grandparents then disappear for a week or sometimes a month at a time. They begged her to move back in and she'd flat refuse every time. Then one time, after I'd just turned four, she never came back.'

'Oh my goodness, I'm so sorry.'

His eyes had misted over and his whole body was rigid.

'I only have vague memories of her, but from what I've gleaned from my grandparents and a few others who knew her, she was opinionated and focused on what she wanted. Sounds very much like Jen, eh? I naively thought that maybe she'd be different, that she would break the mould and change my opinion of that type of woman. Instead of hooking up with a woman like Jen, I should have bloody gone to therapy. I'm sure a therapist would say my relationship with Jen is hideously self-destructive and as damaging as the one I didn't have with my mother. And they'd be right.' He shook his head. 'It was madness to think I could make someone into something they're not. There were warning signs from the beginning – she was all about money, looks and appearances. Everything I'm not.'

'We live and learn. And perhaps this means you'll go into a new relationship with your eyes open and not make the same mistake again. It's what I'll be doing. I think Howard's taught me a lot about what I don't want, but also confirmed that life's too short to waste it not being happy.'

James didn't say anything, but his nod and gentle squeeze of her hand as he took hold of it again said more than words could. His eyes travelled across her face. Sitting together in the middle of the bed, encircled by the pod and the wild beauty beyond, she held his gaze.

There was a moment, just a heartbeat in time when one move would change everything. His words and his openness had moved her. The ache in her heart felt changed, softer, warmer. An altogether different type of ache. In the darkness, with only the faintest hint of the aurora imprinted on the night, Molly tore her eyes away from his before she became lost. The unspoken feeling had been comforting moments before when sharing their grief. Now it felt different. She looked up. The swirls of green and pink had faded, yet the night sky was sprinkled with thousands of stars like tiny glittery lights turning the ebony a dappled silver.

'We didn't tell the others about this,' she eventually said to break the growing silence.

'Maybe they were already awake.'

'Perhaps.'

'I rather like that we shared this experience together.' He released her hand and dropped his gaze. 'I really am going to go to bed now though.' He stood up suddenly, as if he too had realised the intensity of the moment.

Molly remained where she was. 'Thank you for waking me.'

In the darkness she could just make out his smile. She wondered if it reached his eyes.

'Thanks for the chat and the cry.' He shrugged. 'It helped a lot. Night, Molly.'

And he was gone.

The spot on the bed where he'd been sitting was still warm. Molly's head tumbled with a million conflicted and confused thoughts and ideas zipping around as bright as the pinprick stars scattered across the Icelandic night.

23

Molly still found it disorientating to wake to darkness when it was nearly ten in the morning. She yawned and stretched, thoughts from the evening before swirling like the northern lights had during the night. The dusky view was still special even if it wasn't quite as magical as when she'd shared it with James. Snuggled beneath the covers, she allowed herself to wake slowly, with a rare feeling of peace and contentment.

Her rumbling stomach eventually enticed her out of bed. Chucking on her fleece hoody over her pyjamas, she padded along the chilly walkway in her thick socks to the main part of the lodge.

No one was in the communal area but voices drifted from the kitchen, deep and tense as if in mid-argument. Molly spied Elvar outside, trudging through the snow towards the shed where the snowmobiles were stored. She tentatively headed along the hallway.

'You've got it completely wrong!' James's voice filtered from the kitchen.

'What do you expect me to think?' Leifur's reply simmered

with anger. Molly paused outside the door, uncertain if she should disturb them. 'You've just been dumped, so your first thought is a rebound fuck.'

'You're so out of order.'

'I'm out of order! You know I like her.'

Molly's heart raced. The image of James on her bed last night was innocent enough despite their closeness and the thoughts and feelings that had been churning inside. But perhaps it might have looked different to someone else...

Deciding it was best to leave them to it and wait until Kat and Lils were up to have breakfast, she turned to go when Leifur shot from the kitchen, ploughing into her.

'Shit!' His cheeks clenched as his eyes dropped from hers.

'Sorry.' Her voice was small. She wasn't sure if she really wanted to know the answer after what she'd just heard, but she decided to ask anyway. 'What's going on?'

'I came to find you last night.' Leifur folded his arms, his face flushed with rage. 'But you obviously had other ideas.'

Molly frowned and opened her mouth to say something but had no idea how to temper his anger.

Leifur glared at her. 'So, did you? Sleep together?'

James stormed into the hallway. 'Leif, I've already told you what happened.'

'*Já*, that's why you looked so cosy together.' He shoved his hands into James's chest and stalked away.

Molly turned back to James in disbelief. 'What the hell?'

James sighed. 'Apparently he saw me coming back from your room. I wasn't the only one who couldn't sleep. He, um, made assumptions.' James was as red faced as Leifur had been, but presumably for a different reason. 'I'm really sorry if I've inadvertently messed things up between you two.'

'You haven't messed anything up. It's Leifur making assumptions about me and my feelings for him – I mean the feelings I don't have for him. Oh bloody hell, I don't know.' It was Molly's turn to go red. 'It's not that I don't like him in that way. It's just, I'm confused. I don't know what to think. And I'm really sorry if I've caused issues between the two of you.'

'Don't worry, this isn't the first time we've clashed.' James shrugged as if this was normal, expected behaviour. 'He saw what he wanted to see and read way too much into it. He can be fiery and doesn't always think things through first. Gets him into a wee bit of hot water on occasions.'

'Should I go talk to him? Explain what really happened?'

James shook his head. 'Let him cool down first.' He gently brushed his hand against her arm. 'One of us getting bollocked this morning is enough. He can be a dick at times, but he's my pal. He'll come around and realise what an idiot he's been.'

* * *

Molly retreated to her pod and breathed in the calmness of the snow-covered trees and the promise of daylight on the horizon. Twice last night it seemed Leifur had come to find her. Was the weird feeling in her stomach due to relief or a touch of disappointment that he hadn't made it to her room? She liked Leifur, a lot. He made her smile and feel good about herself; he reminded her of a time when life was simple, when snatched kisses beneath the midnight sun were nothing more than a bit of fun, but his demeanour and accusation had shocked her.

Despite longing for coffee and breakfast, she was determined to not go back and risk bumping into Leifur until everyone else was up. She changed into thermal leggings and a fleece and lay on the bed staring up at the sky, which was still star-speckled but with a hint of sunrise. She should have stayed in bed. The more she thought about the conversation and Leifur's hurtful words, the more upset she felt. His choice of language had been as shocking as his rage. She'd never seen him like that before, but then what time she'd spent with him had been fleeting, particularly in recent years. James had seemed less shocked; he obviously knew his temper well. It might not have bothered him, but now she was on her own thinking it through, it bothered her that Leifur had read things into her time with James. Their connection had felt wholesome and it had been incredibly moving to watch the northern lights dance as they shared their grief over losing the people they loved.

'Can I come in?' Elvar poked his head around the door at the rear of the pod.

Molly scrambled to her feet and nodded.

'James, um, told me about the conversation between Leifur and him. And you.' He closed the door behind him. 'Are you okay?'

'I'm fine. I just wasn't expecting to be shouted at by Leifur and accused of something I didn't do.'

Elvar nodded slowly. 'He likes you, that's why he reacted this way.'

'You do understand what he said about me and James isn't true?'

'I know.'

'James couldn't sleep, I couldn't sleep, then when he saw the northern lights he came to show me. That's it. Leifur jumped to a massively wrong conclusion.'

'Leifur can be hot-headed and passionate.'

'That's what James said.'

'He speaks first, thinks later. He's a brilliant father though; he dotes on Birta and will do anything for her,' Elvar said, his tone gentle. 'She's changed him, for the better in many ways. He's more thoughtful and caring. She's brought out the best in him but he still has a long way to go, especially when it comes to his romantic relationships.'

'Why are you telling me this?'

Elvar smoothed down his beard. 'Because his outburst was through jealousy. It's no secret that he'd like to be with you. And you're my sister-in-law and I don't want you to get hurt.'

'And he's your friend.'

'Which is why I know him well. Know him better than you. I know what he's like when it comes to women. I'll put it like this. You're an adult and can make up your own mind, but Leifur is looking for fun and not much more.'

Only days ago Claudia had encouraged her to let her hair down and have a fling, and now Elvar was warning her that a night with Leifur would be just that.

'He talks to me,' Elvar continued. 'Says the truth he might not admit to anyone else – the real reason his marriage ended. You've just been hurt by Howard; I don't want to see the same happening again.'

'I'm sure this is just Claudia filling your head with things – she's been urging me to give it a go with Leifur. But you're right, Howard has just dumped me. Why anyone would think I'd want to move on that quickly and complicate things, I have no idea.' Molly started folding up her night clothes, wanting to focus on something other than Elvar's intense look, her heart thudding with the notion that last night she had been tempted by the thought of Leifur. 'Years ago I probably wouldn't have thought twice about jumping into bed with him.' She glanced at Elvar. 'I mean, I nearly did on that camping trip but not quite in the way he's suggested. I'm sure he's told you. He's told James all sorts of stuff, lots of it embellished.' She shook her head. 'I don't know, my emotions are all over the place.'

'I know they are, Moll.' Elvar folded his arms and sighed. 'I guess all I'm saying is whatever you do, go into anything with him with your eyes open and your heart closed.'

'That's kind of sad though, isn't it?' Molly stuffed her rolled-up clothes into her rucksack. 'To close myself off for fear of getting hurt. I've always liked Leifur. I consider him to be a friend and I don't want to mess that up.' She raised her eyebrows and sighed. 'Perhaps I need a happy medium. Someone with Leifur's passion for the outdoors and adventure but who isn't as clinical and ordered as Howard. I need someone with a smidgen of spontaneity.'

With a start, she realised that description sounded very much like James. Elvar had immediately dismissed the idea that something had happened between the two of them. All he'd seen was Leifur's jealousy, understood what Leifur was like and after hearing James's side of things agreed that Leifur had jumped to conclusions. But something *had* happened between her and James last night, something Molly didn't really understand, but there was a connection, a comfortable familiarity with someone who was going through a similar heartache. A shared moment that had filled her with a renewed sense of peace, a belief that with all the crappy things that had happened, she would get through it and find happiness. Not that her grief would be erased, but she would cope with it and learn to love life again.

'Are you okay, Moll?' Elvar's steady voice cut through her thoughts. 'You look like you're either going to laugh or burst into tears.'

Molly gave him a wry smile and put her hand on his shoulder. Elvar, at fourteen years older, was the big brother she'd longed for when growing up. She hadn't even had the company of her big sister, so she adored the quietly supportive and open relationship Elvar had created with her.

'I was thinking that perhaps it would be better to look forwards, not back. That summer with Leifur has so many happy memories because it was simple and exciting, but sometimes a good thing should remain in the past. The way I'm feeling right now with my emotions all tangled, to pick up where we left off would be a mistake. So you really don't have to worry about me getting my heart stomped on again.'

Elvar nodded slowly. 'Is it because you like James as well?'

Molly looked at him in shock.

'I know something happened between the two of you last night.' He pushed his fist to the centre of his chest as he echoed her own earlier thoughts. 'Sex can be messy and complicated, particularly when it involves friends.' He spoke frankly without a hint of embarrassment. Molly realised he wasn't necessarily talking about her and Leifur, but Leifur and James. Theirs was the friendship that could potentially be compromised.

'I promise you, there was absolutely no sex.' Her cheeks flushed. 'We didn't even kiss.'

'I understand that, but there doesn't have to be sex for things to get, shall we say, confused. Not when feelings are involved...'

24

Molly and Elvar joined the others for breakfast, but after everything that had played out that morning, Molly was hyper-aware of James.

Much to her relief, Leifur had taken cooling off literally with a walk through the snow-bound wood, so he missed out on break-fast. With Kat and Lils unaware of the earlier commotion, they dragged Molly, James and Elvar back to normality as they chatted about their dramatic snowmobiling adventure and their experi-ence of trying to sleep amid the ferocious storm. James and Molly had been the only ones to witness the northern lights, but with the storm now dispersed and clear skies, Elvar was hopeful there would be more opportunities.

Leifur was missing out, doing his moody grumpy thing – he was living up to his reputation as a wild man, hardened and unable to control his emotions. She liked his easy-going friend-ship and she didn't want things to be weird between them. She didn't want things to be weird with James either, but the events overnight had unexpectedly changed things.

As they got up from the table to get ready to leave, Elvar gripped James's arm.

'Claudia messaged,' he said quietly. 'She took Jen to the airport early this morning.'

'She's gone?' James's tone and expression was unreadable.

'Yes.' Elvar certainly wasn't sugar-coating it; not that there was any point after Jen had made her feelings clear in front of everyone.

James gave a curt nod, his lips tightening before he paced away.

Molly understood his upset. Even if them splitting was the best long-term outcome, it didn't take away the immediate heartache and disappointment. Molly had been battling the feeling of failure, as she hadn't managed to save her relationship with Howard. At least she was no longer living a lie.

By the time Molly had retrieved her bag and taken one last look at the snow-strewn landscape beyond her transparent pod, Leifur had returned.

'I was out of order earlier,' he said quietly, so no one would overhear. 'I'm really sorry.'

He didn't say much else but he was certainly less hostile. Molly felt a little more at ease after his apology, but she still kept out of his way. She couldn't help but pick apart the night before, trying to decipher her feelings for James, wondering how Elvar had seen something that hadn't even been obvious to her.

'I put him straight,' James said, his tone hushed as they headed out into the cold to load the 4x4 with their bags. 'About us. Or not about us. You know what I mean.' He laughed nervously, which made Molly wish she could rewind time back to when chatting with him wasn't awkward. Leifur's assumption and his overreaction had completely messed that up. 'My fiancée's just broken up

with me. Honestly, did he really think I'd move on that quickly?'
He shook his head. 'He understands he jumped to the wrong
conclusion, so it should all be good between you two again.'

'And you do understand I've been dumped too? There was
nothing going on between me and Leifur *before* he jumped to
conclusions.' She was annoyed at everyone's assumption about
her and Leifur. Yes, it was flattering to have Leifur's attention, but
she certainly didn't want to be a conquest. And now she'd
snapped at James too.

She was glad they were heading back today. The Star Lodge
was perfect for a night, but the rooms were really only for
sleeping – or star gazing and romance – and she'd begun to feel
hemmed in with James and Leifur. She wanted to be back on
familiar territory with her own private space to escape to.

Everyone was quiet on the way back to The Fire Lodge. The
calm after the storm continued with a clear, winter sun-bathed
sky. Only the snowploughs clearing the roads were evidence of
the overnight storm. When they reached the lodge, Leifur made
himself scarce. He may have apologised, talked to James and told
him that his reaction had been a misunderstanding, but it
certainly seemed as if he was avoiding Molly.

With Jen gone, James was quiet. He went to his room after
lunch and didn't reappear until dinner. Even then he didn't join
them in the lounge afterwards. The joy they'd shared at The Star
Lodge had dispersed as fast as the storm clouds had retreated.

Graham and Maggie chatted to Molly, Kat and Lils about
their trip to Reykjavík with a sullen Jen, although their few hours
at the Sky Lagoon submerged in warm water as they looked out
over the North Atlantic Ocean sounded blissful.

As Molly was getting ready for bed, murky grey clouds
engulfed the clear, star-scattered sky and snow started to fall.
With it remaining resolutely cloudy with little chance of the

aurora making an appearance, no one got woken up in the night.

* * *

Molly slept fitfully, disturbed by the screeching wind and her swirling thoughts. Even a hot shower followed by a strong coffee did little to make her feel more awake. It was Graham and Maggie's last morning, so she said goodbye to them before they left for the airport, feeling a twinge that her own time in Iceland was running out. She retreated to her room to read. She didn't see Claudia until lunchtime when they were joined by Elvar in the apartment kitchen. The moment Elvar headed downstairs to see to the guests, Claudia turned to her.

'What's with all the tension, Moll?' Claudia cupped her hands round her coffee.

'What do you mean?' Molly feigned innocence.

'Oh, come on. Tell me. You've been hiding away all morning. Elvar hinted at there being a bit of a thing.' Claudia looked at her expectantly. 'He said to ask you. So, you and Leifur?'

Molly shook her head. 'Nothing happened.'

'There I was thinking it was the perfect opportunity for you two to get snowed in and loved up.'

'Technically we didn't get snowed in.' Molly was grateful to Elvar for not divulging everything to Claudia, yet annoyed at the need to explain to her sister what had gone on. 'And as for the loved-up thing.' She screwed up her face.

'What is it, Moll?'

'I'm not sure I'm in the headspace for a fling and I certainly don't want Leifur to tick me off his list. I know he's been suggesting that more happened between us ten years ago than really did and I get the feeling he wants to make his lies come true.' She sighed. It was horrible to feel like this. The attention of someone as good looking and as lovely as Leifur should be a huge confidence boost, and until the events at The Star Lodge, a fling had been tempting...

'What do you want, Molly?' Claudia asked gently. 'It's not and shouldn't be anyone remotely like How—'

'I have no idea what I want,' Molly snapped, pent-up emotion threatening to erupt. 'I don't know how to deal with these feelings.'

'Of what? What is it you're feeling, Moll? Is it grief, sadness? Tell me.' Claudia took Molly's hand, an unusually tender gesture.

'I don't know!' All the tension she'd been feeling back home had returned in a wave of confusion. She'd been trying to be strong for so long, when all she really wanted was to be taken care of, for someone to comfort her and tell her everything would eventually be okay. 'Life's just exhausting. As soon as one thing is done and dusted, something else gets thrown in my face, something massive and complicated and bloody emotional that will change everything.'

'You're talking about Howard, right?'

Molly bit her lip and nodded. 'It's not as simple as forgetting about him and having a fling with Leifur – even if I wanted that. I don't want to end up having a messed up relationship with him.' *With James*, she really wanted to say. Doing anything with Leifur now would complicate the hell out of her feelings, feelings she didn't understand. Leifur was sexy, manly, rugged; she'd had first-hand experience of how he made her feel, but that was a long time ago. She'd been a different person with different desires, a whole different outlook on life. What she wanted was someone dependable and loving, someone she could talk to, share her innermost thoughts with and plan a future together with. Her thoughts drifted to the night in the star pod, James's hand in hers, warm and comforting, but not just in a friendly way – the tingles, the anticipation, the possibility, *the what if*, was all there, toying and teasing, the moment full of wonder as much as conflicting feelings.

'Where have you gone?' Claudia's fingers clicked in front of her face. 'You look really worried.'

'I honestly don't know how I feel.' She glanced across the table which was littered with empty plates to the snow drifting past the kitchen window. 'I miss Mum so much.' That was at the heart of everything. A sob caught in her throat and her tears spilt, drenching her cheeks. 'I always had Mum to talk to and I used to tell her everything – well, almost everything – and what I didn't she usually worked out anyway. I've been floundering without her.' She pressed her fist to her chest. 'Keeping everything in here with nowhere for it to go. You're right about Howard, he's been no comfort despite being the one person I should have been able to rely on. He wouldn't have been able to replace Mum, but he was my boyfriend. That should have meant something. Grief counselling has helped me talk things through and understand how I'm feeling, but now I'm having to deal with this… this shitty thing with Howard and, oh I don't know, everything. I just miss her.'

'I know, Moll. I miss her too.' Claudia put her arms around her and drew her close.

Molly's own thudding heartbeat sounded in her ears. 'I can't believe she's gone.'

Claudia didn't say anything; it was only when Molly felt her shake that she realised she was crying too.

Molly wasn't sure how long they remained like that, long enough for her sobs to ebb away, for her shuddery breath to almost return to normal.

'I need to show you something.' Claudia gently released Molly and stood up. 'Come with me.'

They went into Claudia and Elvar's bedroom and Claudia took out an envelope from the bedside table drawer. She sat on the end of the bed and patted the space next to her.

'Mum wrote to me just over eighteen months ago, before she couldn't any longer,' she said once Molly had sat down. 'She worried about being a burden to yo—'

'She wasn't.'

Claudia nodded. 'And she was also worried about you being on your own.'

'But I wasn't.'

Claudia gave her a stern look. 'You were, Moll. I was hundreds of miles away and Howard was no help and Mum knew that. You've just said it yourself – he was no comfort when he should have been the one person you could have relied on. You dealt with so much by yourself.'

She took out a sealed envelope from within the opened one. 'Mum also sent this for us to open together when the time was right. In her letter to me, she suggested it was when we needed her most.'

Tears caught in Molly's throat again as Claudia handed her the cream envelope with both their names written in their mum's spidery handwriting. Molly ran her fingers over the envelope. It wasn't flat. There was something bumpy inside that felt delicate.

'I think now feels about right, don't you?'

Molly glanced from the envelope to her sister. 'She really sent this to you and said that, for when we needed her?'

Claudia nodded, her lips tense, eyes glistening, and Molly knew her hard-as-nails sister was trying to hold it together. 'Go on, open it.'

Molly tucked her finger in one corner of the envelope and gently tore it open. She tipped out three dried flowers into her palm: a miniature rose, a pink astilbe and a sprig of heather. With tears blurring her eyes, she passed the letter to Claudia.

'You read it, please.'

Claudia grabbed her reading glasses from next to the bed and took a deep breath.

25

Dearest Claudia and Molly,

These three flowers mean a great deal to me. Apart from you two, and Finn and Alda, gardening was my greatest love. The rose is from the bush I planted for Molly not long after she was born. I planted the astilbe when Claudia moved to Iceland because the joyful pink colour reminded me of your zest for life. The heather I can see from the kitchen window is my favourite. It reminds me of the two of you, wild and free, living your lives the way you want to, with all the hopes and dreams that young people should have.

I like the sentiment of my ashes being scattered some-where, but it doesn't seem right when I'm such a homebody, so the village churchyard it will be. If I could be buried in the garden, I would, but your father wouldn't want us to be sepa-rated, even in death, so that's not really an option now, is it...

Molly imagined their mum's tinkling laugh and the way she would have smiled to herself as she'd written those words. The subject matter should feel morbid, yet somehow it was anything but. They were reading it as she'd written it, still very much living life as best she could.

I want you to scatter these flowers for me and your dad. I know he wasn't always easy to get on with or understand, particularly for you Claudia, but he loved you both in his own way. Celebrate my life; celebrate your dad's. Claudia, keep doing what you've always done, and Molly, take care of yourself. Please look after each other.

Molly, it might sound selfish to put your own needs, hopes and dreams first, but it's not. Stand up for what you want and go out and get it. It's what Claudia's done. Perhaps it was what I should have done too. Find someone who believes in you, loves you and supports you unconditionally. Don't ever settle for second best, because you deserve more. If something doesn't feel right, then trust your instinct and get rid of it, whether a boyfriend, a husband, even a whole marriage, BUT if something feels right, then hold on to it for dear life and never let it go – at least not without a fight!

When you reach my age life becomes a lot clearer. Of course, facing a terminal diagnosis has made me reflect. It's made me put my thoughts down before I'm physically unable to. I've had a good life and I'm incredibly lucky to have had the two of you – you're what's made it a happy one. But I do have regrets; regrets for things I did, but more than anything, regrets for the things I didn't do.

Claudia paused a moment to take a deep breath. The emotion seeping from the page was almost palpable. Molly was moved and in awe of the thought and strength their mum had put into writing to them when her time had been limited.

They both remained quiet, perched on the end of Claudia's

bed. The fairy lights around the mirror twinkled and Christmas music drifted up from downstairs with a roar of laughter; happy festive sounds that grounded them in reality, while their mum was speaking to them from beyond the grave, somehow still with them, imparting her love and advice long after she'd gone.

The ache that was climbing Molly's chest threatened to overwhelm, yet their mum's words were comforting and uplifting, encouraging and hopeful. They were a warning and a blessing because Howard leaving her was the right path, and her mum had seen that long before Molly had realised it.

'The bit about regret,' Molly eventually said. 'She's talking about her and dad.'

'I think so.'

'And the thing about trusting your instincts, that was for my benefit. It's how she felt about Dad, sticking with him because it was expected of her, but she didn't want to deep down, did she? At least she knew you would be okay. You're with Elvar, the most supportive, loving, encouraging husband you could have wished for.'

'I got lucky.'

'Yet it was something she never truly had with Dad. I just never really saw their relationship from her point of view. She always seemed happy enough.'

'Happy enough is terrible though when you really think about it. I'm happy with Elvar, properly happy.' She glanced at Molly. 'That's not to say we haven't had our difficulties or that everything's been easy, because it hasn't. We've had plenty of arguments; there are times when I want to wring his neck, but I love him, he loves me and we support each other unconditionally. We're equals. Mum and Dad never were. Dad was the breadwinner and had the final say in everything, including what Mum did beyond her domain of being a housewife. It wasn't right and I fought against that; he tried to restrict me the same way he did Mum. We constantly fought because I was adamant I should do what I wanted to do, not what he thought I should do.'

'And Howard and I are...' Molly gazed at the dried flowers cupped in her palm. 'Howard and I weren't even happy enough, at least not over the last year or so.'

'Don't confuse the grief and what you were going through for the reason you weren't happy. You were happy with him at least to begin with, otherwise why on earth did you get together?'

Molly chewed her lip, feeling the familiar lump in her throat forming. 'Yes, we were happy, but you never liked him from the very beginning.'

'That's not completely true; I never warmed to him. There's a difference.'

'Because you saw him for what he really was.'

'Utterly selfish and never had your best interests at heart, only thinking about himself?'

'Tell it like it is, then.'

'Sorry.' Claudia smoothed her hand across the letter in her lap. 'However much it hurts, he's done you a favour.'

Had her mum seen something of Molly's dad in Howard? That restrictive, uncompromising side? Molly wished her mum had said something to her when she was alive, but then, would she have listened? Probably not. Sometimes the truth was hard but necessary.

'Is there more?' Molly asked quietly.

Claudia nodded, picked up the letter and continued.

The village church is the place I'll be laid to rest but I'd like something that means so much to me scattered in Iceland. My favourite place was that waterfall. I'm going to spell it wrong, I'm sure, and I certainly can't pronounce it correctly, but I loved

it there. Skogafoss. Claudia, you'll know where I mean. Please
scatter the flowers and think of me. Your dad too. And then
focus on yourselves. What was so special about that place and
all of our trips to Iceland was the feeling of freedom and possi-
bility that I never had back home. That might seem sad to you
– it does to me as I write it – but there have been many
moments of sheer and utter joy in my life, despite those
regrets. I want your lives to be full of freedom, love and hope,
and no regrets – at least not serious ones. So please, scatter
these flowers, think of me, then look ahead and lead the most
wonderful lives.

   All my love,
   Mum xx

Claudia folded the letter and held it in her lap. She wiped
furiously at her eyes. Claudia rarely cried and now she had twice
in the space of a few minutes; Molly felt numb with their mum's
words weaving their way through her mind. Even faced with her
own mortality, she wasn't thinking of herself but passing on
words of wisdom for them to make better choices – no, not better,
truer choices – than she'd been able to. She wanted them to live
life to the full and be truly happy, something Claudia had been
doing for years. Molly had a second chance; the life she thought
would be entwined with Howard could be rewritten as a new
start.

'Are you okay?' Molly finally found her voice.

Claudia stood, grabbed a tissue and blew her nose. 'We
should go.' She held up the letter. 'See out her wish.'

'Yes, we should.'

'I mean now.'

'Are you serious?' Molly glanced to the window at the heavy

snow. The wind battering the lodge fought against the music drifting up from downstairs. 'It's awful out there, Claudia.'

'There have been reports of the road being blocked from the other direction, so south coast coach trips from Reykjavík have been cancelled. It'll be blissfully quiet.'

'Because only someone completely bonkers would go out in this weather!'

Claudia looked at her, full of mischief.

Molly shook her head, but she felt a spark of excitement. Racing back to safety while snowmobiling in a storm had been scary but thrilling. So much of her life had been influenced by other people's expectations, followed in recent years by adult responsibilities weighing heavy on her shoulders. She'd been longing to be free of that pressure and do something exhilarating. She'd be with her sister, her adventurous older sister who always knew what she was doing, who was strong and confident, who got what she wanted because she was brave and determined. And hadn't their mum's letter been filled with the idea of truly living life? Okay, she might not have meant for them to put themselves in any danger, but she certainly wanted them to live differently to her, to chase their dreams and say yes.

'Fine, let's do it.'

Claudia went to find Elvar to let him know their plan, while Molly layered up in thermals, her fleece, comfy waterproof trousers, thick socks and boots and went downstairs to meet her.

She stood in the doorway of the lounge and gazed in. Apart from Alda, who was in her room, Elvar, Kat, Lils, James, Leifur and Finn were playing a raucous game of Cards Against Humanity in front of the fire. It was tempting to join them.

Claudia tapped Molly on the shoulder and zipped up her rucksack. 'Supplies,' she said by way of explanation. 'Just in case we run into any problems.'

Elvar caught sight of them, left the game and came over.

'Take it easy out there.' He kissed Claudia and squeezed Molly's shoulder. 'Get back in time for dinner.'

He re-joined the others.

James glanced up and caught Molly's eye. 'You okay?' he mouthed.

Molly smiled and nodded, despite a small part of her thinking they were mad to be doing this.

Claudia hefted her rucksack on her back and turned to her. 'Come on, let's go before the weather gets worse.'

With a smidge of jealousy that everyone else was warm and cosy while they were heading out into the wild and freezing day, Molly followed her sister.

26

Claudia took it steady on the drive to Skógafoss, the solid 4x4 gripping the road as snow drifted. Visibility was low, and even in the middle of the day, headlights were needed.

Molly allowed Claudia to concentrate on driving while she ran through their mum's letter over and over in her head. Her heartfelt words couldn't have come at a more perfect time; to know she'd approve of Molly facing the future without Howard was somehow comforting.

They'd been driving for just over an hour when Claudia turned off the ring road and they bumped towards a car park scattered with a few vehicles. Claudia parked up and Molly peered through the windscreen at the snow flurries sweeping across. In the distance, the waterfall was majestic, dove-grey water thundering down between rocky cliffs decorated with ice.

Molly had never been to Skógafoss when it had been this deserted. Only a few people were as brave – or foolish – as them, black ant-like dots struggling against the driving snow.

Pocketing the envelope containing their mum's letter and the dried flowers, Claudia switched off the engine. 'Let's do this.'

The wind was brutal, knocking them sideways and sucking their breath from them. Claudia tucked her arm in Molly's and they staggered across the compacted snow, following the river that sliced through the whiteness.

Mist swirled around the pale grey water as it dropped from the top of the sheer cliff and thundered into the icy pool below. It was much wider and even more impressive than Seljalandsfoss, the waterfall they'd visited during their tour of the south coast when she'd talked to James. Its constant noise mixed with the whistling wind engulfed them. Molly could feel its fine spray on her cheeks. Huge dagger-like icicles clung to the cliff on either side of the waterfall, while in the pool rocks were topped with plump pillows of snow.

Molly remembered standing in the same spot with her mum years before, gazing up in wonder at the waterfall. It had been a cold day with patches of snow and a cornflower blue sky, nowhere near as freezing as this, or wild and blanketed by white. Now chunks of ice topped with powdery snow glazed the black rock and great shards of ridged ice hung down in enormous clumps.

'I'm not sure Mum meant for us to do this on such a wild day!' Molly shouted over the crash of water, the wind snatching away her words.

Claudia tightened her grip and leaned close. 'No, although I think that was her point; she never took risks, never had a true adventure, never did anything for herself. The wildness is perfect.' She waved in the direction of the waterfall. 'It's exciting and freeing. We're doing this for her.'

Claudia unhooked her arm from Molly's, removed her gloves and took out the envelope. Carefully, she tipped the dried flowers into Molly's cupped hands. Claudia picked out the pink astilbe and left the rose and lavender for Molly. They walked away from the roaring waterfall until the icy spray couldn't reach them and stood on the snow-covered edge of the river. It wasn't ashes they were scattering, but the flowers their mum loved that had meant so much to her. Buffeted by the wind, they crouched together by the river's edge and dropped the flowers into the water.

For you, Mum, Molly thought as the flowers were whisked away on an adventure to the ocean. *For you too, Dad.*

They watched until they'd floated out of sight.

'There, she's free.' Claudia tucked her arm back in Molly's. 'Do you know, it's true what Mum said in her letter about Dad. I saw a completely different side to him than you did. You look back on your childhood differently to me, and perhaps that's because with so many years between us, we had such different experiences growing up. I rebelled against him, while you adored him. I do wonder if that has held you back – if he held you back without you even realising. I'm not sure adulthood has ever lived up to your expectations, but it's exceeded mine. I think that's because you had a happy childhood. I didn't.' She looked wistful as she sighed out a breath of frozen air. 'I don't want to destroy your rose-tinted image of him, and I know he's no longer here to defend himself, but he was far from perfect. Much like all of us. We can all do better, be better people, love better, care more.' She trailed off and clutched Molly tighter. 'The reason I'm telling you all this is because I care about you and I'm trying to be a better big sister, particularly now.'

The words their mum had written that had been playing over in Molly's head throughout the journey rang true – they needed to look after each other. Their mum may be gone, their dad too, and sadness and loss had weaved through their lives, but they still had each other. They were family and would be there for each other until they no longer could.

They turned back and took in the cascading water. Molly was

relieved she was standing here with her sister and not Howard. Even if he'd caught the flight and hadn't broken up with her, being here with him wouldn't have felt any more wonderous. They would have feigned romance and gone through the motions but the outcome would still have been the same, days or months down the line. It was better this way; they'd eked out their relationship for long enough. Best to let go and move on before any more time and effort had been wasted.

Involuntarily, Molly tightened her grip on her sister's arm.

Claudia glanced at her. 'Are you okay?'

Molly nodded. 'Yes, I think I am. There's lots to figure out but maybe this is the start of something.'

'This *is* a new start, Moll,' Claudia said firmly. 'Time to move forward and not look back on anything with regret. Mum's words.'

'Speaking of moving.' Molly laughed between chattering teeth. 'Maybe we should get back to the car before we freeze to death!'

They fought their way back against the side wind, the ferocity of the thundering falls diminishing by the time they reached the parking area. They closed the doors on the wild and removed gloves, hats and coats. Molly's cheeks felt tight from the exposure to the cold.

Claudia didn't start the engine. With her hands resting on the steering wheel, she stared out for a moment before turning to Molly.

'As this seems to be a day about letting go of the past and moving on, there's something else I need to tell you. You don't need to know it now, not after what Howard's done, but it might help you to process everything.'

Molly frowned, readying herself for what her sister was about to reveal.

'I saw Howard once, out in a club. It wasn't long after you two had got together. I was back over in the UK for a friend's hen do.' She fixed her firmly with a look that Molly couldn't quite work out. 'He was, um, kissing another woman.'

'He was what?' Molly shook her head in confusion. 'Why the hell didn't you tell me?'

'You wouldn't have believed me and I was pretty drunk; the next day I even questioned what I'd seen. I was uncertain if he'd kissed her or if she'd come onto him and he simply hadn't resisted. You know, if he was drunk and it all went a bit too far. He might have been saying no, laughing it off—'

'While kissing her?' Molly raised her eyebrows.

'Well, yes. A drunken snog. If the woman instigated it, it might have meant nothing and I certainly wasn't going to risk ruining your relationship over something I wasn't certain about. But as the years went by, I wished more and more that I *had* said something. Whether you'd have believed me or not, I should have spoken up. Exactly like Mum said in her letter about being truthful to ourselves and having no regrets. Even if it felt right at the time to not say anything, this is a regret.'

'Is that why you never warmed to him?' Molly stared ahead through the windscreen at the waterfall, the spray of pale grey water looking as if it was falling in slow motion. 'Because you suspected he'd cheated on me?'

'Partly, yes. But there's always been more to it than that, Moll. He's not good enough for you and if only I'd realised it back then, I would have told you about what I saw. But I gave him the benefit of the doubt because I knew how head over heels in love you were. I figured if he was to you what Elvar was to me, then I didn't want to jeopardise that. But the more I got to know him...'

Molly played with the edge of her scarf. 'I've been so naive and foolish.'

'No, you were caught up in the excitement of new love, then the craziness of buying your first house together, starting to put down roots and looking to the future, and then...' Claudia inhaled deeply. 'Then your world was turned upside down. You are anything but naive or foolish, Moll. You're strong and brave, kind and so damn loving. Mum and Dad were lucky to have you there. And as for Howard, he absolutely didn't deserve you.' Claudia's cheeks clenched as she met Molly's eyes.

She was taken aback by the strength of Claudia's words, of the love and passion emanating from her pragmatic sister who rarely showed emotion.

'Thank you for telling me.'

Claudia reached across the gear stick and held Molly's hand. 'What happened to Mum and Dad must have taught you, if anything, that life is fleeting. Waiting for things to get better, for your grief to subside, for Howard to bloody propose or whatever you wanted him to do is just crap. Mum was absolutely right in what she said. Take things into your own hands and actually start living. And whoever you have a relationship with next, go in with your eyes wide open and only commit to someone if they feel right and treat you the way you deserve.'

27

They made it back to the lodge well before dinner. The restaurant had reopened after the Christmas break and early diners were beginning to arrive. Molly felt wrung out, and while Claudia had the guests and the running of the lodge to focus on, she felt at a loss for what to do after yet another emotionally challenging day.

James was the only one in the guest lounge and the warmth of his smile when he clocked her was encouragement enough for her to join him.

'You had fun this afternoon, playing games with everyone?' Molly said as she sat on the opposite end of the sofa. After being battered by the icy wind at Skógafoss, it was a relief to be warmed by the flickering fire.

'Aye, it was good, although we missed you and Claudia.' He reached forward and chucked a piece of wood on the fire. 'How was your afternoon? Elvar told me the reason you went.'

'It was moving,' she said quietly, uncertain how to put the experience into words.

James had kind eyes, although his furrowed brow and the ridged line between his eyebrows suggested he had much to worry about, but there was a sparkle and an openness that was appealing.

'We don't have to talk about it,' he said. 'I understand how hard it must have been.'

'It was needed. It's been a day of revelations and finding out lots I needed to hear. It will help me to figure stuff out.'

'Good, I'm glad.'

Molly glanced round the empty lounge. 'I thought you'd be with Leifur.'

'He was invited to a family meal with Birta; he didn't want to say no, not when he doesn't get to spend much time with her. He'll be back later.'

'Have you heard from Jen?'

'No and I don't expect to either.' He brushed his hands together. 'We're done. When I get back to Edinburgh, I'll move my stuff out of her flat and go live at Karthstone. It's where I belong and where I should have been all this time. Besides a sham of an engagement, we don't share anything. We'll simply move on. How about you? Have you spoken to Howard?'

'Not since Christmas morning when he phoned to have a go because I called him an arse.'

James snorted. 'Aye, I imagine an arse is the polite way to describe him.'

'It's a little more complicated for me to move on from him.' Molly breathed deeply. 'Not that I actually want to go home, but at least when I get back, I can put an end to me and Howard. Take control of my life again.'

'Aye, my breakup's pretty straightforward, but I don't want to return either. I understand your sentiment of a new start. I've loved being here, with Leif, with Elvar, getting to know Claudia and the family more, all the other guests.' He met her eyes and smiled. 'And you.'

An appealing warmth emanated from him and Molly couldn't help but return a smile, her insides doing a little jig as she drank him in.

The arrival of Kat and Lils put an end to their private chat. James caught Molly's eye and gave her a knowing smile as the conversation was hijacked by Kat and her excitement over tomorrow's New Year's Eve party at a bar in Reykjavík.

Once dinner was served, Molly gazed round the table at the familiar faces and realised how much she was going to miss the laughter and camaraderie of her family and newfound friends.

Everyone headed to the lounge for after-dinner drinks as usual, so there was no chance for Molly to continue to talk to James on his own. Her head was a mishmash of emotions and she was relieved when Claudia decided on an early night. With the New Year's Eve's celebrations looming, everyone else was happy to head to bed too.

As Molly went into the dining room, James gestured towards the picture windows and leaned close. 'Leifur's back – just saw him walk past. I'm sure he'll be pleased to see you. Night.' The deep line of worry was back. He shoved his hands into the pockets of his jeans and paced away.

Was he escaping because he thought she'd want to spend the rest of the evening with Leifur? She'd believed that Leifur's misunderstanding about her and James had been resolved, but she hadn't considered whether James still thought that *she* wanted to be with Leifur.

Her eyes trailed James until he reached the entrance hall. She was desperate to follow him, to invite herself into his room, to put him straight about her and Leifur then talk to him late into the night, but after what he'd just said about her and Leifur, he obviously didn't feel the same. She turned away instead and came face to face with Claudia.

'Are you coming upstairs?' Claudia's tone was light but the way she was looking at her was hard to decipher.

Molly nodded and followed her.

* * *

Unresolved feelings flowed through Molly as she changed into her pyjamas. Tension wound so tight within her, she was unable to relax. She got into bed and picked up *The Salt Path* but her attention was hijacked by persistent thoughts and she ended up reading the same paragraph over and over.

Footsteps sounded out in the hallway and the bedroom door next to hers opened then closed. James had been right; Leifur was back.

She closed her book. Today had been filled with truths that had been eye-opening and hard to hear but necessary. Burying her feelings and shutting out those closest to her had felt right at the time, but it hadn't enabled her to move forward. That was what she needed to do now. No regrets.

Molly flung off the covers, slipped from her room and without another thought, rapped gently on Leifur's bedroom door.

'Can I come in?' she asked the second he opened it.

'Of course.' Wide-eyed, he stood back.

The door closed with a click behind her. His room was familiar because it was where she usually stayed, but it was filled with his belongings, with clothes strewn over the armchair, the bed unmade and photos of Birta stuck on the wall above the chest of drawers.

Molly turned to him, words on the tip of her tongue, yet she didn't know the best way to start. Watching her intently, Leifur looked relaxed in comfy trousers and just a T-shirt, his arms crossed, his muscles tense and distracting.

'Elvar said you and Claudia found a bit of peace going to Skógafoss this afternoon?' Leifur broke the silence.

'Yes, we did.' Molly suddenly realised how confusing it must be with her in her pyjamas standing in the middle of his room, her intrusion unexpected even if he'd been suggesting this all along. Well not exactly this. She was only here to talk. She found her voice. 'I wanted to clear things up. I like you, a lot. I always have done, and I *loved* that summer we spent together. Perhaps I wished more had happened, but I think it was for the best it didn't, because we're friends and I kinda like that.'

'Okay...' His frown deepened. 'Why are you telling me this?'

'To make it clear that nothing's going to happen between us, even a fun meaningless fling, despite everyone suggesting that something should.'

'Everyone?' he said with surprise.

'Well, not exactly everyone. Claudia mainly. James's been hinting at it, Elvar's said stuff too but I think that's down to you telling a few little lies about us.'

His cheeks flushed. 'Um, yeah. About that. I'm sorry. I might have said more than I should have, but honestly, I would never intentionally hurt you.' He stepped closer, holding his hands out in a pacifying gesture. 'You're Elvar's sister-in-law. He'd never forgive me. All that stuff I said about us to James, that was years ago. Believe it or not, I'm more aware now of how my actions impact other people than I was when I was younger. I know what I want and don't want. I want you.' His frown twisted into a grin. 'I *wanted* you, but you're right, for nothing more than a bit of fun. I realise that's harder to do at our age, unless of course you have a similar mindset, which you don't.'

'Don't assume you know what I want.' Molly returned a smile. 'But you're spot on. I'm not in the right place emotionally for that, but I once was.'

'I am sorry, for being a shit and saying more than I should have.'

'I know your heart's in the right place, because it all comes down to you putting Birta first. A proper relationship with someone could potentially make things difficult. I get that.'

'I messed my marriage up, I made stupid choices and behaved selfishly. We should never have got married. I've learned that I'm better on my own. I don't mean without Birta; I mean without a partner.' The muscles in his arms clenched. 'Not that I'd have said no to you if you wanted a bit of fun, but I don't want more than that and I'm aware it could ruin my friendship with Elvar, with Claudia. With you. A few nights together isn't worth that.'

'I just want you to understand where I'm at. I value your friendship and I don't want there to be a weirdness between us. The other night at The Star Lodge...'

Leifur waved his hand. 'Ah, that was all my fault. I shouldn't have said the things I did. Again, I'm sorry. I thought I'd try my luck. I read the signs wrong.'

'It's just I get the feeling that James still thinks there's something going on between us.' Heat rushed to her cheeks.

Leifur looked perplexed as his eyes traced her face. He nodded. 'My fault again. I'll put him straight.'

'So we're good?'

'We're good.'

Molly faltered before throwing her arms around him. There was a brief pause before he returned the hug. It felt so good to be held, to be comforted in this way with no expectation of it leading anywhere else.

28

Molly woke on New Year's Eve morning longing to kiss goodbye to the last horrible twelve months and start afresh with a new year that would be filled with challenges but possibilities too. While Leifur and James went out for the day, Molly was happy to spend it with her family, making the most of the time she had left with them. Later on she enjoyed getting dressed up, doing her make-up and heading to Reykjavík for a night filled with celebration.

The rooftop terrace of the family-owned Grey Whale Bar was exposed, but it had unrivalled views across the city with Hallgrímskirkja's iconic spire just visible. The firepit Molly, Claudia, Elvar, Leifur and James were sitting around did little to combat the icy air, but alcohol and plenty of snuggly blankets went some way to warming them up and there was always the option of retreating inside.

Kat and Lils returned from the bar, sweeping back to their seating area full of laughter. Molly was inspired by them, particularly Lils, who'd faced challenges with positivity and good humour. Her own grief was something she needed to learn to live with, yet the other aspects of her life she had control over. The only person to stop her from achieving her dreams now would be herself.

The chatter around the table was good humoured and Molly was relieved that she'd talked to Leifur the night before. It had been freeing to be truthful and she liked that she felt comfortable around him again. James and Leifur were chatting and laughing together like the best friends they were. She wondered if Leifur had remained true to his word about putting James straight about their relationship. A niggling uncertainty remained over her feelings for James and she was unsure what he thought of her.

Around ten-thirty, Elvar and Leifur disappeared inside to watch *Skaupid*, an Icelandic comedy special on TV.

'It's an Icelandic tradition,' Claudia explained. 'Elvar's been watching it every year since he can remember. I'd rather drink and chat.'

Molly, Kat, Lils and James raised their glasses in agreement and took a swig.

'It's a shame Graham and Maggie didn't stay till after the New Year,' Kat said.

'It's not a shame Jen left.'

James's comment stunned them into silence. Lils broke the moment with a snort.

She raised her glass again. 'I'll drink to that! However upsetting it was at the time, she's done you a massive favour. That attitude is the right one. Onwards and upwards!' She glanced between James and Molly. 'A new start for you both.'

Molly caught James's eye over the top of her glass. His expression was lost as he downed his drink.

'I need another!' Clutching his empty glass, he stood up. 'Can I get anyone anything?'

Indicating their nearly full glasses, they shook their heads.

Confused by her feelings towards him, Molly watched James retreat inside. She pulled the blanket tighter, turned back to the others and met Kat's eyes.

The disappointment that Molly felt when James didn't immediately return only added to her confusion; she assumed Leifur and Elvar had enticed him to join them, although perhaps theirs was the company he wanted to keep. Just because a spark of something was ignited whenever she was in his presence, it didn't mean it was reciprocated.

Molly tore her thoughts away from James and turned her attention back to the group. An occasional firework went off, but it had quietened down since *Skaupid* had started, although the conversation, fuelled by Kat and Lils telling funny anecdotes, was raucous. When they started discussing a mutual friend, Claudia shifted closer to Molly.

'It's nice to see you happy and relaxed.'

Molly sipped her drink. 'The alcohol's helping. Also, I'm trying to enjoy the moment and not think too hard about what happens next. The thought of having to go through the stress of selling another house. Ugh.'

'You're thinking about it.' Claudia laughed. She waggled her fingers in front of Molly's face. 'Just stop, empty your mind of anything beyond tonight. But tell me.' She leaned in and lowered her voice. 'You and Leif last night – I heard you sneak into his room. So did you, you know...?'

Molly raised an eyebrow. 'Have sex?'

Claudia grinned. 'You did, didn't you!'

'No! You have the whole me-and-Leifur thing so wrong. I did go into his room to *talk*. Nothing more. I didn't want there to be any weirdness between us.'

'Ah, that's a shame.' Claudia screwed up her nose. 'Not the weirdness bit, just the two of you. I figured a rebound fling with

Leifur would be the perfect way for you to end a shitty year and start a brilliant new one.'

I can think of a more perfect way. Her thoughts flicked to James, but she didn't say anything. She didn't want to go down the route of trying to explain her feelings to Claudia – feelings she didn't quite understand herself.

'The man you rebound with should never be the one you fall in love with,' Claudia said with a knowing tone and a slight slur.

'How on earth, when you've been with Elvar for forever, can you possibly say that?'

'I've had my heart broken too.' Claudia looked wistfully at her. 'I don't think you knew anything about him because I was at uni and you were just a kid. I thought he was *the one*.' She looked sideways at her and shook her head. 'He absolutely wasn't. Cheated on me with half the girls in our halls. Then the summer after I graduated I had a rebound fling with Mrs Greystone's gardener.'

Molly frowned. 'Mrs Greystone, as in Mum and Dad's neighbour?'

'The very one. She was old and doddery and seemed like she was in her eighties for about three decades, but her gardener was fit. You must have noticed him. You were about ten or eleven at the time.'

Molly shook her head; she had no recollection of anyone other than Mrs Greystone with her plaid skirts and ruffled blouses. 'I honestly don't remember but I was into horse riding and baking and wasn't really interested in boys.' She'd been a late bloomer, clinging on to her childhood and happy with her own company, until her teen years kicked in and boys and nights out had come racing to the forefront, but by then Claudia had long left home.

'That summer was lush,' Claudia said with a sigh. 'It was a hot one, so he spent most of it with his top off and I spent most of it getting up to no good with him in the bushes.'

Molly's eyes widened. 'Seriously?' Apart from some teen rebellion that had resulted in numerous arguments with their dad, as far as Molly was concerned, Claudia had gone to university, aced her degree, gone travelling, met Elvar and fallen in love. She was adventurous when it came to her way of life but pretty strait-laced romance-wise. Molly had never really considered her having been with anyone other than Elvar.

'Completely serious.' Claudia smiled drunkenly. 'I have rather fond memories of that summer.'

'I bet you do!'

'But, what I am trying to say' – she patted Molly's arm beneath the blanket – 'is I know you're hurting over Howard, but you will find happiness again. Sometimes having these not-so-great relationships allows us to figure out what we really want. But you don't have to hang around waiting for Mr Perfect – if there is such a thing.'

'Um, Elvar.'

Claudia smiled. 'Yup, Elvar. But I didn't hang about waiting for him, did I? I spent a summer shagging a fit gardener.' She raised her eyebrows. 'But what I'm really saying is live a little and have fun, try and forget about Howard because he sure as hell—' She stopped. 'Sorry. That was going to come out sounding worse than I meant, but you know what I mean, right?'

He sure as hell has been having his own fun for a long time. Yes, Molly knew exactly what she meant.

'It has crossed my mind that it might be good to, um, move on from Howard.'

Claudia nudged Molly's arm with her fist.

'But,' Molly said firmly, 'I don't want to mess up our friendship.'

'Oh, don't worry about that. I'm sure Leifur will be more than happy to oblige if you change your mind on that front. You know the score; he's happily single and I'm pretty sure he wants to remain that way, but a bit of fun...'

'It's not really Leifur I'm talking about.' Molly's eyes drifted across the rooftop terrace to where James had disappeared earlier.

'Oh.' Claudia sounded confused. 'Oh!' she said again as Molly turned back. 'You mean James?'

Molly shrugged. 'I'm uncertain how I feel, but I know I like James enough to not do anything with Leifur.'

Claudia nodded slowly and frowned. 'Something really did happen at The Star Lodge, right? Elvar didn't go into any detail, told me to ask you. You were dismissive. Leifur was definitely off when you got back.'

'Yes, he was. He thought something had happened between me and James when it didn't – I mean something physical.' She was blushing because thinking about James in that way was making her insides go all mushy. She sighed a stream of frosted breath into the night. 'Leifur and James had an argument but are fine now, and I've cleared things up with Leifur too.' Molly sipped her gin and tonic and weighed up how much she should divulge to Claudia. 'It's been flattering to have Leifur's attention, particularly at a time when I've hit rock bottom. He's sexy and good looking.'

'James is a bit of all right too, you know.'

'Yeah,' Molly said quietly. 'I had noticed. But it's not just about the way he looks. He's easy to talk to and I've found myself wanting to spend time with him, just chatting and laughing together; it doesn't have to be any more than that.'

'Oh my,' Claudia sighed. 'You've fallen for him hard.'

Molly frowned. Had she? Were all these jumbled feelings

because she actually really liked him? Or was it because she was hurting and he was too and they'd been drawn together due to their shared heartache? Despite his sadness, he had a way of looking at things in a positive light and she liked that. She needed that. It was the same reason she was drawn to Kat and Lils. Their outlook on life was refreshingly honest and, despite their own individual challenges, they were making the best of what they'd been given, turning disappointment and challenges on their head in an attempt to find the positives. She needed to be more Kat and Lils. She'd been blinkered by Howard's outlook on life; he wasn't one for taking chances, much like her dad. James's outlook, like Kat and Lils's, was the right one for her.

'Perhaps it's best to keep an open mind about everything,' Claudia said thoughtfully, tipping her glass in Molly's direction. 'I know I've been encouraging you over Leifur but then I understand the benefit of moving on from heartbreak both emotionally and physically. It's very soon though and it absolutely needs to be when the time is right for you. My rebound fling is a good memory – a *very* good memory,' she said with a chuckle. 'I just don't want you to miss out on that sort of fun.'

'I am a lot older than you were when you had your heart broken. Early twenties compared to my thirty-five years.'

'Which is not old,' Claudia said firmly. 'Considering I'm forty-six.'

'Yes, but you've really lived. You have a job and lifestyle you love, the best husband, two gorgeous, brilliant kids and you live in the most incredible place, while I don't have—'

'*You can* have all of that, if it's what you want.' Claudia looked at her intensely, her breath fogging between them. 'The husband bit, well, that's down to a bit of luck meeting the right person, but your job and where you choose to live, you can absolutely do something about that. And you should.' She put her gloved hand on Molly's. 'You've been unhappy with your job for so long, Moll. You have the money from the house sale; you have the opportunity to make a new life for yourself without worrying about anyone else. Without anyone holding you back.'

Tears welled in Molly's eyes. The tip of her nose was freezing, the chill breeze giving her the sniffles, while the Icelandic gin was warming her insides nicely.

'New year, new start, remember.' Claudia knocked her glass against Molly's. 'The programme must have finished.' She nodded towards Elvar, Leifur and James emerging from inside.

As they were welcomed back, a firework screeched into the air. It exploded in a shower of gold sparkles. Everyone oohed and aahed, which was followed by laughter. The conversation turned to previous years' firework displays and Lils told them about a disastrous New Year's Eve she'd had in London.

As it neared midnight, they gathered with everyone else at the edge of the terrace to look out over the city's rooftops.

Molly squeezed next to Claudia and leaned close. 'You know what, it's been really lovely talking properly to you. We should do this more often.'

Claudia took her hand. 'We really should.'

With just a few minutes of the old year left, the fireworks started in earnest, the build-up to the countdown and the big moment at midnight. Molly gazed up. It was a clear night, perhaps even clear enough away from the city for the northern lights to show. Reykjavík was lit up by flashes of exploding orange, red and silver, colourful sparkles raining down instead of snow.

Leifur sidled next to Molly and slid an arm across her shoulders. 'I'm glad we talked last night. I just wanted to say how good it's been to see you again. I know you've had a shit time, but hopefully things will get better and you'll be able to visit more often.'

Molly met his eyes. The weight of his arm across her shoulders was comforting, and the twinkle in his eyes that had once sent lustful feelings shooting through her was friendly. She smiled up at him. 'I intend to come back a lot more. I intend to change a lot of things actually. This year will be a whole new start and I'm beginning to look forward to the challenge.'

'I never met your boyfriend, but from the little Claudia's said, I'm rather glad you're no longer with him. You definitely deserve someone better.'

Molly's shoulders tensed. 'And by someone you mean...'

'Not me.' Leifur laughed and removed his arm. He nudged her shoulder playfully with his fist, the kind of way he behaved with James. 'There is someone you're far more suited to.' He gestured to where James was standing with Elvar.

'Oh, I'm not sure he thinks of me in that way.'

'You might be surprised.' Leifur gave a knowing smile. 'Just talk to each other. Spend some time together. He's a good guy. The best. And how do you say it in English? You're a catch?' He winked and manoeuvred her across the terrace in James's direction. 'We talked. It's fine, I promise.'

With her heart pounding, and the fireworks screeching and exploding into the air, Molly allowed Leifur to guide her towards James. She slipped into a snug space between him and Kat.

'Molly!' Elvar slapped a hand on her shoulder.

James smiled and Kat oohed as a huge firework exploded close by, lighting up the sky with a glittery green.

The countdown started in a mix of Icelandic and English.

'*Tíu, níu, átta...*'

The fireworks eased momentarily. Everyone was poised to celebrate the New Year with Reykjavík's very own light show whether the northern lights made an appearance or not.

'Seven, six, five, four, three, two, one!'

'*Gleðilegt nýtt ár!*'

'Happy New Year!'

Cheers and whoops echoed into the night. Kat and Lils hugged; Elvar kissed Claudia. Leifur had his arm around someone. James and Molly turned to each other.

'Happy New Year, James.'

The fireworks lit up the sky in a riot of colour. James leaned close and the hiss, bang and whizz faded into the background. His lips brushed her cheek and their eyes met, a wordless exchange that made her whole body tingle. She wrapped her arms around him and his hands found her waist. Their lips were tantalisingly close. He closed the gap and kissed her. She kissed him back, warmth and excitement pulsing through her. The faded bangs and pops whooshed back into surround sound, along with whoops, cheers and a wolf whistle joining the fireworks screaming into the winter night sky.

James pulled away and laughed. 'Happy New Year, Molly!'

It was a happy New Year indeed. She couldn't think of a better way to start it.

29

By one, the rooftop celebrations began to fizzle out with the fireworks, as the streets below came alive with people heading to bars and clubs. With Finn partying with his girlfriend, Alda sleeping over at a friend's and Leifur deciding to stay and go out in Reykjavík, it was just Elvar, Claudia, Kat, Lils, James and Molly heading back to The Fire Lodge. Elvar, the only sober one, seemed rather amused by everyone else's varying states of drunkenness, particularly his wife's uncharacteristic and numerous public displays of affection. Molly had had just enough to feel happy drunk, the cool air tempering the effects over the course of the night.

Leifur and James hugged goodbye, thumping each other's backs. Molly noticed how Leifur didn't try to get James to stay and James didn't suggest it either. Molly felt a pang of regret as Leifur walked away with a wave to continue partying into the early hours. He cut a lonely figure, but she knew he wouldn't remain lonely. It finally felt as if she'd closed the door on the 'what could have been' with him. The words in her mum's letter about regret flooded back. She hoped that Leifur wouldn't end up being a regret. She still had his friendship, and she was pretty sure him talking to James was the reason their kiss at midnight had happened.

They reached the 4x4 and Elvar slid into the driver's seat with a sleepy, drunken Claudia next to him. Kat and Lils took the seats behind them, while Molly found herself on the back seat with James.

As they drove through the dark streets, still lit by an occasional firework exploding gold and red into the indigo sky, Molly felt completely safe in Elvar's hands as they headed away from the city. She and James sat in comfortable silence, Molly playing the evening over in her head right up to that kiss.

A good twenty minutes out of Reykjavík, Elvar said, 'Look to your left.'

A swirl of shimmering green lit up the sky to the north. Kat's and Lils's sleepy gasps, accompanied by Claudia's rumbling snore, made Molly smile.

She gazed out of the window, mesmerised by the light flickering across the horizon. James took her hand and curled his fingers in hers. A thrill shot through Molly and a tingling heat settled in the pit of her stomach.

'Almost as good as at The Star Lodge,' he whispered.

'Almost,' Molly echoed. That night had been magical for more reasons than just the northern lights. It was that night she'd first felt truly connected to James, when they'd delved deep into their feelings, not about each other, but the point at which they were in their lives. And they'd been alone. Now, even with Claudia snoring and Kat and Lils nodding off, she was aware that Elvar could overhear even a whispered conversation. So they remained silent, their hands entwined, gazing out at the night and the wisps of the northern lights disappearing as quickly as they'd appeared.

It was gone two in the morning by the time they made it back.

They spilled from the vehicle and into the lodge in a haze of tiredness and yawns.

With echoes of thanks to Elvar, a shout of 'buffet breakfast from ten tomorrow' from Claudia and calls of 'happy New Year', they all dispersed: Claudia and Elvar upstairs to their apartment and Kat and Lils towards the guest suites.

Molly and James trailed behind; Molly was aware she was stalling, and she wondered if he was too. She didn't want the night to end, not yet. The sleepiness she'd felt on the drive back had been from the warmth, while the thought of being alone with James now left her feeling very awake. Kat had definitely seen them kiss at midnight, but she was uncertain if Claudia and Elvar had – beyond a wink from Kat and a knowing smile from Leifur, no one had commented.

James turned to her. 'Do you fancy another drink?'

'I was about to ask you the same thing.'

'Inside or out in the hot tub?' Behind his glasses, his eyes glinted.

What the hell. No regrets, right?

'It's a whole new year,' she said. 'We should start as we mean to go on – doing something adventurous and memorable. At least that's how I'd like my new year to be.'

'Mine too. Meet you outside.'

With her heart skipping, Molly crept upstairs to her room and stripped out of her clothes into a bikini. She slipped her feet into boots, threw on a robe and scooped up a T-shirt, hoody, leggings and a towel, before making her way back along the landing. Elvar appeared in the open doorway of his room.

'Claudia's already passed out.' He raised a bushy eyebrow. 'You know what you're doing, right? With James?'

Nothing. Everything. I have no idea.

'Yes,' she said smoothly. She actually meant it. Even if nothing came of it, she was enjoying his company immensely. It was the early hours of New Year's Day and she wanted to continue feeling this alive and free. James was a huge part of that.

'That's okay then.' Elvar nodded and gave her a gentle smile. 'I'm older than you. I need sleep. *Góða nótt.*'

'*Góða nótt,* Elvar.'

She raced downstairs and out into the icy night. She headed towards the hot tubs as James emerged from his room in just his swim shorts. Making her way gingerly along the path, she considered what it would be like if she'd made different choices, if it was Leifur bare chested braving the cold or if she'd remained in Reykjavík and had gone out with him. She would have had fun with Leifur, she was certain of that, but there was possibility with James, a real sense of heading into the unknown on an adventure, mixed with the thrill of getting to know someone she was drawn to. She pushed Leifur to the back of her mind and focused on James – and her footing – as she crunched across the compacted snow.

Laughing at his pained expression, she gestured at his bare feet. 'You're crazy coming out here like that!'

'I figured I'd drunk so much this evening, I wouldn't feel the cold. I was wrong!' His laugh spiralled into the night. 'I also forgot to bring a drink out.' He lifted the wooden cover off the hot tub, releasing the steam. 'Too bloody cold to go back.' His teeth were chattering so much his whole body was shaking. He climbed in and slipped into the water with a moan. 'Och, that's good.'

With her own teeth chattering, she peeled off her robe like whipping off a plaster, dropped it on the snow and kicked off her boots. She tugged her hat down over her ears and joined James. Her sigh as the deliciously warm water caressed her chilled skin made him laugh.

Submerged up to her chin, she bobbed about, her frozen

breath pooling into the night. Away from the lights of the lodge behind them, the valley was dark with just the star-scattered sky and the glistening river visible, the moonlight catching its ripples.

'Amazing, isn't it?' James rested back and gazed up. Molly joined him on the submerged seat. It was too cold to rest her arms along the edge of the tub, so they bobbed together, their shoulders touching.

The snow blanketed everything and softened what little sound there was.

'I've always found the New Year to be a bit odd.' James's voice was hushed, his gentle Scottish lilt drifting into the night. 'Why make resolutions and plans when you have a whole twelve months and plenty of opportunity to transform your life all year round if you wanted to. It's a pressure I've never understood, but after what's happened with Jen, I feel a wee bit different this year.'

'I know what you mean. I've made resolutions over the years, but they've always been silly things, like giving up alcohol for the month – which I usually fail miserably at – rather than big resolutions that require proper commitment. I've thought about making those big decisions, but I've kept them in my head because I was scared to commit to them. I knew Howard wouldn't take me seriously or would discourage me because they were too risky.'

James frowned. 'Like what?'

'Like handing my notice in.' Molly shrugged and sent ripples across the surface of the hot tub. 'I can't tell you how many times I've wanted to do that, and not just at New Year. I've never had the guts and Howard would never have supported me.'

'So he held you back?'

'I've held myself back but he didn't help. He's never encouraged me work-wise and it's only recently, when Claudia pointed out how much Howard reminded her of our dad, that I realised how right she was.'

'Oh?'

'Again, I didn't see it. Me and Claudia had very different experiences growing up. I think Dad had mellowed a little by the time I was born, whereas Claudia took the full brunt of his old-fashioned and sexist ways. She rebelled and forged a successful life away from him and of course ended up with Elvar, the complete opposite of our dad – generous, supportive, sensitive, encouraging, all the things anyone could want in a partner, while I ended up with Howard. He liked our life ordered while I would have loved to be more creative with everything: our house, my job, what we did together.' Now she'd started, it was hard to stop, her innermost thoughts spilling over. 'It's taken the heartache of loss, of understanding the damaging behaviour of my dad and Howard, for me to see the truth. What my mum put in her letter helped too. I think she found it difficult to tell me when she was alive. Writing it down was obviously cathartic for her and she believed it would be helpful. And it certainly was for me, to hear the truth about her regrets and not wanting me to make the same mistake.'

'Aye, regret is a strange thing.' James ran a wet hand over his face. 'I often wonder if my mum ever regretted leaving. It's something I'll never know and it's something I've had to try and come to terms with, not understanding her thought process and how she really felt about me. Although she was well into her twenties, I was an accident. She was troubled and couldn't cope. What I've always held on to is how lucky I was to be raised by my grandparents. For my mother to be strong enough to walk away completely instead of messing up my life benefitted me hugely. There was no love. She went off travelling the world, having adventures, doing whatever she did until she died young. But her decision to cut me out of her life at least gave me the stability of knowing my grandparents were my parents. They were my family, the whole of it. No mother, no father – I have no clue about him. No siblings, at least that I'm aware of.' His breath puffed white between them. 'I could have loads of brothers and sisters for all I know. But my grandparents gave me all the love I needed, and I grew up in the most incredible place.'

'Is that where your mum grew up too?'

'Yep, also as an only child.' He took a deep breath. 'I know my grandma blamed herself. My mum suffered with mental health problems from a young age. She was wild and rebellious, would disappear for days on end as a teen and rock back for food and clean clothes. I think my grandparents thought she'd grow out of that rebellious stage, but she never did. I only have vague memories of her and I don't think my grandparents really knew her either. Everything they told me was more about what she did and her behaviour rather than getting to the heart of *who* she was. Troubled is the only way I can think about her.'

'That's so sad.'

'It is, but I've always looked on the flip side; her instability allowed me to have stability and love, while my grandparents were given a second chance by raising me. I know they were more focused on my well-being and mental health and were aware of the negatives as well as the positives of living in such a unique place miles from friends, from school, from the community. They'd changed their outlook on work and family by the time I was born and got the balance right. It's a little like the different experiences you and Claudia had. You're sisters who each grew up as an only child. By the time your parents had you, it sounds like your dad was a better father than he was to Claudia.'

Molly grimaced. 'Families, eh?'

'A minefield indeed. I think we're both lucky though, that we had happy childhoods.' Beneath the water, James grabbed her arm. 'Look.'

Whispers of iridescent green floated across the night sky, echoes from earlier, teasing them with their beauty. The stars were so dense in places they'd turned the sky silver, while the darker patches met the grey outline of snow-covered mountains, the definition unclear in the depths of the winter night.

Molly marvelled at the peaceful and untainted surroundings, the faint swirls of green tinged with pink painting the darkness. James's hand remained on her arm. They'd moved closer while they'd been talking and their shoulders and thighs were now touching. Their breath frosted together, the rise and fall of their chests syncing as they watched the northern lights dance then fade, until just the faintest trace remained.

'That was something else.' His fingers travelled down her arm and he took hold of her hand.

Molly's senses were overloaded by his touch, the heat within the hot tub and the iciness surrounding them. She wanted time to stop, because moments of pure joy like this were fleeting.

'Do you think being with the wrong person means that when you meet the right one, you'd know without a doubt that it was perfect? That they were perfect for you?' James held her gaze, his blue eyes behind his glasses roving across her face.

Was he suggesting she could be the right person? There was certainly the potential – an attraction and a desire to spend time together. They were both in similar places in their lives. She didn't want to get ahead of herself. She'd made a promise to live in the moment.

'Maybe. I felt that way in the beginning with Howard; I thought we were perfect together. But I do understand what a relationship that's not right feels like now and how damaging it can be. I think I'll know now when something's right.' Beneath the water she ran her thumb along his. She wanted him to understand that right this moment she meant him. 'It's been difficult to judge how I felt when I was miserable all the time. I didn't feel as if I was allowed to be happy and even when I was with Howard, I still felt sad and out of sorts. I put that down to grief but perhaps it was more than that. Even here in Iceland, when I can truly say I've had some wonderful experiences, I still feel guilty when I catch myself laughing. Someone says something funny and I wish Mum was here to share it. It's hard to imagine being properly happy again.'

'You don't have to be happy all the time; no one should expect you to be.' His hand squeezed hers and brushed her thigh, sending tingles through her. 'Just occasionally is okay. For the time being at least. Be patient and those occasions will grow.'

'I'm happy when I'm with you,' Molly said gently, looking into his eyes. 'I'm happy right now.'

James reached up and cupped her face with his wet hand. 'Me too.'

30

Molly's senses were in overdrive as she drank him in. As the steam rose around them, excitement, nerves, anticipation and worry all mushed together in her stomach.

'I'm not sure I can feel my nose any longer.' James broke the intensity and removed his hand from her cheek.

Molly relaxed into a giggle. 'I'm pretty certain I have wrinkled toes and frozen eyelashes.'

'Time to go back inside?'

'Most definitely!'

James braved it first, rivulets of water running down his chest as he stood.

She followed his lead, leaving the warmth of the hot tub and planting her feet in the snow with a gasp. With the freezing air attacking her skin, she didn't waste time throwing on a robe, instead scooping it up along with her clothes, towel and boots, and cold-footed it along the snow-dusted path.

They tumbled into his room in a flurry of icy breath, damp skin and snow. The wood burner was glowing and James shut the glass door on the night. Molly wrapped her towel around her middle, while James grabbed one from the bathroom and they stood shivering and laughing together in front of the fire.

'That... seemed like... such a good idea,' he said, his teeth chattering like crazy.

'And it was,' Molly replied. 'Until we had to get out again.'

'We'll eventually... thaw out.'

He was shivering so much, his whole body shook beneath his towel.

She gestured to him. 'You need to loosen up. Rub yourself dry.'

Laughter escaped through his chattering teeth. 'I literally can't move.'

She closed the gap between them and rubbed her hands up and down his arms, the friction making him laugh even more. Letting go of his towel, he grabbed her hands and pressed them against his chest.

He smiled. 'Ach, you're actually really lovely and warm.'

She focused on her hands and the sensation of his damp skin and the tickle of chest hair beneath them. He dipped his hands beneath her towel, his fingers finding her waist, cold against her skin. Tentatively, she ran her fingers through his chest hair, smoothing upwards across his firm muscles before clasping her hands behind his neck. She met his smiling eyes and realised he'd stopped shaking. His hands travelled even slower, skimming across her goose-bumped skin. Reaching her bikini top, he caressed the curve of her breasts and released the knot in her towel. It dropped to the floor. He tugged her close, her breasts pressing against his chest as he leaned in.

Molly had thought their midnight kiss would be hard to beat, but this was sensual and seductive, and achingly intimate. The embers of the fire glowed, their bodies slowly thawing with each other's touch, awakening a desire in Molly that had long been dampened.

Happiness pulsed through her as they kissed long and deep, while their hands explored and their bodies were warmed by the fire and each other. Right at that moment, in his arms, she felt truly happy, an unfamiliar sensation.

They came up for air, grinning at each other. James released her and opened the wood burner door. Her eyes traced the outline of his muscled arms and chest as he stoked the embers and chucked in another couple of logs.

He pulled the two-seater sofa closer, grabbed the blanket from the bed and beckoned her over. The idea of snuggling up with him was appealing, so she didn't hesitate, sliding next to him and tucking her bare legs beneath her.

'This whole evening has been unexpected but lovely,' James said, adjusting his arm until they were comfortable.

With the blanket covering them both, she nestled her shoulder against his chest, her head resting in the crook of his neck.

'It's been one of the best New Year's Eves I can remember.' Molly sighed. 'It's kinda sad though, that there wasn't one as memorable as this. The last two for obvious reasons have been a write-off, but before that...' She screwed up her face.

'They were either so good you can't remember a thing or so terrible you've erased them from your memory!' His chest reverberated against her cheek as he laughed.

She smiled at his reaction but sadness crept through her. 'They were neither of those things, that's the problem. They were just okay. We went to Howard's parents' once, out with friends a couple of times. Nothing special. I can't even remember what we did on the other years.'

'Throughout my teens and into my twenties, my grandparents

used to host huge New Year's Eve parties. They were the talk of Perthshire.'

'What made them stop?'

James shrugged. 'I never really considered why at the time. I guess you don't think too much about other people when you're a teenager, but looking back it coincided with my grandma having a few mobility problems and I think the loss of my mum. Everything became a bit too much. I don't think it helped that I wasn't around as much. It's funny, isn't it, looking back on things through older, wiser eyes.'

'Yeah, I've been doing a lot of reflecting recently. It's like I'm seeing things for the first time. Things I couldn't see when I was with Howard. The reality of our relationship and how he treated me. Personality wise we were so incompatible. And when I think back to how I felt when I arrived.' Molly shook her head. So much had happened, it was hard to believe she'd only been in Iceland for a little under two weeks. 'Talking to Claudia has helped me to see things clearly. Howard dumping me actually feels as if a weight's been lifted.'

James stroked his thumb along her arm. 'He did you a favour. I feel the same way about Jen. The way she went about it was shite mind, but it's the right thing. I just wish I'd had the guts to say no to her long ago. That enough was enough. I gave her too many chances.'

'You were decent; this way you'll have no regrets.' Molly lifted her head from his shoulder and shuffled upright until she was facing him, the blanket still covering them both, soft against her skin. 'You did everything you could to save your relationship and in the end the decision was made for you. You can move on. It's scary but exciting. At least that's how I'm beginning to feel about it.'

'What are you going to do with your newfound freedom?' he asked.

Molly breathed deeply and gazed past the flames flickering in the wood burner to the cold darkness. Swept up in family life and the Christmas festivities, ideas had been bubbling during the last few days as she'd mulled over her situation. Her usual feeling of trepidation had been trumped by a renewed determination to make massive changes. Now all it would take was courage and belief in herself to make them happen.

'I might actually hand my notice in.'

'Are you serious?' James was wide-eyed.

'Do you think that's a mistake?'

'No, absolutely not.' His astonishment morphed into a smile. 'I think it's bloody bold and brilliant! So, that's step one. What comes after that?'

'I mentioned something to Kat and Lils, but you're the first person I'm properly telling this to. My dream has always been to have a taco truck. I make incredible tacos, even if I say so myself.'

'Like Taco Bell.'

'More like Taco Bliss.'

'I love it.'

'Claudia usually insists I make them, but she hasn't mentioned it this time. I think she's wanted to give me a complete break. I never had any ambition to do a nine-to-five office job, but it happened and I got stuck. It was only supposed to be a fill-in job, but fast forward goodness knows how many years and I'm still there. All the dreams I had, I put on hold. I've always wanted to do something creative. My dad owned a stationery company, and when I was little I had this grand idea of taking over from him, but it was the design side I fancied doing, you know, designing notebooks, not the day-to-day running of a big company. He never encouraged that creative side and was determined I study something "proper" like business studies. As it turned out, he sold the company when he retired and never once encouraged Claudia or me to work in the business and certainly not to take over from him.'

'But cooking became your passion?'

Molly nodded. 'I didn't want to be a chef or work in a restaurant though. For a while I catered for friends and then friends of friends at birthday parties and even a couple of weddings, but that trickled off.'

'Let me guess, not long after you met Howard?'

'I stopped when we became serious, and buying a house and renovating it took over.' She stared wistfully at the flames flickering scarlet and amber, thinking back on all that lost time. 'I like the idea of focusing on a few incredibly delicious and creative dishes, of being able to travel around to festivals or markets instead of having a base. It's risky and unpredictable, which is why I've never done anything about it. Howard would have scoffed at the idea.'

'Well, I think it's brilliant, inspiring and motivating.' Slipping his hand beneath the covers, he ran his fingers over her bare thigh, while looking intently at her. 'I've always loved talking to people who have a passion for something; it makes me feel that my dreams are achievable. I just need to be focused and work harder – probably think smarter too, to make them come true. It's having belief in ourselves.'

'Yeah, absolutely, and that's what I've been lacking. Other people not believing in me or supporting me in the way I'd hoped ate away at my confidence. It made me question why I wanted to do it and how hard it would be.' She felt fired up talking to James. He wasn't belittling her or dismissing her ideas, and his enthusiasm bubbled as much as hers. 'I'm fed up of leading a boring life; I want some adventure and spark.'

'Like soaking in a hot tub at three in the morning when it's minus eight outside?'

'Exactly!' Her heart soared with joy at the freedom she was experiencing, both physically and emotionally. *This* was what her mum had wanted for her – to truly feel alive, to be happy and follow her dreams as much as her heart. 'I don't want to be held back any longer, and I'm not just talking about Howard; I've held myself back. I want to say yes and to feel like I can do anything.'

'There's nothing stopping you any longer. There's nothing stopping either of us.'

Now her parents' affairs were settled and once Howard was out of the picture, there really was nothing preventing her from changing her life. Even her dad's influence with his flippant comments of 'oh, you can't possibly do that, Moll' or 'what does Howard think?' was long gone. Unlike Claudia, she hadn't been wise to its damaging negativity, but years and years' worth had ground her down, and then she'd been in a relationship with someone with similar traits. Howard had most definitely been the wrong person for her.

James was gently caressing her thigh, his touch a confusing mix of sensual comfort. Now the alcohol had worn off, she was overly aware of him.

'What about you?' She wanted to take the focus away from how she was feeling. 'What are your plans for the new year?'

'Karthstone is going to be my priority. I need to think outside the box. I can easily Airbnb the part where my grandparents lived and I'm happy to bunk elsewhere while I work on the rest of the castle. But the grounds...' His eyes lit up. 'They're something else. Acres of woodland with a stream and a lake. The formal garden needs tackling, but there's a massive lawn with views down the valley to the woods that are spectacular. I grew up there, but I have to pinch myself every time I go back. My dream, like yours, is to completely quit my job, then I can focus on the castle full time. Along with Alistair, the groundskeeper, I already manage the woodland. It's a lot.'

'It sounds like you work all the time.'

'I do, but I love it. Jen never did though. She's a workaholic too, just with different priorities. Not my problem any longer.' He removed his hand from her thigh and reached behind the sofa for the bottle of wine and glasses that he'd forgotten to bring out to the hot tub. 'Maybe we should toast to that.' He handed Molly a glass and poured the wine.

'What, to hard work and crappy exes?'

He raised his glass. 'Indeed! To hard work, crappy exes and an exciting future.'

They knocked their glasses together and swigged the wine, which was smooth and warming with a hint of spice.

'It sounds like there's so much potential with the grounds and the castle. While you're working on the inside, how easy would it be to set up a camping area?' With her free hand, Molly grabbed his arm as ideas bounced around her head. 'Or, even better, what about glamping tents – individual private havens nestled among the woodland?'

'Aye, it would take a bit of investment but it could end up paying for itself, and that would give me time to work on the castle.'

'Along with the Airbnb bit where your grandparents lived. And didn't you say you already rent out a couple of cottages and some land?' Molly shifted closer as James nodded. 'And what about a festival in the grounds? You could start off small, something that grows over time and even expand into the castle as and when it's ready. It would work perfectly alongside the glamping too.'

James placed his wine glass on the floor and nodded enthusiastically. 'A festival of nature. Or of food. A festival of nature and food!' He laughed. 'You know I'd need a food truck to keep punters happy. Taco Bliss sounds perfect.'

'It's a deal.' Molly shook his hand. 'If you get a festival going, I'll rock up with my food truck.'

'I'm going to hold you to that.'

Actually, I want you to just hold me.

Molly sensed her smile matched his as their eyes traced each other. His eyes were a deep blue, twinkling behind his glasses, the line between his eyebrows less pronounced. *What now?* Her heart was racing, the deliciousness of being this close to him leaving her whole body tingling. Yet uncertainty crept through her about where it would lead.

'I have no idea what time it is, but it's been so good to talk to you.' She tore her eyes away from his and sipped the warming wine. 'I might have to try and get some sleep though.'

'You don't have to go if you don't want to... This was your room, remember.' His tone, the hint of colour in his cheeks and the way he was looking at her suggested he was thinking a lot more could happen between them.

She placed her hands on his chest and gazed at him. 'I'm not sure I'm quite ready for that.'

'I'm not sure I am either, but I'd like to be.'

Molly leaned close and gave him a long lingering kiss. There was temptation, but her head was as scrambled as her heart and she didn't want to rush into anything. His hands on her skin were electric. He kissed her deeply. She didn't want to pull away, but she forced herself to. She sensed his eyes on her as she shoved her fleece hoody over her bikini, pulled on leggings, put on her fleece-lined boots and picked up her towel.

James wrapped the blanket round his shoulders and walked with her to the door. A waft of cool air snuck in as he opened it.

'I'll see you in the morning, Molly.' He laughed. 'Later in the morning.'

On tiptoes, she gave him one last kiss, not wanting her resolve to head to bed on her own to desert her.

As she walked along the empty glass walkway, with the darkness spreading in both directions, she mulled over why, when Howard had dumped her and had been cheating for months, she still felt tied to him. She could imagine what Howard had been getting up to over Christmas with his pretty brunette work colleague. *His lover*, she reminded herself.

The shadowed restaurant was empty, with only the moon and stars visible through the windows, along with the river glimmering silver. Tonight with James had been freeing and wonderful, stirring feelings that had been dormant for so long, but surely it was too soon to act on them?

She crept upstairs, not wanting to disturb anyone, although only Elvar and Claudia were home. The apartment was dark and quiet. Finn was with his girlfriend; Alda at her friend's. She wondered if Leifur had hooked up with anyone. She hoped he had, with someone like-minded who wasn't after commitment. She hoped he'd one day find happiness, although perhaps he already had. With the support of Elvar and Claudia, he was rebuilding his life, happy on his own, his love solely focused on his daughter. He was doing just fine.

She closed her bedroom door quietly. She was almost completely dry; the heat of the wood burner, the blanket and James's body warmth had worked wonders. Standing in the middle of the room, looking at the empty double bed, she realised she didn't want to be alone. This wasn't how she wanted the night to end or the new year to begin, not without James. Why was she willingly depriving herself of the feeling of self-worth, the gentle love, hope and contentment that being with him had given her?

The tingling was back, pulsing through her, the thought of a nearly naked James leaving her breathless. She dumped the damp towel on the floor and snuck out of her room, anticipation jangling in the pit of her stomach as she retraced her steps through the lodge. What did she have to lose?

She reached his room and knocked.

For a horrible moment, she thought he'd already gone to sleep and wouldn't answer, but then she heard footsteps. James opened the door and his brief confusion morphed into a smile.

'I didn't want to be on my own,' she said.

Without a word, he pulled her inside, shut the door and kissed her passionately. Any early hesitation dispersed as they landed on the bed together. He'd changed into a dry T-shirt and pyjama bottoms and Molly made quick work of removing them, his skin now warm beneath her fingers. He tugged off her clothes and laid exploratory kisses on her lips downwards, lingering over her breasts, while his fingers teased lower to where she ached for him, her arousal leaving no doubt in her mind that coming back had been the right choice. She lay back on the pillow gasping, the feeling that had been building all evening heightened by his touch and intoxicating presence.

31

The sun had long risen by the time Molly and James stirred. After their revealing heart-to-heart, the gentle exploration of each other had left them satisfied and happily exhausted. They'd eventually fallen asleep snuggled up together.

The New Year was a new start and it had begun with James, but it also meant facing Howard. After last night, flying home would put a halt to something that had the potential of being so right, that initial spark and connection with James having grown during their time together.

'I'm glad you came back last night,' James said sleepily. He yawned, stretched and wrapped his arms around her, pulling her close.

'Me too.' Molly revelled in his warmth and the utter contentment of being in his arms. 'I wonder if Claudia and Elvar have realised I'm not in my room?'

'I'm sure Kat and Lils will have noticed our absence at breakfast.'

'What time is it?'

James reached for his phone. 'Gone midday.'

'We've definitely missed breakfast then.' Molly groaned, then realised it didn't matter. Both she and James had been heart-broken and had found comfort in each other. They were free to follow their hearts and the more they'd got to know each other, the more obvious it had been that being together was what they wanted. At least, it was right now. She'd absolutely made the right decision to return last night; she'd have been punishing herself if she'd stayed in her room and slept alone. Whatever anyone else may think about their liaison, the desire that had awoken within her suggested just how right it was.

No regrets; that's what her mum had urged. And she wouldn't have any, she was certain of that. Talking with James had cemented decisions and her mind was made up. The way forward had become as clear as the Icelandic nights when the aurora borealis had decorated the sky. However sad she'd be to say goodbye to her family, to everyone here, to James most of all, part of her was itching to get home and put an end to her life with Howard. Then she'd have her new beginning. It was time to move on. It was *her* time.

Knowing their absence would really be noticed if they ended up missing lunch too, they dragged themselves from bed. Every-thing had been said the night before, through words and actions. So, with a long, lingering kiss, and still with her bikini beneath her hoody and leggings, Molly left his room, bracing herself for the inevitable questions, but apart from hearing Kat and Lils chatting together in the lounge and nodding hello to the restau-rant staff, she made it to her room without seeing anyone else.

After a heady few hours with James, and with only one day left in Iceland, time was slipping away. Elvar and Claudia were around but Molly didn't see them until after she'd showered, changed and had joined Kat, Lils and James in front of the fire in the lounge. Finn and his girlfriend returned from Reykjavík with

Alda and, after a night partying until the early hours, Leifur rocked up a little later. It was a communal and fun-filled afternoon and evening, many of them nursing hangovers as they took it easy reading, playing games and eating. It was the perfect last day, and it seemed that James and Molly's night together had gone unnoticed, or maybe no one was bold enough to mention it in front of everyone else.

Tension crackled between Molly and James though. Her whole being was filled with thoughts of him and the memory of the hours they'd spent together, sharing their innermost thoughts and exploring their feelings for each other. Whether anyone else noticed it or not, the looks between them conveyed so much; a silent dialogue with a longing to pick up where they'd left off that morning. The way they sat apart was telling too, as if sitting together would show how obvious it was that their relationship had developed into more than it had been just the day before.

The evening ticked on and Molly was drawn into a conversation with Kat and Lils. They swapped numbers and friended each other on Facebook. She noticed James and Leifur talking quietly together, felt their glances, caught James's smile, Leifur's too and she knew James was divulging what had happened between them.

After the previous late night and little sleep, it was to Molly's relief that the evening drew to a close early. Leifur instigated it, bidding them all a good night with a kiss and hug for Kat and Lils in case he didn't see them again before they left. He stirred Claudia and Elvar into moving too; both of them had been yawning for the last hour at least.

'Night, Molly.' Leifur winked at her on his way past.

'An early start tomorrow,' Claudia announced as she stood up and flashed a sleepy smile at everyone. She placed the guard in front of the fire. 'I'm going to be sad to say goodbye to you all.'

Disappointment washed across her face as her eyes landed on Molly.

Elvar squeezed Molly's shoulder. 'Coming up?'

'Um, in a bit.' Molly met James's eyes and he gave an indiscernible nod.

The moment Claudia and Elvar left, Kat turned to Lils and gave an overly dramatic yawn and stretch. 'Don't know about you but I'm dog-tired.' She flashed Molly and James an almighty grin. 'We'll let you two have a bit of alone time...'

As Lils hugged James goodnight, Kat leaned close to Molly. 'I saw you go past the lounge earlier today.' She gestured towards James. 'I put two and two together. I'm so pleased. You both deserve happiness... Right!' She stood and hooked her arm in Lils's. 'Have a good last night, you two.'

They left the lounge in a whirl of laughter.

The fire creaked and smouldered in the grate, the clock's rhythmic tick tock tick loud now quietness had descended.

'So, Kat and Lils know about us. Leif does too.' James smiled shyly. 'Are you, um, going upstairs or do you want to come back to my room?'

Molly stood up and held out her hand. She'd never been more certain about anything. It was depressing to even contemplate leaving Iceland and saying goodbye to everyone. It was the end of something, yet the beginning of so much more. She'd only just turned thirty-five and she was getting the opportunity to start afresh, and however hard that would be, she would embrace the challenge and move forward. But for now, she had one more night with James, and boy was she going to make the most of it.

* * *

Molly and James woke up together again but early this time, well before the sun had risen so they could say goodbye to Kat and Lils. The final morning. Molly sensed James's sadness as they tore themselves away from each other, because it mirrored hers. They were all heading home, but at different times to different destinations. Elvar dropped Kat and Lils at the airport first thing for their flight to Manchester before collecting two new guests, while James and Molly left the lodge later in the morning with Claudia for their separate afternoon and early evening flights to Edinburgh and Bristol.

After a tearful goodbye with Elvar, Finn and Alda, the journey to Reykjavík was subdued. Molly sat in the front with Claudia and it was hard to know what to say, so she didn't try. Instead, she watched the snow-covered landscape zip by, aware of how much she was going to miss it and everything that had made her time in Iceland so special. Time that had begun to heal much of her hurt.

All too soon they reached the bus station. Claudia unloaded James's luggage and hugged him goodbye. She glanced between them before getting back inside.

'I've been dreading this moment.' James reached for Molly's hand. 'These last couple of days. They've meant so much.'

'The thought of going home.' Molly shook her head as she fought back a wave of sadness. 'I'm going to miss you.'

'You're not doing this on your own, Molly. Neither of us are.' He wrapped his arms around her and hugged her tight. 'We've got big plans, remember. Let's make them happen.'

Molly nodded; there was so much more she wanted to say but her words got choked.

'Right.' James heaved his rucksack on his back and firmly gripped the suitcase handle. 'My coach... I'd better go.' He leaned in, kissed her and walked away.

With tears in her eyes, Molly got back in the 4x4. Claudia started the engine and turned to her. 'Are you okay?'

'I don't want to talk about it.' Molly kept her focus on James. However, not talking to her sister was the old Molly, and she understood how much it had helped to open up and share her feelings. She turned to Claudia. 'Actually, I do. I'm going to miss him. I'm going to miss all of you. I'm going to see you all again, but James...' She sighed.

'You have his number, right? He has yours. Keep in touch; you never know where it will lead.' Claudia pulled out of the parking space. 'You seemed rather cosy back there. And, um, I couldn't help but notice you weren't in your room last night and maybe the night before that. I take it something happened between the two of you?'

Molly tried to catch sight of James as they left the bus station, but he'd been swallowed up by the swarm of people queuing for the coaches. 'Something definitely happened, although it mostly involved us talking into the early hours.'

Claudia snorted. 'Mostly! Please tell me you at least kissed?'

'Yeah, we kissed.' That warm, fuzzy feeling was back. 'And then some.'

Claudia raised an eyebrow.

'Actually, we did everything but have sex.' Laughter escaped as she caught her sister's surprised look.

'Molly Bliss! No wonder you've both looked so bloody happy.' Claudia reached across the gearstick and squeezed her hand. 'Right, before I take you to the airport, let's have lunch. Then you can tell me *everything*.'

32

Molly arrived home to a dark and empty house. It had been quite the day, and hugely emotional saying goodbye to her family, to Leifur, Kat and Lils. And to James. He hadn't been far from her mind the whole way back, but thoughts of him didn't keep the dread at bay as she neared home. She dragged her suitcase inside and closed the door on the damp January evening. A pile of post lay on the mat; bills and unopened Christmas cards. With no lights on and the heating off, she knew Howard wasn't back. So much for his promise of being home when she returned. The warmth and love that had emanated through The Fire Lodge was most definitely missing here.

Neither of them had been in touch with each other since their argument on Christmas morning. Howard obviously hadn't wanted to and Molly had felt there was little point. The longer they'd spent apart, the easier it had been to get her head around the situation. What she'd wanted to say needed to be said to his face. He knew what flight she'd been on and when she should have arrived, and yet he'd made himself scarce. It was yet another way to put the power into his own hands, by leaving her waiting and wondering where he was and when he'd return. Except her heart was filled with James and her head was resolute in what she was going to do. Howard's absence, behaviour and lack of understanding about everything she'd been through only made her more certain of the path ahead.

Molly turned on the hallway light and checked the rest of the house. They'd never bothered to put up any Christmas decorations, so it seemed even more bleak after the magic she'd left behind in Iceland.

After locking the front door and unpacking, Molly headed to bed alone. Apart from the last two nights with James, it was no different to when she was in Iceland, yet it felt more meaningful to be alone in the house she shared with Howard.

She'd only just got into bed when her phone pinged. Her heart skipped at the message.

Not sure phoning would be a good idea if you're home with Howard, but wanted to check you're okay? Had an almighty row with Jen so in a hotel for the night and going to Karthstone tomorrow. Hope you're having a better evening than I am! Thinking about you and miss you x

Molly's fingers hovered over the message. He was alone, she was alone... She closed WhatsApp and rang him.

He answered within seconds. 'Hi, I wasn't expecting you to call.'

'And I was expecting Howard to be here, but he's not, so what the hell.' And ever since they'd said goodbye in Reykjavík she'd been desperate to speak to James. 'I was primed for an argument but I guess he anticipated that.'

'He's avoiding you?'

'Presumably. I'm not sure if he's playing emotional games or is just a coward, but his behaviour is actually making it easier to think about moving forward.'

'And put your plan into action.' James's deep, lilting voice was soothing, wrapping around her like a hug. What she would give to be in his arms right now. Just the thought of him and the memory of his hands on her skin erased the hurt. To be able to talk so intimately with someone, to feel that loved and desired, had sparked something deep inside.

'Yes, first thing tomorrow I'm on a mission to get my life sorted. I'm home but it doesn't feel like home. I don't want to be here any longer. I don't want anything of my old life. Honestly, after spending the last couple of days with you, then getting back here, it's like I've had a lightbulb moment, a clarity about all that's wrong and the way I can change it. The things I'm thinking of doing are drastic, but they're actually a simple way to completely reinvent my life.'

'You sound excited.'

'That's because I am. I've not felt this hopeful for so long. I was scared of everything before, that changing anything would be too difficult, but I honestly feel like I've been handed an opportunity to take charge of my life and finally make something of it.'

'Jen has made moving on really easy for me too,' he said. 'I was blinkered by what I thought I wanted. Time to rock the boat, Molly.'

'Oh, I'll be doing plenty of rocking.' She wondered if James could hear the amusement in her voice. 'There'll be no stopping me.'

* * *

Molly woke early. It was the third of January and a weekday, but she wasn't back at work until tomorrow and after talking to James

long into the night and sharing their innermost thoughts, their
hopes and dreams, she had an even clearer plan than when she'd
left Iceland. James remained at the forefront of her mind as she
went through the motions, showering in the walk-in shower
Howard had insisted on getting which left no space for a bath;
making coffee in the Nespresso machine – *his* pride and joy –
before having breakfast alone at the kitchen table looking out on
their small but neat garden. So much of his influence had infil-
trated her life and there was so much she'd do differently –
painting the living room a deep sage green for starters, instead of
the clean and modern off-white.

The second it turned nine, Molly phoned the estate agent
who'd sold Ashford House to book in a valuation. She ticked the
first thing off her list. Then she went food shopping and spent the
next couple of hours trying out a new taco recipe with spicy pork,
jalapenos, roasted tomatoes, three different types of cheese,
guacamole and a cooling sour cream dressing.

The result was a lunch that was spicy yet delicious and a
messy kitchen, something Howard would hate, but it left Molly
feeling satisfied and tingling with excitement. Apart from in
Iceland, it had been a long time since she'd actually relished
cooking, rather than it being a necessity to fuel her. She stacked
the dishwasher and cleaned the kitchen before typing up the
recipe she'd scribbled down on the back of a used envelope. She
needed to buy a laptop for herself. She needed a website too and
to revamp the Taco Bliss Facebook page she'd created years ago
but had never been brave enough to publish. Possibilities fizzed;
she was so used to feeling a heavy ache in her heart that this
newfound excitement took her by surprise.

She was sitting at the kitchen table drafting her resignation
letter when Howard arrived home. She didn't go to the door to
meet him. It wasn't hard to imagine where he'd spent last night

and probably all the nights since he'd got back from his parents', whenever that was. She knew so little and yet she no longer cared. So she waited for him in the kitchen.

He sauntered in, placed his wallet on the table and finally looked at her. If he was feeling any remorse over how he'd behaved, it wasn't obvious.

'Nice of you to show up,' she said calmly.

His jaw clenched. 'I wasn't sure when you'd get back.'

'Of course you were; please don't take me for a fool.' She didn't even feel upset that this was the end; she didn't feel anything when she looked at him, smart as usual in trousers and a shirt, neatly shaven, his hair slicked back. She'd never liked it styled like that, preferring a more natural look, but then he was rather particular about everything. So incredibly different to James. She felt nothing for him any longer, not even anger or hatred. With her mind made up, she wanted to articulate her plans without breaking down. 'But it's fine, you've just given me more time to get my head straight.' She folded her arms and held his gaze. 'The first thing we need to do is sort out this house. You need to either buy me out or we sell up.'

'We need to talk about this first, Molly.'

'No, we really don't.' The fire in her chest was stoked; for the first time, she felt sure of herself and could visualise a way forward, one not without its scary moments, but one with so much possibility. '*You've* been having an affair and *you* broke up with me. *You* chose not to discuss how you were feeling. You weren't here when I got back and you're the one who no longer wants to be around me. It's quite obvious we need to move on. You already have, now it's my turn. Actually, I've already moved on from you in every way possible.'

'What's that supposed to mean?' He glared at her.

She challenged him with a look of defiance; let him make of

that what he wanted. If the thought of her being with another man upset him, then good, he'd have a little understanding of how he'd made her feel. 'It means I want a clean break, so either buy my half of the house or we sell it. I've booked the estate agent to come round next week to value it, then we take it from there.'

God did it feel good to look him in the eye, to stand up for herself and tell him *her* plans. For too long he'd been the one in control, dampening her resolve. An idea had been formulating over the last couple of days, fuelled by James's encouragement and his belief in her, an idea that filled her with optimism that left her head buzzing with a million thoughts. With no one holding her back, she needed to make her life count for something; she needed to be the one to inject happiness into it through the choices she would now be making.

No regrets.

Howard was looking at her in disbelief. What had he expected? For her to beg for him to stay, for them to give their damaged relationship another go? Her eyes had been opened to who he really was and how stale and pedestrian her life had become. There was so much more she wanted to do and achieve and it no longer involved him.

'Fine, we sell up.' His jaw clenched.

'Great. Might be an idea for you to move out too. You could move in with Emma Hastings – unless of course your bit on the side isn't that serious about your relationship?'

'My God Molly, you're being unreasonable!'

'I'm unreasonable!' Molly laughed. 'You either move out or into one of the spare rooms. Your choice.'

She left him standing in the kitchen. Let him mull it over; she had things to do.

On the way to the churchyard, Molly stopped off at a garden centre to buy a pot of heather and a small trowel. The familiar drive to the village she'd grown up in whispered of a time gone by. She passed Ashford House, its familiar stone walls giving her a brief pang of longing. So many memories were here, but her future wasn't. Her future wasn't in Cheltenham either, she was certain of that.

The sky was painted a dull grey with a streak of silver where the weak winter sun was attempting to strain through the clouds. The churchyard was empty and bare branches creaked in the breeze. It wasn't as cold as it had been in Iceland but there was a chill dampness that permeated her coat. She reached her parents' grave. The headstone had already weathered a little. Positioned on the edge of the churchyard with only a low stone wall to separate it from the open fields bordered by a wood, it bore the brunt of the weather. In spring, everything would come alive, the grey headstones scattered throughout the graveyard offset by the pop of fresh greens and the warmth of pink blossom. Snowdrops were already appearing, decorating the grass beneath a cluster of trees like patches of snow.

Molly knelt on the ground in front of the grave, took off her gloves and traced her fingers over her mum's name chiselled into the headstone. With a deep breath, she dug a hole in the hard soil and eased the heather from its pot.

'I thought this heather would brighten things up. It's like the one you had outside the kitchen window. I know you found this time of year hard and always looked forward to spring, but I think this will take away some of the bleakness.' The words began to tumble from Molly, along with a desire to release her pent-up emotion and convey her feelings to her mum. 'It's a lovely spot though; not quite as wild or as breathtaking as Iceland, but it has its own beauty.' She gazed beyond the wall to the soft grey-green of the copse on the far side of the field, before turning her attention back to the grave. 'I'm no longer with Howard. I'm not sure you'd be too surprised by that, but I expect you'd be relieved. We're going to sell the house *and* I wrote my resignation letter earlier. I'm going to send it tomorrow. I need to stop being afraid and just do it.' Molly laughed, the sound echoing into the peaceful churchyard. 'I'm doing first and thinking later. Actually, that's not technically true, I've been thinking about it for so flipping long. I know what I want to do – I'm going to start cooking tacos for friends again and set up a website. I'm going to buy a van with my inheritance money. Thanks to you and Dad, I have the means to make my dreams come true. I'm taking charge of my future and focusing on what I want. Everything you said in your letter, Mum, was spot on and it couldn't have come at a better time. I wish I'd talked to you more back then, but perhaps I wouldn't be where I am now without this whole cycle of events showing me the way.'

She placed the heather in the hole and patted down the soil around it. She sat back. The tiny pale-purple flowers added a splash of colour into the otherwise dull winter landscape.

'I've met someone too.' She thought of James back at Karthstone, back at his family home where he belonged. He'd messaged her earlier when he'd arrived and she'd call him before she got home, just in case Howard was still there. 'His name's James and he owns a castle in Scotland. I actually first met him in Iceland ten years ago, but I only got to know him over the last two weeks. We've been good for each other. I think you'd like him. Because I do. I like him, a lot.'

A robin flew down and landed on the gravestone.

'Hello,' Molly said, watching as it looked around, its fluffed up feathers giving it a jolly roundness. 'Sorry, I don't have anything for you. I'll bring something next time.'

She wasn't going to keep running away from her grief, or from anything, however challenging. She made a silent promise to visit the grave more often. Although returning to the village evoked sadness, and kneeling by her parents' grave accentuated the reality of her loss, there was also a sense of peace and the feeling that she was slowly beginning to work through her grief and would come out the other side finding a way to live with it. She kissed her fingers and pressed them to the headstone.

'Love you, Mum and Dad. I'll visit again soon.' She stood up and breathed in the fresh, cold air. 'And Mum, I'm absolutely going to do what you said in your letter and lead the most wonderful life.'

EPILOGUE

TWO AND A HALF YEARS LATER

Karthstone Castle had stood for at least five hundred years, nestled in its own slice of Perthshire countryside, its stone walls and mullioned windows overlooking a wooded valley of ancient oaks and graceful beech trees. Nearly three years since first setting eyes on it, Molly still found it a thrill to call it home. She understood why James had never lost his awe of arriving back to the place he'd known and loved since he was a wee child, because Molly was certain she'd never take the sense of history, the breadth of space and the natural beauty of the landscape for granted.

The well-worn trail through the wood was sun-dappled, the shade beneath the dense canopy a respite from the hot June day. As Molly wound her way back towards the castle, she reflected on just how lucky she was, her whole life so far removed from the sedentary nine-to-five routine she used to have.

A squirrel scampered across the path. With a nut clutched in its tiny paws, it paused to look around. A branch snapped and it shot up the closest tree.

Molly searched the wood on either side of the leaf-strewn

path, watching for movement. She stopped where a patch of sunshine had managed to squeeze through the tightly entwined branches of the tunnel of trees. Apart from birdsong and an occasional branch creaking, there was only silence. The woodland was the perfect place to escape to and get lost in, and it was hard to believe a festival was taking place. Not that she'd get lost any longer; she was now adept at navigating her way round Karthstone and its acres of grounds.

A rustle in the undergrowth caught her attention. She turned and whistled. 'Flóki! Here boy!'

A black Labrador shot from the bushes, bounding towards her, his tongue hanging out as he panted. Skidding to a halt, he nudged his wet nose into her hand, sniffing for the treats in her shorts pocket. She got him to sit and fed him one. They set off again, Flóki racing ahead, while Molly strolled. It was cooler beneath the trees, but out in the sun, the June day shimmered. After weeks of being constantly on the go in the run up to the festival, her back ached and her feet were sore.

Flóki was a blur, streaking through the long grass they'd left to grow wild. The splashes of mustard yellow and poppy red wildflowers added to the varying shades of green that spread in every direction. This walk was part of her daily routine and one she and James usually took together. The view from the hill down to the castle, its garden and the lawn with the wooded valley beyond was Molly's favourite, although it wasn't usually filled with quite so many people.

Domed tents and gleaming white trucks peppered the lawn and the final day of the Karthstone Festival of Nature was in full swing. For the last three days, James had been in his element, emersed in the natural surroundings of his beloved family home, sharing it with people in a way that made so much sense. While he was running a forest school for children and adults, Molly had been busy feeding festival goers from her Taco Bliss truck, one of a handful of food trucks catering for the hundreds of people who'd descended on their usually peaceful part of Scotland. With wild storytelling in the wood, iron working in a makeshift forge and wood carving in another tent, the festival celebrated nature and local crafts and had grown since its inaugural year, the second festival welcoming four times as many people through the gates.

While much of the castle remained a work in progress, many of the ideas James and Molly had bounced around that New Year's Day morning in Iceland had come to fruition. Although Molly had wasted no time in changing her life, the January when she'd arrived home had felt eternal, the dreariness of the weather accentuating the strain of dissolving her life with Howard. After handing in her notice, she had a month before she was jobless, so she'd put all her focus into selling their house and getting Taco Bliss up and running. Howard had moved in with Emma Hastings; whether they lasted or not, Molly hadn't cared. With him gone, she was free. She hadn't missed Howard one bit, but James had been far away. They'd spoken every day, the plans they'd hatched in Iceland evolving and developing as they'd slowly put them into action. And yet, even though she was free of Howard, it hadn't taken away Molly's heartache of packing up their home and her life, particularly when it had been reminiscent of the emotionally draining task of selling her parents' house just months before. Keeping busy helped and she'd made herself scarce for the dozens of house viewings. Even an offer at the asking price, although welcome, had been tinged with sadness. A chapter of her life was over, but the thought of leaving her job and the freedom she would have after years of dreaming about doing just that had kept Molly going, along with long chats late into the night with James.

He'd been the first person she'd phoned after finishing her last day of work.

'I'm officially unemployed!'

'How does that feel?'

'Scary. Exciting. Like I need to get my arse in gear and buy a truck.'

'Well, now it's official and you have a wee bit of time on your hands, how about coming to visit me?'

A couple of weeks later, on a dreary, rain-streaked February day, James had met her at Edinburgh Airport. Laying eyes on him again with his dark windswept hair and smiling blue eyes half-hidden behind his glasses evoked such good memories. She had an overwhelming sense of having made the right decision about everything. In the middle of arrivals, he'd engulfed her in a hug, their kiss interrupted by other travellers knocking their elbows and suitcases into them.

Leaving behind the city and driving deeper into the country-side had helped to banish much of the grey day, because the dullness hadn't mattered by the time they'd reached Karthstone. Even in winter, the privacy, space and beauty had been apparent. The long drive swept through woodland that Molly imagined had been there for centuries, hinting at the vastness of the grounds. The approach had revealed the castle in all its glory, its stone turrets the first to become visible, followed by the remainder of the elegant grey stone building as they'd emerged from the trees.

'You own a castle, James.'

'Aye, I own a castle.'

They'd picked up right where they'd left off, as if they'd known each other for years, old friends so comfortable with each other that it didn't matter how long they'd been apart. Their conversation had flowed, the looks between them or the brush of an arm electrifying, the anticipation of what was to come crack-

ling between them as James had showed her around. His grandparents' apartment took up one wing, and although dated, it
mostly needed cosmetic work and was what James planned to
tackle first. The potential that Jen had scoffed about was apparent
in the high ceilings, polished wooden floors and large stone fire-
places. With two bedrooms, a kitchen, bathroom, living room,
dining room and a library, it had left Molly buzzing with ideas.
The rest of the castle, which remained as it was when James's
grandparents had run it as a hotel, needed a lot of work but the
bare bones were there.

After a two-hour walk through the woods to explore the far
reaches of the grounds, they'd returned to the castle just before
dusk, when the setting sun had bled into the horizon and the
view across the valley had been bathed in a soft lilac light. Molly
had been glad of the warmth and solidness of the castle, but she
couldn't remember ever feeling this way about someone; she'd
loved talking to James as much as she'd longed for them to head
to bed and revisit those two nights in Iceland.

They'd cooked crispy jacket potatoes, made chilli con carne
and eaten in front of the fire in the library, chatting about their
plans for the rest of the week before James went back to work and
Molly returned to Cheltenham to put her own plans in place for
her Taco Bliss dream.

The journey, followed by miles of walking and a copious
amount of fresh air, had left Molly exhausted, but it was a good
kind of exhaustion, where she felt as if she'd actually done and
achieved something. It also reaffirmed how much she'd needed
her life to change. In a short space of time it already had; quitting
her job and selling her house had just been the beginning.

After taking their plates to the kitchen and grabbing the
bottle of wine she'd brought with her, Molly had faltered in the
doorway of the library. The fire sent flickering light across dark

wood walls lined with hundreds of books. Apart from an armchair and a battered chesterfield facing the stone fireplace, the room was empty. Leaning forward and resting his elbows on his knees, James looked at home – thoughtful and reflective too. There were an awful lot of emotions and memories tied up in Karthstone. Molly understood how conflicting they could be, even if it was his home and a place he loved.

Molly had stirred herself and joined him, deciding she didn't want to continue putting off what had been on her mind all day. Placing the bottle and glasses on the stone hearth, she'd pushed James back on the sofa and straddled him. 'It's been a long few weeks.' Even hushed, her voice had filled the room.

His wide-eyed surprise had quickly been eradicated with a kiss. His hands had reached beneath her jumper and smoothed across her skin. With the fire warming her back, Molly had never felt a desire quite like it, an urgent longing that had grown over the weeks apart, an ache that could only be shifted by James. His beaming smile and eager fingers as he unzipped her jeans had showed he felt the same. As she'd manoeuvred closer and brushed kisses across his neck, the realisation of how much she wanted him to be a permanent fixture in her life had made their first night together since Iceland all the more meaningful.

One week was too short, and it was obvious that James had similar feelings, because the day before she'd returned to Cheltenham he'd asked her to move to Scotland to live with him. It had been the easiest yes she'd ever uttered. So that spring, after buying a truck to turn into Taco Bliss, Molly had driven it all the way to Karthstone and their adventure officially began.

Their first few months together had been spent grafting with James working out his notice with Forestry and Land Scotland, then they'd spent long days together renovating James's grandparents' part of the castle. The effort had been worth it when they'd welcomed their first paying guests that summer. They'd moved into the east wing and worked on converting that into a home for themselves while Molly got her taco business up and running and James had liaised with the local primaries and started a forest school in the grounds. They had been happy to spend all their time together, their hard work offset with evenings spent bouncing around ideas, Molly experimenting with different recipes and trying them out on James, before they'd work off the calories with passionately energetic nights.

Once the house sale had finally gone through, her tie to Howard was severed. There were no regrets, only an occasional sadness that she was a long way from where her parents were buried, although from time to time she'd return to see friends and visit the churchyard to tend to the heather that was flourishing, while updating them on her life that had changed beyond all recognition. Her grief had remained, but it had been soothed by a happiness she hadn't dared believe she'd ever be able to find again.

In memory of her parents, she and James had planted an apple tree at Karthstone, which they could see from their kitchen window. It was covered in blossom in the spring and laden with fruit in the autumn that Molly had turned into crumbles, pies and chutney. She was certain her mum would have approved. Whenever she'd felt the need to reflect, to talk to her mum or longed to visit the grave, she'd stand by the tree and trace her fingers across the plaque attached to the trunk.

In loving memory of Alan and Gertrude Bliss.

Other changes had included Molly and Claudia talking at least once a week, sharing their thoughts and feelings, celebrating achievements, catching up on gossip and what Finn and

Alda were up to, while being a sounding board for ideas or simply talking about the past and their parents. Sadness still weaved through their lives, although less acutely than it had, particularly for Molly.

Welcoming her family to Karthstone Castle the following Christmas had been a highlight, culminating in Hogmanay celebrations to see in the New Year. A whole twelve months had gone by without seeing them, everyone too busy with their individual lives and projects to make the trip. Leifur, along with Birta, had joined them for a few days over the New Year and although it was a little strange to think back on the brief but intense time in her life when she'd been consumed by lust for him, how she felt about James was altogether different. Somehow they'd seamlessly navigated their changing relationships and had managed to remain friends. Leifur was still single but he certainly wasn't lonely and after nearly two years of living with Elvar and Claudia, he was about to move into his own place, although he'd continue to work for them. Everyone was managing to adapt and move on, the challenges of life only making them stronger while helping to shape their futures.

* * *

Desperate for a drink, Molly stirred herself from her swirling thoughts and picked up the pace down the hill. The long grass tickled her bare legs, while the sun blazed, making her wish for a breeze and long for a cooling drink. She reached the castle and paused in the shade to catch her breath while Flóki lapped at a bowl of water. He followed her across the gravel drive and they skirted the formal garden that was ablaze with late spring colour. Thoughts of her mum rose to the surface at the sight of the purple heather she and James had planted, before they continued towards the far side of the festival and the area of woodland where the forest activities and wild storytelling were taking place.

Flóki spotted James before Molly did, capering over and flopping on the dry earth next to him. James's face was flushed as he ran a hand through his wild curls and then stroked Flóki. Molly watched him from afar. His enthusiasm was infectious as he showed a group of primary-aged children a collection of different leaves from the trees that grew in the castle's grounds.

'I think he's having as much fun as the kids.' A familiar voice broke Molly's trance.

Molly turned and smiled at Kat. 'That's because he is.'

'I hoped you'd have your feet up by now,' Kat said, handing her a bottle of raspberry lemonade.

'I'm fine,' Molly replied smoothly. 'This is needed though, thank you.' She took a swig of the chilled drink and smacked her lips together. 'Have you lost Lils?'

'She's joined that campfire cooking demo.'

'I'm glad she's enjoying herself.' Molly nodded towards the castle. 'Her historical walking tour around Karthstone went down a treat earlier.'

'She loved it. It's massively boosted her confidence, so thank you for giving her the opportunity.' Kat tucked her arm in Molly's. 'She's talking again about running a series of historical talks back home and I think she really will this time. She's adored the experience here.'

They wandered arm in arm along the edge of the woodland, the dappled shade and refreshing drink exactly what Molly had needed. She was in her element as much as James and Lils were. Kat too, and the festival goers, judging by all the smiling faces enjoying the sunshine, workshops and events.

'I'm finished.' James's voice was deep and lilting in her ear as he appeared behind them. Kat let go of Molly as James slipped his arms around Molly's waist, gliding his hands across her neat bump. He nuzzled into her neck, while his hands remained supporting her tummy. She leaned back into him, aware her lower back was beginning to ache now she'd stopped.

'Did you feel that?' Molly took James's hand, moving it up to where a tiny fist or a foot was jabbing at her insides. 'There, again.'

James beamed. 'Aye, I felt that.'

'At least it's not my bladder that's getting a pummelling.'

'I've been telling her all day to sit down,' Kat said with a motherly tone that Molly appreciated. It wasn't a regret, because it was completely out of her hands, but there was an underlying sadness to her pregnancy that her parents weren't around to hear the happy news, that they never got to be grandparents again or would meet her baby. She held on to the thought of what she did have; she was closer to Claudia and her Icelandic family than she'd ever been and she had new friends in Kat and Lils who'd very much become a part of their lives. She adored Lils's positivity and the way Kat had stepped up to be a surrogate mum, offering pregnancy advice and support because she'd been through it all before with her own, now grown-up children.

'There'll be plenty of time to put my feet up once the festival is over.' Molly wafted her hand in front of her face. 'It's the heat that's getting to me.'

Kat nudged her arm. 'Imagine you're in Iceland, being battered by the wind on black sand beach.'

'Just a few degrees cooler would suit me fine,' Molly said, resting her hands over James's where he cradled her baby bump. 'Although in six months we'll be there.'

That was the plan. With the baby due in October, Claudia had suggested Christmas at The Fire Lodge with the promise of cosy days in and plenty of sleep for Molly and James while Claudia got to spend time with her new niece. Alda, who was going to apply for university places for the following year to study environmental science at either Dundee, Edinburgh or Glasgow, had already offered to babysit in her free time.

Everything had come together beautifully. The last couple of years had been filled with new experiences and welcome challenges. Molly had finally found someone to share her hopes and dreams with, while the future promised even more excitement. After James's New Year's Day proposal, Molly's much wanted pregnancy had put their plans to get married on hold, at least until after their daughter arrived. The prospect of motherhood was what Molly was most looking forward to.

She tightened her hold on James and rested her head back into the crook of his neck, relishing his warm embrace. It was hard to believe how consumed by heartache and grief she'd once been. Her life had been transformed, first by James and a move to Scotland, then the joyful addition of Flóki and now of course with the promise of baby Bliss. Life really was wonderful.

ACKNOWLEDGMENTS

Iceland is a place I've always wanted to visit, so it made sense to pitch it as a location for one of my romantic escape books for Boldwood. Then, after signing the contract, I realised that Iceland would be a challenge to write about without ever having been there. In the middle of the COVID pandemic, travel at the time was out of the question, but when the situation eased towards the end of 2021, we took the chance and booked a holiday there over the February 2022 half term. Little did we know that the Omicron variant would raise its ugly head and with cases increasing, the lead up to travelling to Iceland was rather stressful, as first my son, then me, then my husband came down with COVID.

But somehow, despite the worry and stress, the day before we travelled our PCR tests came back negative and in a flurry of last-minute excitement we made it to the land of fire and ice. It did not disappoint. I hope I've managed to weave some of its beauty and magic into the book, and that Molly's story, despite starting with loss and dealing with grief, has ultimately been uplifting. Without a doubt, the loss of my own dad at the very end of 2020 and then my mum subsequently selling and moving out of the family home influenced the storyline.

Moving on, looking to the future and focusing on all the wonderful experiences and people in your life is at the heart of *One Winter's Night*, and although it was hard to write at times, it's a book I'm proud of.

As always, my thanks go to the brilliant team who make what

I've written a whole lot better, design the most beautiful covers and get the book out into the world! Team Boldwood are the best. My thanks in particular to Amanda, Nia and Jenna, and extra special thanks to my brilliant editor Caroline, whose insightful and encouraging editing notes without a doubt elevated the novel. Thanks to Candida for her spot on copy edit and Jennifer for the final polish – it's a pleasure to work with you.

My thanks also to my friend Judith for her continued encouragement, support and for loving *One Winter's Night* so much (snow and ice are definitely romantic!), and to Kristófer Dignus for generously answering my questions about Iceland and its culture. And a big thank you to all the bloggers, reviewers, friends, fellow authors and readers who are encouraging, supportive and kind enough to champion my books.

Thanks and love as always to Nik, Leo and Mum – we had quite the adventure in Iceland and made some wonderful memories.

ABOUT THE AUTHOR

Kate Frost is the author of several bestselling romantic escape novels including *The Greek Heart* and *The Love Island Bookshop*. She lives in Bristol and is the Director of Storytale Festival, a book festival for children and teens she co-founded in 2019.

Sign up to Kate Frost's mailing list here for news, competitions and updates on future books.

Visit Kate's website: www.kate-frost.co.uk

Follow Kate on social media:

facebook.com/katefrostauthor

twitter.com/katefrostauthor

instagram.com/katefrostauthor

bookbub.com/authors/kate-frost

ALSO BY KATE FROST

Boldwood

Boldwood Books is an award-winning fiction publishing company seeking out the best stories from around the world.

Find out more at www.boldwoodbooks.com

Join our reader community for brilliant books, competitions and offers!

Follow us
@BoldwoodBooks
@TheBoldBookClub

Sign up to our weekly deals newsletter

https://bit.ly/BoldwoodBNewsletter

Printed in Great Britain
by Amazon

28494242R00175